Searching at Jimmy's

K.M. Higgins

Clara Evans Series

Book 2

Searching at Jimmy's

First printing July 2019

ISBN: 9781072235606

Edited by: Emma Shinnick, Kara Farewell, Kelley Oliver
Cover Design concept: John Shinnick of JS Designs LLC
Cover Created by: Kelley Oliver, Harvest Design
Cover photo & Author photo by: Cara Bailey Photography
Printed in the United States of America.

To my mom and dad, thanks for supporting me as I pursue my crazy dreams.

Chapter One

Things I Love About Winter

1. Cute, cozy clothes – sweaters, scarves, boots, etc.
2. Good excuse to curl up under a blanket with a book
3. Lots of hot chocolate
4. Snow is pretty, when it happens
5. It's not summer. Summer is hot and gross

As I drive to work, I mentally run through my "Things I Love About Winter" list that is written in the small, pocket-sized notebook in my purse. The one I use to jot down random thoughts, things to remember, sermon notes, and anything else that comes to mind. I keep that last item—about it not being summer—rolling through my mind as I shiver in my seat and triple check that the heat in my car is set as high as it can go. I don't like summer; it gets entirely too hot and humid in Missouri. I would rather be cold than hot any day. Although, with my glove-covered right hand wrapped around the steering wheel and my other hand tucked under my leg, I am beginning to wish it was at least a little bit warmer.

My car was covered in ice this morning when I left for work, so I had to stand in the freezing temperatures and scrape it off. Not fun. Then again, working on a Saturday morning isn't exactly fun, but I don't have to be there as early as the wait staff so I can't complain too much.

Jimmy's Diner isn't terribly far from my house, which means I'm two blocks away from work by the time my car actually warms up to a cozy temperature. I pull into the busy parking lot and maneuver my car to the parking at the back of the building, not quite ready to brave the cold again, but knowing I have to.

I hustle inside and quickly pull the back door closed behind me and pause for a second, trying to catch my breath in the much warmer kitchen. Unzipping my coat, I pass the storage and dish pit area on my left and the staff lockers on my right before getting to the main part of the kitchen, where Nolan, one of our lead cooks, is moving around the prep area with considerable skill.

"How's it going this morning?" I call over the hum of the bustling kitchen.

"Pretty busy. Not overwhelming or anything, but busy." Nolan's focus stays on the food he's making, as if he barely noticed I'm in the room.

I should know better than to expect anything more than a basic answer. Nolan is not much for small talk, which is why I know next to nothing about him. He sure can cook though, which is why our primary cook, Danny, brought Nolan on as one of our lead cooks a couple months ago.

"Alright." I give up on pulling any more conversation out of Nolan and turn to head into the office to deposit my coat and purse before I head out front.

I emerge from the office as Wendell makes his way from the dish pit to rejoin Nolan in the food prep area. "Morning, Wendell."

"Good morning, Clara. How's it going?" Wendell is pretty much the opposite of Nolan, always friendly and up for a chat—to the point that he forgets to work sometimes because he's talking with other employees or customers. I always feel a little bad when I have to be the boss and tell him to get back to work.

"I'm good. A little cold, but good."

"You'll warm up fast. Today has been busy." He says before turning to jump back into helping Nolan with food.

Two of our servers come through the swinging door that leads to the dining area and grab a couple plates on the prep table. A head nod from each of them is all the greeting I get before they disappear back through the door.

I follow them out the door and step between the counters that are just to the left of the kitchen door. The counter that runs along the wall holds our drink machines—a couple coffee makers, tea brewers, and a soda machine. The cabinets underneath hold backup dishes, napkins, salt & pepper shakers, serving trays, aprons. Basically, a little bit of everything. Directly in front of the drink counter is a taller counter that has eight barstools on the other side and the POS cash register system on the end closest to the kitchen.

To get started, I decide to make another pot of coffee on the industrial coffee maker on the back counter and take the partially full pot off to pour refills. I turn to serve the closest customers first.

"Good morning, gentlemen. How are you today?" I flash a smile at the three regulars seated at the front counter.

"I'm doing well, but Paul here is a mess." Gary is the first to respond, and as usual, he's throwing his buddy under the bus.

"I am not! But I am doing better now that you're here." Paul, who I would guess is at least seventy, winks at me.

"Aww…shucks." I give him a smile while I finish filling their drinks.

"Now, now…" Rich, the last member of their trio, chimes in. "Quit forcing her to put up with your lame lines."

"You're just jealous because the ladies have always loved me more." Paul launches into a speech about how he was such a catch back in the day and how many women wanted him when he was young. I laugh as Rich heartily disagrees with every one of Paul's arguments.

Gary leans towards me and tells me something he's told me many times before. "They've been arguing like this since I met them fifty years ago. One of these days, they're going to have to realize I'm better looking than both of them."

"Good luck convincing them." I lean over to interrupt the other two. "I should get to work now, so you guys behave yourselves."

"No promises." Paul grins and waves me off.

I smile as I walk away to offer coffee refills to other customers. Those old guys are some of my favorites. They're here at least twice a week, and they're always entertaining.

When I return to put the coffee pot back where it belongs, the back wall above the counter catches my eye and makes me smile. It has an assortment of old photographs, mostly family photos from the Harpers' long history in this town. Jimmy Harper opened this diner almost sixty years ago, and his family had already been living in Rockton for a generation or two at that point. This place was Jimmy's pride and joy for over thirty years.

Eventually though, he wanted to retire and passed the restaurant on to his son and daughter-in-law. Dean and Sharon moved back to Rockton with their three sons to run the business, which they did successfully for more than twenty-five years. They loved this place and they were amazing to work for—I know that for a fact. I spent three years waiting tables here when I was in high school, and another few months waiting tables after I graduated from college last May. It was during that time Dean and Sharon decided they were ready to retire and passed the reins over to their youngest son, James.

James and I grew up going to church and working here together throughout high school with a bunch of our friends from youth group. When he took over running the diner last fall, he asked me to be the Assistant Manager. We spent the first few months learning everything we could from Dean and Sharon before they stepped away from the day-to-day.

The Harpers were like a second family when I was in high school because I spent so much time at Jimmy's, so it's pretty weird to be here all the time and not have them around. Especially on a Saturday. Dean used to love being here on Saturday mornings to make the rounds and chat with all the regulars. I'm not the only one who's noticed how strange it is without him here. Almost every Saturday, someone laments over the fact that Dean isn't around to talk to when they come in for breakfast. Clearly, talking to me just doesn't quite cut it.

I know James was right when he decided one of us should be here on Saturdays to work the crowd and be a friendly face to the regulars, but it's going to take some time before it feels normal for one of us to be here instead of Dean.

From my spot behind the counter I can see almost every table in the diner is full. Spotting an empty but not cleared table, I grab a rag from the sanitizer bucket under the counter and head over to clear it. It takes almost no time at all for me to get it cleaned up and ready for the next group, who just walked in the door.

The next couple hours pass quickly as I move around the room filling drinks, greeting customers, and clearing tables—I even spend some time in the dish pit to ensure the cooks have enough dishes and silverware to use.

With the early breakfast rush dying down, we move into the part of the morning where the number of people is steady, but not overwhelmingly busy, which is why I end up staring out the window at the dreary, gray sky when I should be clearing off tables in the front section. The sound of the door opening pulls my attention back to the stack of plates on the table in front of me. I hurry to finish cleaning the table and motion to the couple coming in the door to go ahead and take it.

"Hello, welcome to Jimmy's. Have a seat, and I'll send Scout out to take care of you." I say as cheerfully as I can, despite the stack of dirty dishes in my hand. The couple nods and takes their seats as I head back to the kitchen to dump the dirty dishes I've collected into the long, metal dishwashing sink at the back of the kitchen.

I address our newest server, Scout. "I just sat a couple in your section. They still need menus."

"On it, boss." Scout smiles as she heads out to the front of the restaurant.

I flinch at the title. It doesn't matter that I've been the Assistant Manager here for almost six months, being the "boss" still weirds me out sometimes.

"I saw that." A voice from the office draws my attention. I spot James' tall, fit frame leaning against the office door frame. I shake my head. Maybe one of these days he'll learn how to stay away from this place on his days off. I don't have proof, but I'm pretty sure he comes in and works on Sundays sometimes. We're not even open on Sundays. I opt to use the fact that he's not supposed to be here to distract him from what he saw.

"What are you doing here?" I ask, even though I know the answer.

"I have a few things I want to get done today." He grins from his place in the doorway. "Now back to what I was saying. I saw you flinch when she called you boss. What was that about?"

I shrug. "I don't know."

"You don't like being in charge? I thought you of all people would enjoy it." He turns and heads back into his desk.

I follow him into the office, annoyed with his statement. "What's that supposed to mean?"

"You have two younger brothers. I thought bossing people around would be right up your alley. Allen and Tanner always loved it."

Allen and Tanner are James' two older brothers. We grew up in the same church, but they had both moved out of the house by the time I really started hanging out with James in high school, which means I don't know them super well. Although, I've gotten to know Allen a little better recently because he and his family live in town and come in semi-frequently.

"So, you're insulting me because your brothers were mean to you when you were kids?" I challenge.

His brow furrows as he studies me, eventually shaking his head. "I didn't insult you."

"You said I was bossy. I don't think a single woman on the planet would take that as a compliment."

"I did not say you were bossy. I said I thought you would enjoy *being* the boss. There's a difference." He leans back in his chair and crosses his arms in front of him, eyes locked on mine. He's not backing down on this.

I hold the eye contact. "Not really. I still think it sounds like an insult."

"That is your prerogative. But I only meant I don't understand why you get all weird about being the boss."

"Whatever." I turn and maneuver around to my desk. I'm sure this felt like a large office when Jimmy first built this place and only had one desk in it, but at some point over the years, Dean and Sharon added a second desk and a couple filing cabinets, which makes the space a bit tight.

"That was a very well-articulated argument, Clara. I'm impressed." James shoots me an ornery smile, and for a second I see the fun guy I grew up with instead of the business man I work with every day.

I hold in my desire to stick my tongue out at him like I would have when we were in high school. I go with a slightly more mature response: an eye roll he can't see and headphones so I can ignore him while I do some work on my computer until the lunch rush begins out front.

The last six months of being the Assistant Manager here have not been what I expected when Dean and James offered me the job last summer. Even though I worked here for a few years in high school, I didn't have a clue how much time and energy it takes to run a restaurant. Even a well-established place like Jimmy's Diner takes a ton of work.

Plus, neither James nor I had ever done anything like this before, so it was quite the learning curve starting from scratch. At least he had the knowledge gained from growing up watching his parents run the diner. We both put a lot of time and effort into figuring things out though, and by the time the holiday season rolled around, Dean and Sharon had completely stepped away from all things business related, unless we had questions.

They were still in town though. Spending time with their grandkids, prepping for the massive Christmas they were hosting for Sharon's side of the family, and planning their next steps. Somewhere during that time, Sharon managed to convince Dean to spend a month or two in Arizona. He has a lot of extended family down there, and she thought spending a couple months of winter in the warm, dry weather of Arizona sounded great. They left right after the New Year. I think the fact that they left town and aren't around for backup is one of the reasons James has been spending all his down time here. Although he was working a lot even before they left town, so maybe he's just a workaholic.

Either way, this new side of James is definitely something I'm getting used to. I'm hoping the longer we work together, the better we'll understand each other. But on days like today, I think he'll drive me crazy long before that actually happens.

ᒍᒍᒍ

My feet are sore by the time the lunch rush is over, and all I want to do is curl up on my couch for the evening, but I can't. Luckily, I do have a couple hours to relax before I have to be somewhere. I was planning to run to the store to pick up shampoo and a few other miscellaneous items when I got off, but I don't think that's going to happen now. I ended up staying at work longer than I planned, which means I have less downtime than I thought I would.

"Do you have any fun plans for the rest of your day?" James looks up at me as I pull on my coat and gloves.

"I'm going home to relax for a little bit, and then the boys have a game, so mom and I are going. Nothing super exciting, but it beats working all night." I give him a pointed stare along with my response.

James looks up from his computer to meet my gaze. "I won't be here all night."

"Ha-I'll believe that when I see it." I pull my purse strap over my shoulder and fish my keys out of the outside pocket.

"I won't." His eyes narrow. He officially looks annoyed.

I guess it's time to drop this subject. "Fine. Have a good evening. I will see you tomorrow."

His head snaps up to look at me again. "You don't work tomorrow."

"Neither do you. It's Sunday. I figured I would see you at church. Obviously, I know you won't be working, since Sunday is supposed to be a day of rest and all." With that, I head out the office door before he can protest. I toss a wave to Wendell and Nolan and head out to brave the cold.

Once I get back to my house, I'm more than happy to burrow down in the covers on my bed with my chocolate Lab, Albert, curled up next to me. I pull up Netflix and hunker down for a nap with a show I've already seen on for noise.

A few hours later, I'm still lying in bed, even though I'm not sleeping, when I hear my mom calling to me from the bottom of the stairs. "Clara! Are you almost ready?"

With a glance at the clock on my nightstand, I hop off my bed and start searching for something other than sweats to wear. I wasn't paying enough attention to the time. Cameron and Carter, my almost sixteen-year-old twin brothers, have a basketball game starting in less than thirty minutes and my mom always wants to be there early.

"I'll be down in a minute!" I hurry to swap my sweatpants for jeans and pull on a Rockton High School long-sleeve t-shirt over the tank top I've been wearing. Without another thought, I grab my purse and head downstairs where my mom is wiping off the kitchen island as she waits for me.

"Sorry, I lost track of time." I offer the pathetic excuse, but Mom doesn't look upset.

"It's fine. We'll still be there before the game starts, and that's what matters." She tosses the rag into the sink and heads to the garage where her SUV is parked.

"Do you think we'll see Henry tonight?" Mom's gaze is on the house next door as she backs out of our driveway.

Henry McKinley was my best friend and neighbor growing up. We spent pretty much all of our time together as kids until Henry started getting really involved in sports in middle school. Then we sort of lost touch despite being neighbors. His parents still live next door, so the two of us reconnected last summer when I moved home. He still enjoys Rockton High School sports enough that it's not uncommon for him to show up to a basketball or football game when he can get away from work.

I shake my head. "I doubt it. Saturday's are normally busy for him at work. Although, I would bet he'd rather be at the game."

She smiles as we exit our neighborhood and head toward the school. "He's always loved sports, whether he's playing or watching. I'm actually a little surprised he didn't end up coaching."

"Me too! I suppose there's still time for him to try."

I can totally picture Henry coaching. He would love it. When we were kids, he worked with me night after night during the summer, trying to get me to be better at whatever sport he was obsessed with at the time. Unfortunately, I inherited my father's love of sports but not his athletic ability—all of that went to my brothers. Given how much time Henry spent trying to help me, I imagine he would enjoy coaching kids who actually have some skill.

When we get to the school, Mom and I make our way across the commons area and down the corridor to the gym. A small smile spreads across my face. I have some fun memories of making this trek with her when I was a little kid. My dad started teaching and assistant coaching at Rockton High straight out of college, and he's been here ever since. We came to a lot of games when I was little, just me and Mom hanging out in the bleachers. After the twins were born, it was a bit challenging for Mom to bring all three of us to a high school basketball game by herself, so there were a few years when we didn't attend many games. The older I got though, the more I could help her with the boys and the more games we got to attend.

Of course, when I was in high school, I didn't really like having to help her keep an eye on elementary age versions of Cam and Carter. Thankfully, most of my friends thought the boys were adorable, which meant they were willing to help me keep track of them.

Walking into the gym, there's an immediate and dramatic change in both volume and temperature. The music pumping over the sound system is a little obnoxious, but I've been told it helps the guys get excited while they warm up. I would bet the gym is a bit warmer than the hallway because of the large number of people packed inside. The student section is crowded. Directly next to the student section is the visitors' section, which has a respectable number of people. On the opposite side of the gym, parents and friends fill the bleachers in their Rockton blue. Mom and I climb almost all the way to the top, near the center of the bleachers and take our usual seats. Most of the people seated around us are other parents, many of whom my mom clearly knows. She jumps right into conversation with them, catching up since the last game, talking about their kids.

I listen, but most of my attention is focused on the crowd. I enjoy people watching, and a high school sporting event is such a fascinating place to do it. From where we're sitting, I have a pretty good view of the student section on the other side of the court. As usual, I see a number of teens, mostly guys, lining the front few rows decked out in crazy outfits and holding posters with words of encouragement for our team and mockery for the other team. I was never really in that group of kids. I think I was a little too nerdy for them. The only athletic activity I was involved in was cross-country because even though I didn't have enough skill for other sports, I could run.

"I don't see Hannah." I mumble once my mom has taken her seat next to me again.

"What?" She leans closer to hear me over the noise.

"I don't see Hannah anywhere." I nod to the student section where I normally spot Henry's little sister Hannah, who's a senior.

"I haven't seen her at the last couple games. Stacey mentioned the other day that Hannah has been more of a homebody the last few months." Mom replies. I shouldn't be surprised that she's talked to Henry's mom recently. The two of them have been good friends since I was little, even during the period when Henry and I weren't.

"Because of her dad?"

Mom nods. "Stacey says it's almost like Hannah's afraid to leave because she's worried she'll never see him again."

"Poor girl. I don't blame her. I would probably feel the same way." Last July, Mr. McKinley went to see a doctor about the constant headaches he was having, and they found a brain tumor. Less than two weeks later, he had surgery at a hospital in St. Louis to remove the tumor. The doctors were able to remove most of the tumor and test results showed it wasn't cancerous, but the invasive nature of the surgery left

Mr. McKinley struggling with his mobility and motor skills. He's been doing physical therapy for months now. About a week before Thanksgiving, he took his first unassisted steps since before the surgery. He keeps improving, but it's been a long, drawn out process that's been really hard on the entire family.

Mom reaches over and squeezes my hand. "Well, we'll just have to keep praying for her as well as for John's continued healing."

"Yes, we will." I agree as the buzzer sounds to start the game.

Chapter Two

After the game, I'm sitting in bed pulling my Bible onto my lap when my phone rings, interrupting my devotional time before I even start.

"Hey." I answer cheerfully when I see who's calling me.

"Hi. I hope I didn't wake you!" My good friend Eleanor says quickly.

"Nope." I glance at the clock and realize it's almost eleven, so I guess she has good reason to be slightly worried about me being asleep. "We got home from the boys' game a little bit ago, and I haven't made it to bed yet."

"How was the game?" She sounds entirely too energetic for how late it is. I may be awake now, but that probably won't be the case much longer.

"It was stressful. And they lost in the last minute, which was a bummer."

"How are your brothers handling the loss?"

I smile. El's seen them after they lose a game, so she knows how they get. "Like they normally do. They talked and argued about the game the entire way home and have been taking their frustration out on their Xbox ever since."

"Sounds about right." She laughs lightly.

"Aren't you normally in bed by now? What are you still doing up?" I'm a little annoyed she doesn't sound tired. El is a fifth-grade teacher, and she's always saying she needs as much sleep as she can get just to keep up with her students.

She laughs. "Normally, yes. I would be at home in my lovely bed, but alas, I'm still on my way home. When I get there, I plan to fall into bed and possibly not wake up for several days."

"On your way home from where? Did you have a hot date tonight you failed to tell me about?" I ask the question as a joke, but the silence on the other end makes me wonder if I'm actually right. I wait a few more seconds before trying again. "El, seriously. Were you out on a date tonight?"

"What?" From the tone of her voice I can tell she wasn't paying attention to me. "Oh…no. Sorry. I was distracted. I just dropped someone off and got a little turned around getting out of this neighborhood."

Now I'm really confused. "So, where were you?"

"Do you recall me talking about Elise? She teaches fourth grade."

I rack my brain trying to connect the name with a story I've heard before. "Is she the one you don't like or the one who thinks she's the next American Idol?"

A chuckle sounds on the other end of the phone. "Elise is the singer."

"Okay. Got it. I do remember you talking about her. Were you hanging out with her?"

"Sort of. She was actually performing tonight, so myself and a couple other teachers went to support her. We all met at eight to eat some food before she performed at nine. Anyway, we ate and hung out and cheered Elise on once she hit the stage. I know I complain about her singing sometimes because she drives me crazy with it, but she does have a great voice."

"Sounds great. Did you have fun?"

"I did. Like I said, she did great. She's very country in style, which you know isn't my favorite, but she really came alive on stage and gave a good performance. I honestly think she could make it as a singer if she actually pursued it and applied herself."

"Cool. So, where was she performing? I don't think you said."

"At Langhorne's."

That catches my attention. I sit up a little straighter in bed. Langhorne's is a local bar on the edge of downtown, which in and of itself is not super fascinating. What interests me is that Henry manages Langhorne's, so I bet she saw him tonight. "Really? How was it?"

"They have good food. We haven't been there in a while; I had forgotten how much I liked their food. Especially their fries."

I roll my eyes. She knows I was not asking about the food. "It's the brown sugar."

"What?"

"The fries. They put a mixture of salt and brown sugar on the fries, which sounds kind of weird, but it's delicious as you have already pointed out."

"Oh. Well, however they do it, I really enjoyed them."

"So, did you see Henry while you were there?" I correctly predicted he wouldn't show up to the basketball game tonight, meaning he was most likely at work.

"You mean my new best friend? Yup, I saw him." The way she says 'new best friend' sounds sarcastic enough that I get the impression she's not feeling very friendly toward him.

"What do you mean? Was he rude?" I don't care if I've known Henry way longer, if he was rude to El tonight, he's going to get an earful from me whenever I see him next.

"No. Quite the opposite. He was so friendly and outgoing. He was walking around talking to everyone, treating them like his best friends. I've never seen him like that before. It was intriguing."

I nod knowingly. At some point during the years when Henry and I weren't friends, he mastered the art of being the life of the party, especially anytime alcohol is readily available. "I'm not totally surprised. He was like that in high school."

"It was kind of fascinating in a watching-a-train-wreck sort of way."

"It is a little weird to see him like that since that's not how he is normally, but I suppose it's his job to be friendly and outgoing."

"Probably. Anyway, all my friends loved him." A thud in the background followed by what could only be wind across the microphone tells me El has gotten out of her car and is now making her way inside.

"I'm sure they did. Everyone always does." I try, and fail, to stifle a yawn.

"I heard that." El laughs. "But I don't blame you. I'm super tired myself."

"Have you made it safely inside?" I do my best to hold back another yawn.

"I am walking in my front door as we speak."

I stare at my open Bible still on my lap. I want to get at least a little bit of reading in before I go to sleep. "Okay. I'm going to go. I'll see you tomorrow?"

"Bright and early." She confirms before adding a yawn of her own.

We end our call, and I reach over to my nightstand to grab my little notebook and a pen. Someone once told me to always be ready to take notes when reading the Bible because the anticipation of learning something will help you pay attention, and you'll pick up more as you read. I'm not sure if it's true or not, but it always stuck with me. Most of the time I think it really does help me focus.

I open my Bible to Matthew 14 and start reading. Toward the end of the chapter, I come across one of my favorite Bible stories: when Jesus walked on water.

Jesus sent his disciples out on a boat so he could have time to pray by himself, and when he's done praying, he decides to join his disciples by walking on the water to where they are in the sea. His appearance struck fear into the hearts of the disciples.

> But immediately Jesus spoke to them, saying, 'Take heart; it is I. Do not be afraid.' And Peter answered him, 'Lord, if it is you, command me to come to you on the water.' He said, 'Come.' So Peter got out of the boat and walked on the water and came to Jesus. But when he saw the wind, he was afraid, and beginning to sink he cried out, 'Lord, save me.' Jesus immediately reached out his hand and took hold of him, saying to him, 'O you of little faith, why did you doubt?' And when they got into the boat, the wind ceased.

When I was a kid, this was my favorite story because I was never a strong swimmer, and I liked the idea that Jesus could walk on water and enable someone else to walk on water. As I've gotten older though, I've grown to love this story because it shows the importance of continually trusting God.

Peter heard the voice of his teacher and was willing to climb out of the boat. He trusted Jesus to empower him and to protect him. I've always been amazed by his faith. Mainly because I'm not sure I would've had the courage to step out of the boat. I hope I would, but even Peter faltered in his faith.

He took his focus off Jesus and began to sink. The part of this story that jumps out at me tonight is the question Jesus asks Peter. "Why did you doubt?"

Tonight, I feel like Jesus is asking me this question. Why do I doubt him?

The question reminds me of last summer, after I graduated from college. I had a hard time trusting God the first few months after I finished college. It felt like he was sitting by idly watching me struggle to find a job without caring or helping. Then came the job offer at Jimmy's and I realized God had a plan the whole time. I just couldn't see it.

In that situation, the answer to why did I doubt would've been fear and insecurity. I was so scared of being a failure and feeling like a failure compared to my friends, I was trying to figure out life on my own. All I focused on were the wind and waves.

With that in mind, I open my notebook and jot down a quick prayer.

Lord, I want to trust you. I don't want to focus on the wind and waves of life. Help me to keep my eyes focused on you.

ꟷꟷꟷ

Sunday afternoon comes more quickly than I expected, and I'm grateful. Both my Sunday school class and the main service at church this morning were good, as was lunch with a bunch of friends afterward, but I could use some down time today.

Pulling up to my house, I park my car on the street because the driveway is otherwise occupied—Cam, Carter, and Henry are playing an intense game of basketball. The game comes to a halt when they spot me walking up the driveway with leftover donuts from my young adult Sunday school class this morning.

"Donuts!" Cam shouts.

"Have one for your favorite brother?" Carter shoves Cam out of his way.

I laugh at their reaction. I was just as excited about getting donuts when I got to Sunday school this morning. They rotate what sort of food is set out during our class.

Donut days are always my favorite. Apparently, loving donuts is a family trait.

Cam collects himself and hustles over. "Shut up, Carter. We all know I'm her favorite."

"Whoa…all this time, I thought I was your favorite brother?" Henry pushes in between them, resting his arm on Cam's shoulder. Cam and Carter have grown quite a bit in the last year, surpassing me, but Henry's six foot frame still has a couple inches on them.

"First of all," I point to Henry, "you're not even my brother. You're the annoying neighbor kid we can't seem to get rid of. Second, there are only two donuts left, which means only my actual brothers get one. Third, you have a job and money. Go get your own donuts. And fourth, you're old enough to come to the Sunday school class these came from. If you want some so bad, you should come sometime."

Henry ignores the invitation to my Sunday school class by turning to shoot the ball. He came to my small group with me a few times last summer on the occasional night when he could leave work for a while, but he hasn't come in the last couple months. At first, he was busy helping his parents after his dad's surgery. Then he seemed to have plans every Tuesday night. Now, since our small group is moving to Thursdays, he says work is too busy for him to get away long enough to come. I'm not sure how much I believe him, but I'm trying to be respectful about it while still making sure he knows he's invited.

"Yes!" Carter pumps his fist in the air.

"Thanks!" Cam snatches the box from my hands.

"I can't believe you would gyp me." Henry complains as the twins each down their donuts in about two bites.

"You know what they say, blood is thicker than water…or sweat, in your case." Despite the fact that it's barely in the mid-thirties, Henry is wearing shorts and a t-shirt, and he's still dripping sweat.

"It's two on one. I have to work twice as hard as them." He reaches for his bottle of water on the grass. "Plus, they have that whole twin-mind-reading-thing going on. It's surprisingly hard to follow."

I smile. They've teamed up on me before, so I understand his complaint. "I'll give you that."

"So, what do you say? You want to be on my team?" Henry gives me a pleading look.

"We both know I'm no good." I respond honestly, hoping it's enough to get me off so I can go inside and maybe take a nap.

"True. However, I'm planning to use your lack of talent and affinity for clumsiness to my advantage because at least you'll be in their way, hopefully slow them down a bit." He holds the basketball out toward me, expectantly.

From anyone else, this blunt description of my poor athletic skills might be offensive, but Henry spent a lot of time trying to help me improve, which earned him the right to mock my lack of talent.

"But it's cold." I try to argue, still wanting to go inside.

"It's not cold once you start moving around." He dribbles the ball as he jogs around the driveway in a small circle and smirks. "You know there's no way out of this, right? You might as well give in now."

"Fine." I admit defeat. "But I need to change."

"Yes, you do. Hurry though. You have as long as it takes us to get more water before we come looking for you."

"Okay, okay, okay."

His voice gets quiet as I make my way to the front door. "By the way, I know I really am your favorite brother!"

I roll my eyes as I hurry off. It only takes me a few minutes to dig out some sweatpants, a t-shirt, and a hoodie to wear. The guys seem to think it's warm enough for shorts, but I don't plan on exerting enough energy for that to be a good idea.

"Clara, don't make us come up there!" Henry shouts from the bottom of the stairs right as I finish tying my shoes.

"I'm coming!" I yell back as I grab a ponytail holder to corral my too-long, chestnut brown hair and rush down the stairs to follow them outside.

The next half hour passes as I do my best to help Henry against the twins. Unfortunately, Henry's plan of me getting in Cam and Carter's way only partially worked. It was enough to help him keep the score close but not enough to win the game.

"Losers put the ball up." Carter calls as the two of them head in the front door.

Henry laughs. "Is it me, or did he just make that up?"

"Probably. But it's not like it's hard to open the garage and put the ball inside." My actions follow my words as I enter the garage and toss the ball into a bin in the corner. "How's your dad doing?"

"Pretty good. He's planning to go back to work this week. Not full-time or anything, but he's desperate to get out of the house."

Mr. McKinley hasn't worked since his surgery in August. Or at least, he hasn't gone to the office since then. In the last few weeks, he started to resume some simple duties that can be done remotely to help him stay sane as he recovers. He works for the local office of a large bank based in St. Louis and has branches all over the Midwest. From what Henry's told me, his bosses have been extremely supportive and told him to take his time recovering, but the last time I saw Mr. McKinley, he was chomping at the bit to get back to work.

"Awesome!"

He nods. "I think so. Mom isn't so sure, but she worries too much. The important thing will be for him not to wear himself out trying to do too much too quickly."

"I'm sure your mom is worried, but maybe him going back to work will be a good thing for her. It will give her some time to rest. She's been working so hard to take care of him. She definitely deserves it."

"No argument here. She's been amazing through all of this." Henry sounds like he's legitimately in awe of his mother.

I nod in agreement. "So, can he drive?"

"No, his doctors haven't cleared him yet. Mom will still be on chauffeur duty, even if she's losing some of the caregiver duties."

"Gotcha." I nod for Henry to join me inside the house. It's too cold to stand out here and chat. We enter through the kitchen and are immediately greeted by Albert, who seems to be more interested in Henry than me.

"Your dog is really weird." Henry laughs behind me.

I glance back at him to see Al licking Henry's legs. "Oh, sorry. He likes the salt."

"What?" He shoots me a confused look before looking back at Al, who is still licking his legs.

"You're sweaty. Sweat contains salt, which he apparently really likes. It's a whole gross thing…Al does it to the boys too." I pull Al away from him and lead my ridiculous dog to the back door to put him outside for a while.

Thankfully, Henry just laughs.

"I saw your friend El last night." He informs me when I return to the kitchen.

"She told me. Apparently, you are quite a popular guy when you're at work."

"What do you mean?" He refills his water bottle at the sink.

I peel off the hoodie and toss it toward the stairs to take up later. "The way I heard it, you were the life of the party. Mr. Personality if you will."

He gives shrug. "Oh…yeah. It's part of my job."

"I figured. I think it just threw El off a little. She's never really seen that side of you."

"Hmmm. What's her deal anyway?"

Now it's my turn to be confused. I shoot a raised eyebrow his direction. "What are you talking about?"

"Well, it was a Saturday night, there was good music, pretty decent food. Everybody was…having a good time."

"And by that you mean they were drinking." I clarify, trying to hide my annoyance at his notion that someone has to be drinking to have a good time.

"Yeah…and I know you're not a fan. We've talked about it, but with El it was different."

"Why do you care that she doesn't drink? You've never cared that I don't."

He leans forward to rest his elbows on the kitchen island, and I make a mental note to wipe that area off when he leaves because he's still all sweaty. "You're always chill about it, plus like I said, we've talked about it. When I offered to get her something, she got tense and super adamant. So, I was wondering if you knew what her deal was."

I think about it for a moment. "Honestly, I have no idea."

"Alright, fine. But I would bet anything there's a story there." He finishes off his bottle of water, again. I think that's the third bottle of water I've seen him drink in the last hour and a half.

"Thirsty much?" I take a seat on one of the chairs that line one side of the island.

"I've been trying to up my water intake the last couple weeks. It's one of my New Year's resolutions."

"Random, but okay. You have any other New Year's resolutions?"

He nods but doesn't say anything.

"And they are…?" I wave my hand in a circular motion trying to urge him to continue.

"None of your business."

"Ouch. That's a bit harsh."

He simply shakes his head and redirects. "What about you? Any New Year's resolutions?"

I pause, trying to decide whether or not to push him, but I opt to answer his question instead. "Yes. First off is to find my own place and move out."

"Yeah? Finally going to spread your wings, huh?" He smirks. He's baiting me, but I'm going to ignore him.

"That is the plan. I have good job, and I've been able to save some money since I moved home. But I'm really ready to be out on my own again." I deliver this statement with confidence, ignoring the doubts about my job rolling around in my head.

"Cool. How's the search going?"

I bite my lip. "Uh…"

"You haven't even started looking have you?" He laughs.

"Not really, but we're only a few weeks into the year, so I have plenty of time to make it happen."

"True. So, what else is on your list of resolutions?"

"I…um…I want to travel." The words come out slowly because this one is a little harder for me to share. It's not as obvious as wanting to move out, and I haven't really talked about it much with anyone, but it's been something I've wanted to do for a while.

"Cool. Where you going to go?" He sounds supportive, which surprises me for some reason.

"I have no idea. I just…I'm…twenty-three, and I've barely been out of the state. I want to see things. Go places. It doesn't have to be crazy or even super far away, but I want to go…somewhere…" I trail off, not sure if I'm making any sense.

"Then you should go." He says this simply, as if it's an obvious fact. "Make a list of places you want to see. Pick one and go."

"By myself?" I voice one of the concerns holding me back.

Henry shrugs again. "If you want. Or you could probably get El or Leah or what's her name—your crazy friend—to go with you."

The description makes me smile. "Kenzie isn't crazy! How many times do I have to tell you that?!"

Henry's only met Kenzie once: when she came to visit for my birthday back in October. Kenz and I were roommates and best friends in college, but she stayed in Kansas City after graduation and I moved home.

"I beg to differ. She was bouncing off the walls at your party."

"There were no walls, we were outside." My birthday party was just me hanging out with a bunch of friends in the backyard around a bonfire. It was a lot of fun, and miracle of all miracles, Kenzie managed to get time off from her job as a nurse to come out and visit. She stayed for three days and we had the best time. I was super bummed when she had to head back to KC. It's only a couple hours away, but between my work schedule at the diner and her schedule at the hospital, in addition to our commitments at church, it's been hard to find weekends where we're both free to get together. Most of the time we have to settle for phone or video calls to keep up with each other.

"A minor detail. You know what I meant." He shakes his head at me.

"I know what you meant, and I still disagree. Kenz was excited to be here. Plus, she's pretty outgoing. I don't think that's enough to call her crazy," I argue. Then, another thought comes to mind, and I continue a little more forcefully. "Also, I don't think someone whose list of best friends include Maddox Lee and Trey Coleman has any right to call my best friend crazy!"

Henry's mouth opens in protest, then closes for a moment before he actually responds. "You may have a point there."

I smile triumphantly. Maddox and Trey played football with Henry all through middle and high school, and they've always been tight. They're nice enough, but they're a bit on the wild side for me.

Henry waves off my success and circles back. "My original point was you have plenty of friends who would be up for going with you if you invited them on a trip."

"As much as I hate to admit it, you're probably right." If she could get the time off, I'm positive Kenzie would go with me because I know she loves road trips. I don't really know how El feels about travel, but I should find out.

"I know. I should get going. I'm starting to gross myself out over here." He waves a hand in front of his nose.

Thankfully, I'm too far away from him to tell how bad he smells, but given how hard he was playing, I imagine he's pretty ripe. "Sounds good. See ya later."

He gives me one last wave as he makes his way out the front door. Despite the fact that Henry is returning to his former status as one of my best friends, I'm not sad to see him go. I'm ready to go veg on the couch for a little while and relax for the rest of my weekend because I'm not mentally prepared for Monday yet.

Chapter Three

I walk in the back door of Jimmy's a little before eight Monday morning and offer a wave of greeting to Danny who is stationed at the stove, completely in his element.

"You need something to eat, Clara-girl?" Danny calls over the hum of the refrigerators and whir of the dishwashers running as I enter through the back door. Danny is pretty much the nicest, most encouraging human I've ever met. He also happens to be a total genius in the kitchen. I love getting to work with him.

"I could go for an omelet. With cheese, ham, and green peppers?" I give him a pleading smile.

"Coming right up." He flips the pancakes he's making on the stove before transferring his attention back to the oatmeal he's preparing for a different customer.

I duck into the office to drop my purse and shed my coat, then return to the kitchen to wait for my food.

Watching Danny cook is one of the more entertaining parts of my job, not just because he's so good at it but because he enjoys it so much. He hums and sings and dances around the kitchen while he works his way through the list of order tickets up on the wall. Currently there are only two, so he's not super busy, which is good because he's all on his own for the next little while. Monday mornings are one of our slowest times, so Danny can usually handle the orders by himself. It's James' responsibility to help Danny out if he needs it. I can help the staff cover things out front, but I'm not the person you want cooking the food. James is a lot better at cooking than I am.

I stand and chat with Danny for the few minutes it takes him to get my omelet together.

"Thank you!" I take the delicious looking breakfast back to the office and sit at my desk.

I spot a note taped to the top of my computer screen that I didn't see when I first came in a few minutes ago.

- Marketing ideas???
- Next week's schedule
- Inventory
- Place food order

I roll my eyes and resist the urge to crumple the To-Do list James left for me. I swear, he writes some items on my list just to make sure he doesn't forget to do something. He knows if it's on my list, I'll remind him to do it. I don't understand why he doesn't make his own list.

For instance, I've placed our food order once in the last six months, and the only reason I did it was because Dean thought it was an important thing for me to know how to do in case I need to do it in the future. Ever since James and I started working together, the ordering has been one of his responsibilities, which means I'll remind him when he gets back.

"Where is he anyway?" I mutter when I finish my omelet. I make my way over to his desk to see if there's anything to give me a clue as to where he's disappeared to this morning since he has clearly been here already.

Nothing.

I duck back out to the kitchen to check with Danny. "Have you seen James?"

Danny glances up at me while prepping a plate. "I think Jamie walked through a little while ago, but I don't know where he went. Check the front."

I proceed to the front of the diner and a quick scan of the room tells me James is nowhere in the building. Unless he's in the bathroom. I peek down the hallway to the bathroom door. No light. No James.

"Hey, Peyton?" I reach out to stop one of our servers as he heads into the kitchen.

"What's up, Clara?"

"I'm looking for James. Have you seen him?"

"Bossman was in the office when I got here to open, but I haven't seen him since."

"Alright. Thanks."

Peyton takes my response as permission to head back into the kitchen, leaving me out front by myself.

Well, not all by myself. It's slow this morning but a handful of people are seated around the spacious room. I politely smile at the older couple taking up the booth closest to the door. I can't remember their names right now, but they come in a few times a month.

It takes a moment for me to realize standing here staring out the front window isn't going to solve the mystery of where my co-worker has disappeared to this morning. I shrug off my confusion and head back to my desk. Going over the list of tasks on my desk, I opt to work on doing inventory. My brain isn't fully functioning yet this morning, so simple counting and note-taking sounds like my best option. I quickly print off the inventory sheet and head to the storage area, clipboard and pen in hand.

Our cooks try to keep a running list of items they need us to order with the next shipment. They add items once we are down to only one or two left in stock, depending on the item. However, we also do a detailed inventory every other week to ensure we don't run out of anything. It helps us keep track of which items we go through quickest. We try to keep an eye on expiration dates when doing inventory. It takes a little more time, but I think it's necessary. Which is why James finds me sitting on the floor, bent over, reaching for a jar on the back of the shelf in the food storage area an hour later.

"Why are you sitting on the floor?" His voice startles me, causing me to drop the clipboard and pen and smack my head on the shelf.

"Shoot! James! You can't sneak up on a person like that!" I rub the sore spot and sit up so I can see him.

He raises an eyebrow. "I didn't sneak up on you. I simply walked into the room."

"Well, I still don't like it."

"You'll live. Why are you sitting on the floor?"

"My obnoxious boss wanted me to do inventory, so I'm doing inventory."

"Your boss is obnoxious, huh?" He raises an eyebrow.

"Totally. He's the worst. I should quit." I keep counting and writing.

"That would be unfortunate."

I toss him a smug smile. "I know. He would be lost without me."

"I meant it would be unfortunate for you. Since your obnoxious boss brought back a treat he was going to give you."

"Really?" I turn toward him excitedly, noticing for the first time that he's holding one hand behind his back.

"Yes. But you only get it if you behave." He pats me on the head.

I swat his hand away. "I'm not a dog."

"Are you sure? The way you got all excited at the word *treat* would indicate otherwise. You looked like Albert. Maybe you're spending too much time with him."

I laugh. Al definitely does get excited when someone says the word *treat*. Mentally, I admit James may be right, even though I would never say it to him.

"I'll take your lack of smart-aleck response as agreement." James reads my mind.

"Whatever." I pretend to be annoyed, even though I'm loving that James is in a good mood today.

"So, do you want this or are you staying on the floor?" He pulls his hand forward so I can get a better look at this *treat* he brought.

It's a drink holder from Friska—a local juice and smoothie shop. I'm not normally one to enjoy super healthy foods, like smoothies and fancy juice drinks, but Friska has some delicious combinations I actually enjoy.

"You got me a smoothie?" I hop up from the floor.

James is already leaving me behind, so I have to hurry after him. I hurry a little too much though and run smack into the back of him when he pauses to open the office door.

"You seriously are like your dog!" He chuckles as we enter the office and I swipe my drink from the holder in his hand.

"What kind did you get me? It looks great." I crack the lid to smell it and maybe identify the flavor I got. All I can tell is, it's fruity.

"Try it and find out."

I take a long swig and find I was right about it being fruity, but I still can't tell what's in it. I'm sort of horrible at distinguishing flavors from each other once they've been mixed together. You would think working in the food industry would help me develop a super sense for how different foods are made and whatnot, but I'm a lost cause. James on the other hand is pretty good at it.

"I have no idea, but I like it." I shrug and step back to lean against my desk.

"I don't remember the name of it, but it's their berry energy boost smoothie. I went with their green energy boost one. It's pretty good." He swirls his around a bit before taking another sip.

"So, why did you get smoothies? Is this your way of apologizing for being obnoxious?"

"No." He gives me an annoyed look before continuing, "I drove by Friska on my way back here from dropping the deposit and thought it sounded good."

"And you got one for little ole' me? How thoughtful." I feign a southern accent and a look of surprise.

"Well, it was either get you something or listen to you complain all morning about how horrible I am for not getting you something. The monetary cost seemed more endurable than the verbal harassment you would inflict."

The look of grateful innocence on my face is quickly replaced by annoyance. "Oh, quit being so dramatic. I'm not that bad."

"Please!" James leans back in his chair and laughs. "The last time I picked up a snack for myself while I was out, I heard about it for days. Trust me, this was easier."

"Only because you got ice cream! You know how much I love ice cream. I couldn't help myself."

"Whatever." He shakes his head, but he's still smiling. "You should try to show some gratitude for this one."

Smoothie in one hand, I put on the sincerest look I can muster. "I appreciate you getting me this berry energy boost smoothie…even though my favorite smoothie is the peanut butter and banana one."

"Don't you have work to do?" He's looking through a stack of papers on his desk, but I still see a trace of a smile on his face and decide it might be best to leave him alone since he appears to be in a good mood.

"Now that you mention it, I do need to finish doing inventory since someone interrupted me." I step out of the office and head back to the storage area before he can argue with me. Obviously, it was nice of him to get me something. I definitely appreciate it, but sometimes, I think James needs someone around to help him find the humor in life.

My smoothie is gone before I finish doing inventory. Eventually though, I make my way back to the office and drop the sheet on James' desk. I double check that he is planning to put in the food order, and he is.

A little before noon, my ringtone breaks the silence in the office where James and I have been working quietly for the last few hours. I shoot a glance across the office and see James has headphones in, so I go ahead and answer the call at my desk.

"Hey, Kenzie." I answer the phone call from my best friend with a bit of guilt. I feel like I've kind of dropped the ball where our friendship is concerned lately.

"Hi." Her response is more of a whimper than an actual word.

Oh no. "What's wrong?"

"I just want one day. One day. One single day where I can go to work and not feel like a complete outcast and the mortal enemy of my co-workers."

I sigh. Kenz was so excited about the job she got at one of the hospitals in Kansas City after we graduated. However, things haven't gone the way she expected. "I'm sorry. Today's been a bad day, huh?"

"One of the worst." I can tell by the quiver in her voice that she's close to tears. A surge of dislike for her co-workers courses through me again.

"What happened? I thought your boss was going to take care of things?"

"He tried. He talked to them last week. It helped for like a whole two seconds. Then he left for a conference this week and it's gone back to the normal barrage of blatant hatred for me. I don't know what to do. I'm not sure how long I can keep this up."

"I'm sorry. I don't know what to tell you. Have you thought about transferring to a different department?"

"Yeah. I was hoping it wouldn't get to that. Plus, I don't really want to work in a different area. I like what I do. I just don't like the people. I don't know what to do."

"Is there anything I can do?" I know there isn't, but I want her to feel like someone's on her side.

"You could come visit. It feels like it's been forever since we got to hang out last. A little best friend time might make life feel less terrible."

It's a good thing Kenzie can't see my face when she says this. The involuntary grimace probably would've been a bit offensive. It's not that I don't want to go see her. I do! I just haven't been able to find a good weekend when we both have time off for me to go visit. "I'll see what I can do. Maybe I can come out for one of your free weekends this month."

"Please. Please. Please."

"Text me your days off, and I'll see if I can get them to line up with one of my off weekends. Okay?" Maybe, just maybe, we'll actually be able to see each other soon. After Kenzie and I became friends my freshman year of college, and eventually roommates, we rarely spent much time apart. The longest we were apart was Christmas break when we would both go home for three weeks. It's been over three months since we've seen each other. I don't like it. At all.

"Will do." Kenzie's side of the phone goes quiet for a second. "Thanks for listening to me complain."

"Always." I look up to see one of our servers standing expectantly outside the door, like he needs to talk to me. "I have to go, Kenz. I'll talk to you later."

"Okay, bye," she says quickly before I disconnect the call.

I wave Peyton into the office. "What's up?"

"Sorry to interrupt." He shoots a hesitant glance over at James. Then Peyton walks as close to my desk as he can and leans forward. I would be weirded out by how close he is if I hadn't seen it before. For reasons I completely understand, though I would never admit it out loud, some of the staff find

James a bit intimidating, and therefore come to me and try not to disturb him.

"Oh, it's no problem." I try to give him an encouraging smile.

"So, I need a day off next week." Peyton starts, but I stop him before he gets very far.

"Did you fill out the request online?" James and I recently decided to switch from the manual/hardcopy scheduling system his parents always used to a web-based system. The new system allows our employees to view the schedule as long as they have internet access and it makes my life easier because I don't have to keep track of people's availability or time-off requests—it's all in the program.

Peyton shakes his head.

"Do that first. If I have any questions or issues, I'll let you know." The trick has been getting everyone used to the program, which clearly hasn't quite happened yet.

"Okay." He slips back out to the kitchen.

With Peyton taken care of and Kenzie pacified for the time being, I turn my attention back to working on ideas for a redesign of all the Jimmy's marketing material. Actually, there wasn't a lot of marketing material when I started, so I'm mostly creating new material. Or at least, that's the plan. It's still in the brainstorming stages. James and I had a discussion last week to try and nail down the feel and come up with some basic ideas for me to work with. We came up with a few good ideas. Now I simply have to do the design work that will make them a reality.

That's my goal for the week: get two or three design options for marketing materials made. Whether or not I'll be able to make it happen is another story, but I've been told it's good to have goals.

Toward the end of the afternoon, a second visit from Peyton before he left for the day reminded me I needed to check in on the scheduling system. I got a little bit of design work done on the marketing material, but not nearly as much as I wanted. I'm not actually a designer. Did I take a design class or two in college? Yes. Does that make me a great designer? Not necessarily. So, the process is taking longer than I had hoped.

I've been staring at the scheduling software on the computer for what feels like forever. When I logged in to see what Peyton's request was, I found the inevitable had happened. He's not the only one who needs a change made. Another one of our employees needs a few days off at the end of the week for a family emergency.

She even included an extra comment with the request to give me an idea of what's going on and when she will be back in town. I feel terrible her family is going through a hard time, so I'm not upset with her by any means. Things like this happen, so we'll adjust.

It simply means instead of accomplishing what I had planned to accomplish today, I'm sitting here trying to find someone who will be able to cover the shifts on Thursday and Friday. If I can't find someone, it will be up to me to cover front.

Once again, I don't mind doing it, but it wasn't what I had planned. Last I checked, I only have about half an hour left in the day, and I'm still waiting to hear back from a couple of our servers about the open shifts. Hopefully, one of them will respond to the request sometime tonight, and I'll have the schedule fixed.

Suddenly, movement on the other side of my desk catches my attention. I blink and notice James is looming over my desk staring at a stack of papers, his head cocked to the side.

I pull my headphones off. "Do you need something?"

"Yes. I can't tell what this is supposed to say." He holds out the papers in his hand and points to a specific spot on the top sheet. It only takes a quick glance for me to realize it's the inventory sheet I filled out earlier. Clearly, he's putting in the food order.

"That's a four."

"A four? Seriously?" His eyes scrunch as he pulls the paper back to look at the notation more closely. "How is that a four?"

"What do you mean how is that four? It looks just like a four." At least, I'm pretty sure it's a four. It was a bit difficult to read.

He shakes his head as he takes a seat at his desk. "No, no it doesn't, but now that I know what it's *supposed* to be, I can get this order finished."

"Hey, have you talked to your parents in the last few days?"

James answers without looking up from the computer. "I talked to them Saturday. They were going hiking somewhere with one of mom's cousins."

"Hiking, huh?" I can't really picture Dean hiking.

James looks up at me. "Weird, right? My dad has never been the most outdoorsy guy in the world, but I think he's actually enjoying the down time."

As weird as it is to think of Dean hiking, it's even weirder that he's not here. They're gone. They're off in Arizona for months, doing things like hiking. It makes me sad to think about.

"So, we're really on our own now, aren't we?"

James chuckles as he continues to work on his computer. "Clara, we've been running this place on our own for months."

"I know, but that was different. They were around if we needed something or had questions."

James looks up at me and raises an eyebrow. "You do realize it's not the 1800s, right?"

"Um…yes. Why?" I don't understand the sudden change of topic.

"I wanted to make sure you knew that we've moved well beyond using the Pony Express to communicate. It no longer takes 10 days to send a message to someone in Arizona. Nor do we have to wait another 10-plus days to receive a response. We have all sorts of communication options now, most of which are virtually instantaneous. *Even if* we needed my dad's signature on something, between emailing, faxing, and overnight mail, we could take care of it in 24-48 hours, depending on the situation."

I stare at him.

"What?"

"That is so not helpful." It's not a very good comeback, but it's the best I can do at the moment. I'm too surprised by his complete lack of emotion about the situation.

"But I'm not wrong." He gives me his award-winning grin.

"So, you don't miss your parents at all?"

"We weren't talking about missing them. We were talking about running the diner without them, which we've been doing successfully for months. So, no. I'm not worried about our ability." He shrugs.

I think about it for a moment. "Fine. But you still didn't answer my question."

"About missing my parents?" He pauses for confirmation. After I nod, he continues. "I suppose I miss them some. We've been having family nights with them on Sundays at Allen and Grace's house, so those have been different without them."

Yet again, I sit and stare at him with unbelief. I don't understand why I'm so much more upset about not getting to see his parents than he is.

"What did I do now?" He sighs.

I take a moment to think about it. Honestly, I'm not even sure what to say, so instead of offering an actual answer, I simply shake my head. "Guys are so weird."

James laughs in response. "That's probably true. But I would argue that women are super confusing, which is worse."

"No we're not…" I start to disagree with him but interrupt myself. "Wait a second. What woman is making you so confused? Is it someone I know? What did you do?"

I stare him down. The possibility of James having a lady in his life, especially a confusing one, is extremely intriguing to me. He had a girlfriend when we were in high school who worked with us here at Jimmy's. I wasn't a huge fan of her because she was a bit of a slacker most of the time, which is downright frustrating even if she was super nice. I have no idea how much he dated in college because we were at different colleges and didn't stay connected. Although, I did run into him once in KC and he was with this beautiful girl, but every time I've mentioned it, he insists she wasn't a girlfriend. I haven't heard him mention anyone since being back, so I'm curious.

"I didn't…that's not what I meant." He stumbles over his words. "I wasn't talking about anyone in particular. More like, women in general are confusing. You included."

I sit up, surprised by the allegation. "Me? When am I confusing?"

"Pretty much every time you say something." He smiles.

My eyes narrow and I level him with a glare. "Rude."

"The truth hurts."

Feeling slightly annoyed, I decide to turn my attention back to working on the schedule.

"Clara?"

I glance at him and see he has a serious look on his face.

"I meant what I said about how we've been doing a good job running this place. You know? I think we've really gotten the hang of things, and while I'm sure there are still things we'll learn, I think we're ready to move forward."

"You do?" I have to say, that was not what I was expecting him to say.

He gives a quick nod. "Do you disagree?"

I pause before responding to think for a minute. One of James' primary goals when he took over for his parents was to open a second location of Jimmy's Diner. We never really talked about what his timeline was though, but I guess I was thinking it would be a little longer before we got started on it.

"Um…not necessarily." I offer the weak response.

"So, you're okay with moving forward on this?" He seems hesitant.

"I guess." I shrug, mentally deciding to go ahead and support this idea. "What exactly do we have to do to move forward?"

I don't know much about business—outside of the marketing and social media used to promote a business.

James leans forward. "Well, we start with a business proposal."

"Which is what?"

"A document I've been compiling that will list our objectives as a business and how we plan to achieve them, including a lot of records from this location. Then, I'll take it to the bank and convince them to give me a loan to get the new diner started. From there, we find a location, do a bunch of work to get it ready, hire staff, and open the place."

I nod. That makes sense. "What can I do to help?"

James gives me a kind smile. "For now, keep doing your job and maybe give me a second opinion when I need one. Later, once we're closer to opening, you'll obviously have a big part in the marketing and promotion of the new location. You know, helping me get the word out so it doesn't totally flop."

"It won't flop. It will be great. And I'm happy to help with whatever you need." I give him the most reassuring smile I can muster.

"Thanks, Clara."

I finish the day mostly pretending to accomplish things. In the back of my head, I'm too distracted by the news that James is ready to open a second location. I was just beginning to feel like I've gotten the hang of my job here and now that's going to change.

Chapter Four

Wednesday nights are one of the rare times when I have the house to myself. Cam and Carter have youth group, and my parents started doing some twelve-week class at church. The class is a new thing for them this year, so I'm reveling in this new-found freedom of having the whole house to myself at least one night a week. It makes the fact that I'm still living with my parents a little less frustrating, but not enough to keep me from wanting to move out ASAP.

After work, the first thing I did was take Al for a walk. A short walk because it's still pretty chilly outside, but he's been acting a little ornery lately because he's sick of being in the house. Apparently, being out in the freezing cold doesn't bother him nearly as much as it does me. We did a lap around the block to the park where I let him stretch his legs for as long as I could stand being outside, and then we practically ran home. It made for a good workout for Al, but now all I want is to be curled up inside for the rest of the night.

I take a fast shower once we're back inside to serve the dual purpose of warming me up and getting the smell of diner food off of me. One of the biggest downsides to working at a diner is it leaves me smelling like burgers and fries for the rest of the night. I'm not a fan.

By the time I'm out of the shower, my stomach is loudly and painfully reminding me of its existence. I'm standing in front of the fridge, door wide open, when I hear my phone buzzing.

I swipe to answer, but I don't get any words out before El's panicked voice comes through the phone. "I'm almost there. Please tell me you're home?"

I lean back against the kitchen island, still looking through the fridge. "Uh…yeah. I'm here. Did I know you were coming over?"

"I texted you a little bit ago saying I was picking up some pizza and coming over."

I shut the door to the fridge and amble over to the front door to unlock it. "Oh, I was in the shower."

"No worries. I'm just glad you're there. See you in a few." She disconnects the call the same way she started it: abruptly.

Her actual entrance into my house a few minutes later is much more graceful and proper than the hasty phone call. Despite the fact that I've told her on numerous occasions she can come in without knocking, she stands out in the cold on my porch waiting for me to come to the door.

"The door was unlocked." I let her in and almost start drooling when I catch the scent of the pizza.

El shakes her head as a response. "It goes against the rules of polite society to barge into someone else's house."

"Does it also go against the rules of polite society to show up without being invited?" I argue and head for the cupboard to get some plates out. I almost feel bad for giving her a hard time about coming over, but it's too much fun to harp on her for her love of decorum and 'the rules of polite society.'

She pauses for a moment before answering. "Technically, yes."

"Ha!" I like being right.

"However, you've told me to come over anytime I want, which would be considered a blanket invitation. Since I did tell you beforehand and I brought food, it's probably fine." She shoots me a haughty smile while opening the pizza box. Clearly, she doesn't mind me questioning her love of the rules of polite society, seeing as she's ready to defend them.

"Okay, fine. You can stay." I offer her a plate, which she happily accepts. "Now that my confusion over rules of etiquette have been answered, what's up?"

"I've been going a bit stir crazy this week, holed up at home grading. I wanted out of my apartment."

"Well, thanks for bringing pizza." I slide a couple pieces onto my plate and offer her a drink as she grabs a few pieces for herself.

It only takes a minute for us to get all the food and drinks we need and get settled onto the couch to hang out. Once we're settled in, I take a closer look at El. Ever since she walked in, something seems different.

"Is your hair different?" I finally have to ask since I can't put my finger on exactly what the change is.

The curly hair in question bobs when she nods. "Yes. It's a little bit lighter."

"That's it!" I nod as I dig into the deliciously cheesy pizza in front of me. El's hair is a lighter shade of brown than normal.

"Does it look okay?" She bites her lip, waiting for my response.

"Yeah, I like it. What made you decide to change it?"

She shrugs. "I figured it was about time."

I raise an eyebrow and take another bite of pizza.

"It's about time to return to my natural color."

"Wait, your hair isn't naturally dark?" I'm a bit surprised by this revelation since I've never seen it any color than dark brown.

El shakes her head again. "Nope. My hair is naturally more of a dark-blonde."

"Serious?"

"Yeah. I've been dying it dark since my freshman year of college, but I've decided I'm sick of keeping up with it. So, Jules is helping me slowly change it back. I didn't think I could handle it if I went straight to the blonde, so I'm easing myself into it."

"Well, it looks good."

"Thank you."

I take another bite of my pizza. "How's school this week?"

"Eh…the kids are still settling into a routine after the holidays. Plus, we had a day last week that was cancelled because of the ice storm that never happened, which definitely didn't help anything."

I nod. At the beginning of last week, the supposedly all-knowing weather people were predicting an ice storm would hit our area hard mid-week.

We've had a few of these ice storms over the last ten or so years. Some of them are really bad and cover the entire region in a thick layer of ice, leaving downed trees and power lines, roofs collapsing because they couldn't bear the weight of the ice, and horrible multi-vehicle accidents.

The worst ice storm happened when I was in middle school. It left over thirty thousand people in the area without power, caused millions of dollars in damage, and a number of people died—and that was just in the Rockton area. The rest of Missouri was just as bad if not worse.

So, when the weather forecasters predict a big ice storm, the city tends to go into end-of-the-world mode. Stores sell out of water, non-perishable foods, and generators. Businesses shut down. Traffic gets terrible. It's a bit of a mess.

The one they predicted last week was supposed to deposit a good amount of ice on the city mid-afternoon Tuesday, so most of the area schools dismissed early and cancelled school for the next day. In reality, we barely got any snow or ice and the roads probably would've been fine, but the threat is enough to send people here into panic mode.

"Hopefully, you won't have any more unexpected breaks and the kids will calm down a bit."

"That is my hope too!" El takes another bit of her pizza. "Hey, did you see Dana at church on Sunday?"

I shake my head as I try to swallow the massive bite I just shoved in my mouth.

"Me either. We'll have to corner her at small group tomorrow night."

"Yes, we will."

Our friend Dana got engaged recently, and El and I are still waiting to hear all the details of the proposal. Tomorrow night is actually our small group's first night back after the holidays. We were technically supposed to start last week, but because of the weather closures earlier in the week, the guys that lead our group ended up being swamped at work and had to cancel.

El and I are sitting on the couch, eating and chatting, when the front door opens again. I glance at the door, surprised my family is home so soon, only to see Henry not my parents. I turn back to El, "Maybe you're on to something with that whole not walking into someone else's house unannounced thing…"

She laughs.

Henry walks toward us until he spots the food on the island. "Oh…pizza!"

I open my mouth to tell him he can't have any because it's not his, but El beats me. "Dig in, there's plenty."

I roll my eyes as he grabs a piece out of the box without a plate. She's entirely too nice.

"What are you doing here?" I yell back to Henry.

"Thought I would swing by my parents' on my break. Saw you guys were here, so I thought I would say hi." He takes a seat in the overstuffed chair at the end of the couch and holds the already half-eaten piece of pizza in the air. "Thanks, by the way."

I'm a little tempted to throw the pillow on my lap at him to express my annoyance at his interruption of our hang out time; however, my mom would not be happy if I got pizza grease on her pillows. So, Henry gets off easy this time.

"How's work going tonight, Henry?" El seems less annoyed than me, or she's simply better at hiding it behind a polite smile.

"It's good. Fairly busy. The boss decided we should start running food specials each night of the week to draw in more business. So far, it's been working."

"That's good."

"I thought you were the boss?" I ask the same time El responds.

He nods as he finishes off his pizza. "I'm the manager, but the guy who owns it is the real boss. My job is to keep him happy. He doesn't come by very often, so for the most part all I have to do is keep it running smoothly, and he leaves me alone."

"Gotcha."

Henry hops up and heads back to the kitchen. "You have anything to drink?"

"No. But I bet you could find something at your parents' house," I respond, knowing full well he's going to ignore me and raid our fridge. Sure enough, he returns with a blue energy drink and a second slice of pizza and proceeds to have a nice chat with El while he consumes both.

As soon as he finishes them, he stands to leave. "I'm going to head next door really quick and say hi before I head back to work. I'll see you ladies later. Thanks for the pizza."

"Sorry." I say to El once he leaves. "Maybe I should lock the door just in case he changes his mind."

"No worries. I figured your brothers would eat whatever we didn't anyway, so I'm not upset." She waves it off.

"Want to watch a movie?"

"Not really. I've seen so many movies and binged so many shows this last week while grading, I'm a bit sick of it."

"Fine by me." I shrug. "Oh, hey. Did I tell you James has decided we are officially doing well enough on our own to start working on the new location? He's still in the preliminary stages, so I don't think he's really telling anyone yet."

"Well, that's exciting! Why do you look…not excited?"

"I don't know. I mean, I was pumped about the idea for the new diner when he first offered me the job, but he started talking about it the other day and it just feels like a lot. I was finally starting to feel like I've gotten the hang of things there. I was getting comfortable with my job, and now he's all ready to dive in to this whole other project that's going to take a ton of work and be super stressful, and I'm not sure I'm ready for it." My response spills out before I have a chance to really notice what I'm saying, and I'm a little surprised by what I hear.

This is the first time I've had the opportunity to talk about the new diner with anyone other than James, and I hadn't realized how I was feeling about all of it.

El gives an understanding nod. "I can see how you would feel like that. But it is a pretty cool opportunity to get to help with the whole process. That's not something very many people get to do, so that's good. And you like working with James…do you not like working with James?" Her statement changes to a question when she notices my face.

"Uh…well…" I bury my face in the pillow on my lap for a few seconds. "Some days I enjoy it. Some days I don't. It's so much different than I thought it would be."

Her head tilts to the side. "How so?"

"We had a lot of fun working together in high school, so I guess I thought it would be more like that. I know it can't be exactly like that now because we have more responsibility, but I was expecting to enjoy it more. Sometimes it seems like he's a totally different person."

"Well, it has been, what…like, four years? He's probably changed and grown a bit in the last few years, which isn't a bad thing."

"Yeah…"

"I imagine you've changed some as well, right?" She probes.

I nod slowly, processing El's point. "Sure, I guess."

"So, maybe make an effort to get to know him again—or at least to figure out the ways he's changed and grown in the last few years. Maybe that will help you enjoy working with him more?" She suggests with a shrug.

"I'll think about it." I nod, considering her suggestion. She may actually be onto something.

ᘏᘏᘏ

"And those are the words of a gentleman. From the first moment I met you, your arrogance and conceit, your selfish disdain for the feelings of others made me realize that you were the last man in the world I could ever be prevailed upon to marry."

"Forgive me, madam, for taking up so much of your time."

I sigh as I watch Mr. Darcy walk away from Miss Elizabeth Bennet. It doesn't matter how many times I read *Pride and Prejudice* or watch the movies, I always feel a little sad for Mr. Darcy the first time he proposes. I mean, I totally get why Lizzie turns him down—at this point in the story he's not a great guy—but her rejection is a bit harsh. The poor guy just put his heart on the line.

"Um…what the heck just happened?" Jules interrupts my mental commentary.

This is not her first inquisitive outburst, so I go ahead and pause the movie before responding. "What do you mean?"

"Why the heck would he propose? He didn't really think she would say 'yes' did he? Who in their right mind would want to marry him? He's terrible!" Jules cries in response to my confused stare.

Dana and Leah start to laugh. Before I can compose myself and offer Jules an explanation, El, our resident Jane Austen expert, takes over explaining the movie to our very confused and slightly irritated Austen newbie.

The only downside to having a Jane Austen newbie watch the short version of *Pride and Prejudice* with Kiera Knightley and Matthew Macfadyen is it moves so quickly and skips over some important plot points, so it's easy to get lost in the complex storyline if you've never read the book before.

Normally, this stop-and-start way of watching a movie would drive me nuts, but tonight I'm just glad to have all the girls together. It's been at least a month since the five of us have been able to spend time together because of everyone's busy schedules during Christmas and New Year's.

While El explains, I make my way to El's kitchen in search of a refill and maybe more snacks. Dana and Leah, who have both seen this version of Pride and Prejudice before, follow me with their empty glasses.

"Do you think we should have picked something else to watch?" Leah asks sensibly while refilling her drink.

"Maybe, but it's too late now. We're too far in." Dana shakes her head before dropping her voice to a whisper and saying, "Plus, I love the ending. The second proposal is so much better."

I nod in agreement. "I bet you're glad Adam got it right on the first try."

At the mention of her recent engagement, Dana holds her left hand out in front of her and gets a dreamy look on her face. "It was perfect."

Leah and I both wait for her to continue, ready to hear the proposal story. I keep getting snippets about how beautiful it was without hearing all of it. Hopefully, this is my chance.

"Are you guys ever coming back so we can finish this ridiculous movie?" Jules hollers from the living room.

I guess we'll have to wait to hear the full story of Adam and Dana's proposal until the movie is over.

"Yeah, we're coming. You want anything?" I call back as I grab a bag of chips.

"Yeah. I want to get through this movie." Jules settles back into her previous movie watching position and pulls her blanket around her. Clearly, she's not kidding about wanting to get this movie over with.

"Okay, okay, I'm coming." I follow Leah and Dana back to the living room. They fall into their spots on the couch with El. I take my seat in the recliner on one side of the couch. Jules is sitting on the floor with her back against the couch on the opposite end. As soon as we're all resituated with our blankets properly covering us, El hits play, and we fall back into the world of Miss Elizabeth Bennet and Mr. Darcy.

As much as I enjoy Jane Austen books and movies, I'm pretty happy to be living in the twenty-first century instead of the nineteenth century. I smile to myself remembering the list I have written in a notebook somewhere.

Why I'm Glad I Live in the 21st Century:

1. Professional Baseball – I would miss my Cardinals
2. I'm also a fan of the whole indoor plumbing thing.
3. Bloodletting is no longer a common practice.
4. Modern medicine in general.
5. TV, Radio, Computers, the Internet – pretty much all technological advancements.

6. Corsets are the worst. At least, they seem like they would be.

I also had a list about what I would've enjoyed about the Regency Era. If I remember correctly, that list wasn't as long.

As the movie continues, my focus shifts from the screen to the ladies around me. Eleanor Rimes has quickly become one of my best friends since I met her last summer. We have a lot of similar tastes and her engaging personality drew me to her from the beginning. I particularly love the fact that she is always willing to host girls' nights or just have me over to hang out when I need to escape my parents' house. I'm so grateful El is willing to share her space until I find my own.

My eyes drift over to Leah who is sitting with her legs tucked under her. Leah has been a complete gem since we were kids in Sunday school together. The long, blonde hair, kind smile, and petite frame that made her so noticeable in high school have hardly changed any. I wasn't surprised when our fellow youth group attendee, Stephen, married her a few years ago. The two of them had always been a good team.

The fact that they lead the young adult group was one of the major reasons why I was willing to check it out last summer, and I'm so glad I did. She's been such an encouragement to me the last few months since we reconnected.

Dana is newer to the church, but I'm so glad I've gotten to know her. She has an effortless sense of joy that's absolutely infectious. Simply spending time around her has helped me to become a more positive person.

Jules is the one who pushes me out of my comfort zone. Not in a bad way, but she has a unique way of looking at life that helps me see things differently. Although, she does keep pushing me to let her put a few streaks of color in my hair like the vibrant red she has throughout her long, dark locks.

I've been able to dissuade her on that so far, but she's one of the most passionate people I've ever met, which makes it hard to disagree with her.

I settle back in my chair and try to focus on the movie, feeling incredibly grateful for all of these amazing ladies.

We make it through the rest of the movie without too many more breaks.

"So, what did you think?" El asks Jules excitedly once it's over.

"It was good, I guess." She shrugs in response. "At least it had a happy ending."

El's eyes about pop out of her head at Jules' response. Since I met El last summer, I've come to learn that she adores Jane Austen. So much so that I'm a little impressed she keeps her mouth shut when Jules says this, but she's probably just practicing the good decorum you would find in the Regency era. El tends to get a little more proper when she's recently read or watched something from that time period; luckily, it doesn't last too long. She'll be back to normal in an hour or two.

Our conversation quickly turns from the love story in the movie to a real-life love story we've enjoyed watching unfold.

"So, how are things going with you two?" Leah questions, her eyes locked on Jules.

Jules fidgets a little in her seat before responding, "Things are good. Sam's a great guy."

"That much we already knew. Come on, give us a little more." Dana chimes in.

Jules laughs. "Okay. Um…I love the way he pushes me to grow in my faith. I've never really had someone who asks me the kinds of questions Sam does."

A calm quiet falls when she finishes talking. I don't know about anyone else, but I wasn't expecting such a serious answer.

"Plus," Jules flashes us a goofy smile, "he's so cute and funny, and I really love hanging out with him, whatever we end up doing."

"I'm glad. We want you to be happy." This affirmation comes from El.

"What about you, El? Any special guys in your life these days?" Leah, our happily married friend, seems to think everyone should be in a relationship.

El glances at me with a grin, "As a matter of fact, someone asked me out the other day."

"Really?" Dana jumps into the conversation with rapt attention.

"Who's the guy?" Jules leans in closer to El, as if being closer means she'll be the first to know.

"Yes." El says definitively. "Unfortunately, he's only eight-years-old, so I don't think it's going to work out."

The look of disappointment on their faces is almost too much, but El and I get a good laugh out of her story. Being that she's a teacher, and absolutely gorgeous, El gets asked out a lot by adorable little boys. She often has students offering their older brothers, uncles, and friends to her as an option for marriage. So far, she hasn't taken any of them up on their offers.

"So, Clara…" Leah pauses, opting to stare me down before asking her inevitable question.

"Yes?" I prepare to answer the same question she asks at least every other week.

"Are you sure there's nothing going on between you and Henry? Because…"

I interrupt her before she can get any further. "How many times do we have to have this conversation? There is nothing even remotely romantic going on between us. Not now. Not ever."

"But he treats you differently than he treats everyone else. We all see it. Don't we?" She turns to Dana, Jules, and El for confirmation. Dana and Jules give a quick nod.

El gives me a sympathetic look and shrugs. "Sorry, Clara, but I have to side with Leah on this. He acts different with you."

I sigh. "He's just comfortable with me because he's known me for so long. Trust me, he treats me the same way he treats his little sister, Hannah. What you're seeing is familiarity, not romantic interest. Now can you *please* drop this? I don't need everyone jumping to wrong conclusions here."

El gives me a short nod. Leah on the other hand looks less willing to give up on this particular subject.

"How about this?" I start in an effort to pacify her. "I promise you guys will be the first to know if anything ever changes in my non-existent love life. And I'm certain any developments in that area won't be with Henry."

"I suppose I can live with that." Leah concedes and moves on, much to my relief. "Dana, will you please tell us how Adam proposed? It's been almost two weeks, and I still haven't heard the full story."

With a laugh, Dana sits up and pulls the blanket a little tighter around her and starts her story.

"Well, we spent Christmas Eve and Christmas Day here with Adam's family, and it was so fun. They are such great people. But if I'm being honest, I really thought he would propose on Christmas day. When it didn't happen, I was pretty bummed. I tried to distract myself with the fact that we were about to go visit my family for a few days, which would be really fun. And it was. We had a blast hanging out with my siblings and my extended family. My dad is one of eight kids and most of them still live in the area with their families, so I have a lot of aunts, uncles, and cousins there."

"Okay, okay. We get it, you love your family. Get to the proposal." Jules has a bit of an impatient streak.

"Fine. Being around my family really helped me get past the disappointment left by the lack of a Christmas proposal. Our last day there, I said I wanted to take a walk around my parents' property one more time. Apparently, I played right into Adam's plan with my request. His proposal plan included asking me to take a walk, but he wanted it to feel spur of the moment so he hadn't said anything yet. It ended up being perfect that I wanted another walk down to the lake. When we got down to the lake on the back side of my parents property, I was in the middle of telling him some random story from when I was a kid. All of a sudden, he took my hand and got down on one knee."

We all let out squeals of excitement.

"He said all sorts of sweet things about how he wanted to start the New Year off right and the only way that could happen was if I would marry him. Then he told me he had talked to my dad, which was important to me, and my dad had given us his blessing. Obviously, I said yes, even though I was pretty much a sobbing mess by then."

"We knew that already…we've seen the pictures." Jules chimes in with a smile. She's right too. One of Dana's siblings posted a bunch of engagement photos a few days ago, and there are quite a few where Dana is crying pretty hard.

"Right. It was so sweet of Adam to have my brother take photos. I'm really happy we have them, even if I'm a mess in some of them. Anyway, we walked back to the house, and my mom had some food set out and a bunch of family was over to help us celebrate. I loved it."

El reaches over and gives Dana a side squeeze. "It sounds beautiful. And perfect."

"I'm so excited for you!" I do a weird little hand clap to release some of my excitement.

"Do you guys have any idea when the wedding will be?" Leah asks.

"After Adam graduates in May. He doesn't need the added stress of a wedding before then. So, probably sometime in June. We haven't figured out an exact date yet. When we do, I will let you guys know."

The conversation about wedding details continues for at least an hour. Leah has a lot of suggestions and tips she learned during her wedding. Jules, the hair stylist in the group, wants to talk about how Dana is doing her hair for the big day. And El and I get swept up in the fun of looking at different potential venues, dresses, and cakes. Eventually, we each start yawning and remember we have church to get up for in the morning, so we part ways knowing we'll see each other in a few hours.

Chapter Five

Sunday and Monday slip by quickly, as does the first hour of work Tuesday morning. I've been focusing on creating promotional material for February. James and I decided to offer special discounts for Valentine's Day. Now it's up to me to create materials to advertise these specials—table top displays, window signs, and all the social media posts we will need. This is the part of my job I've enjoyed the most.

This morning has been pretty quiet, allowing me to make some serious progress designing the materials. It's actually been a little too quiet. James hasn't showed up yet. He's almost always here early, so for him to be running late is strange.

It's a little past nine thirty when James finally comes into the office with a determined look on his face.

"Where've you been all morning?" I take a break from the work I'm doing to figure out what's up with him today.

"I was at the bank." He says simply as he drops his man-bag onto the floor by his desk and lowers himself into his chair.

"Were you really at the bank for an hour and a half? Or are you making that up because you don't want to admit you overslept?"

James stops shuffling papers on his desk and looks up at me. His face is broadcasting how annoyed he is right now. "Actually, I got up at five. Went for a run. Got home. Showered and got ready. Then I came here for about half an hour to finish some things up—you weren't here yet, so you obviously wouldn't know. I also picked up the cash deposit to take with me to the bank. I made the deposit, like I normally do, and then went on to have a meeting that lasted a little over an hour. It probably should have only taken half an hour, but sometimes things go long when the person you're meeting with has known you since you were a kid and wants to catch up about everyone in your family before bothering to talk about business."

His words end but he's still staring at me, annoyance visible.

"So..." I give him a hesitant smile, "...that's a 'no' to the oversleeping question?"

A frustrated sigh comes from the other side of the room. He is clearly not in a joking mood today. I will have to adjust accordingly.

I hold my hands up in surrender. "Sorry. Other than the fact that it went long, how was the meeting at the bank? What was it about?"

James' look softens a little with these questions. "It went well. Remember what I told you last week about putting together a business proposal?"

I offer a nod so he'll keep going.

"Well, I've been working on it for a while and finished it up the other day. This morning I met with Mike, the guy who oversees our account, and one of their loan specialists to talk about getting the financing for the new location. They thought the plan looked solid and gave me the preliminary go-ahead. We'll still need their final approval once we find a property, but it was an encouraging step."

"Cool." I force the one word answer out and try to make the expression on my face a pleasant one, but my brain has gone into shock. I can't come up with another response. I had no idea he was so close to actually looking at properties. I obviously knew the business proposal was in progress, but this is moving a lot faster than I expected since he's now ready to look for property.

Before my brain has a chance to catch up and ask him about his thoughts on choosing a location, he switches the subject. "Where are you on the website process?"

Sitting back in my chair, I answer him honestly. "Not very far. I've been looking into a few different website host options, but it's not really my area of expertise."

"Should we hire someone to build it for us?"

"Maybe. I was thinking about asking Leah to design the site for us, but I'm still researching."

Leah does a lot to help Stephen with the young adult group at church, but she's also a freelance graphic designer. I know she's designed a number of websites in the past—I have no idea how much she knows about the process though. I'll have to ask her the next time I see her.

"Okay. Do you have a timeline for when you want to have it up and running?" James is jotting something down on his notepad.

"We hadn't really talked about a timeline. I guess I've just been thinking we should have it ready by the time we open the new restaurant. Since we haven't really been moving forward with that, I haven't been stressing about the website."

"Got it. Go ahead and talk to Leah and start putting a little more effort into that process. I'm hoping we'll be able to get the new location up and running before summer."

"Okay." I nod and make a note to work on the website process more.

James settles in and turns his attention to his computer, headphones on. It looks like any questions I have about finding a location, or really anything to do with the new diner, will have to wait.

Thankfully, I only have to wait a few hours until the end of Danny's shift.

"You two ready for me?" Danny stands in the doorway of the office, one hand on the doorframe the other holding a glass of soda.

James waves Danny into the room. "Yeah, come on in. Shut the door behind you, if you don't mind."

Danny lowers himself onto a folding chair he grabbed from the corner.

James turns to Danny. "Alright. I mentioned to both of you that I got the preliminary approval to move ahead with plans for the new diner. Now, I need find the right property. Before I meet with a realtor, I wanted to pick your brains a bit."

"Pick away." Danny leans back and props his left ankle on top of the opposite knee.

"The goal is to find a building larger than this one. We want more seating, plus enough space to add a party/meeting room toward the back. So, what I need to know from you is how big the kitchen would need to be to effectively serve more people."

"Okay. How much bigger are you thinking? In comparison to what we have now. Is it going to be slightly bigger? Are we doubling in size?

"My goal is between one and a half to two times the size of what we have here. It will depend on what kind of properties are available, but that's my hope."

Danny leans forward and sets his cup of soda on the floor. He grabs a pen and paper off my desk and starts talking and writing at the same time. He and James discuss square footage needs and how to design the kitchen in a way to allow for better flow and help the cooks be as efficient as possible.

The two of them bounce ideas off each other while I mostly listen because I know basically nothing about kitchen design or square footage, plus I think it's fun to listen to what they're coming up with during this little brainstorm session. It's obvious, even to me, that some of the ideas they come up with won't happen because they're too crazy and expensive, but it's cool to see them dreaming and imagining about the new diner.

They continue throwing ideas and suggestions back and forth for almost forty-five minutes before James redirects the conversation a bit.

"That gives me a much better idea of what to look for and how the kitchen will work. Now, I would love both of your opinions about the rest of the diner as well. Things you like about our current setup, aspects that would need to be different—I want to hear your thoughts."

"We will need more space for bathrooms." I say simply, thinking it's the most obvious area that will need to change. At least, it was the first thing that came to mind as I've been sitting here listening to them talk about how much bigger they want the new diner to be.

"Go on." James is ready to take notes if he decides my idea are worth it.

"The single-occupancy bathrooms we have here are sometimes not enough for this building. They're good-sized and handicap accessible, which is great, but there are a lot of days when we could use a few more stalls. So, if the new diner will be larger, we will definitely need more stalls in each bathroom."

"Makes sense." James jots it down on his list.

"And we have to make sure the bathroom is designed well. Nothing is worse than when they put the toilet paper dispenser down so low you have to be a child to reach it. Or when the stalls are super tiny because they were trying to cram more into the same amount of space. We need multiple stalls, but we have to make sure they aren't too cramped. And please don't make us use automated hand towel dispensers. Those things never work right. Do the ones you pull the towels out or the air dryers…Why, why are you looking at me like that?" I pause my rant when I realize James is staring at me with a peculiar look on his face. "What…what's wrong?"

Instead of responding, James begins to chuckle and shake his head. I turn to Danny for an explanation to find him trying to contain his laughter as well.

When James' stare first interrupted my train of thought, I was confused. Now, I'm getting more frustrated and self-conscious by the second as the two of them continue to laugh at me. Crossing my arms in front of me, I wait for an explanation while I nervously chew on the inside of my bottom lip.

Danny must sense my discomfort because he quickly regains his composure. "Sorry, Clara-girl. We don't mean to laugh at you."

"No, we don't." James calms his laugh down to an exuberant smile. "You have such strong opinions about the bathrooms, and for some reason, it struck me as really funny."

I think it over and decide everything I said was good advice, even if I got a little carried away in my delivery.

"Come on Clara, you have more ideas. What are they?" James is trying to make up for laughing at me by asking for my opinion and offers me his award-winning smile to prove he's listening. "Maybe about something other than the bathroom this time."

I narrow my eyes and stare at him, refusing to smile. "Make sure there's enough storage. I know Danny mentioned the proper amount of food storage, but I'm talking about everything that's not food. For instance, I know we don't necessarily need a front counter like the one we have here, but I think it would be great if we could have one in the new diner because it provides a good amount of storage."

"Okay." James is making notes on his piece of paper.

"What about you? What do you think?" I pose the question to James.

"I think both of you have given me some good ideas." He smirks. "At least, most of them were good."

I crumple a piece of paper on my desk and throw it at his face. "Whatever. Where do you want the diner to be? I assume you have some actual thoughts."

"I do. Um…let me pull up a map of Rockton." He clicks a couple of times and turns his computer screen toward us. Danny and I both move closer to see it better. "Obviously, our current location is in the northeast part of the city, so my goal is to go further south, probably more toward the west side of town. That way the two locations end up being in very different sections of the city and draw their customers from different pools of people."

"Makes sense to me." Danny claps him on the back. "I was a little nervous about this at first, but the more I hear you talk about it, the better it sounds."

"Thanks, Danny."

"You need me for anything else?"

James shakes his head. "Nah. I think we're good for now. You can head out. Thanks for sticking around."

"No problem. I'll see you kids tomorrow."

Feeling pretty good about how our conversation went, I venture to ask the question that's been forming in my head since our first chat this morning. "So, you're going to look at some properties, huh?"

"Yeah. I think I'm going to look at a few places later this week."

Again, wow. This is so fast. But that's not really what I'm wondering about right now. "By yourself?"

"No. You know Mr. Simmons from church. He does commercial realty. I talked to him a couple weeks ago about helping me out and gave him a call on my way back from the bank. He told me to get him some ideas about size and location," James waves the paper he was taking notes on during our chat with Danny, "and he would have some options for me later this week."

"So, it's just going to be you and Mr. Simmons going to look at these properties?" I continue to prod, hoping to get an invitation to join them.

"Yeah. Once we find some good options, I'll probably send them to my dad to see what he thinks about them."

"Got it." And I do. I get it. I'm not invited. My opinion about the locations is not wanted or needed.

ꝏꝏꝏ

I've never been more grateful to leave work early than I am when I take off at 1:30 Friday afternoon. As soon as the bulk of the lunch rush is over, I head out because tomorrow is my Saturday to be here. This whole week has been so frustrating for me. James has been looking at properties online and he even went out with the realtor to check out a few in-person yesterday. No matter how much interest I show in being involved in the search, James seems determined to keep me out of it, which made for some seriously aggravating conversations.

I try my best to push all thoughts of Jimmy's and the new location out of my head when I leave. Lunch was pretty busy, so I spent about an hour out front helping the servers. I was honestly a little relieved to be out with the customers because it makes time go by faster.

Now, I have a few hours to kill before I'm supposed to go over to hang out with El at her place for the evening. I head home to grab some food and relax, but after getting a quick snack, I really want to get out of the house and decide to go see an afternoon movie. A new faith-based film came out last week that I was interested in seeing, and going on a weekday afternoon means it will be half the price.

As I'm walking to my car after the movie, which was fairly decent, I get a text from El saying she's picking up food and heading to her apartment. She has perfect timing. I skipped getting popcorn at the theater because it's so expensive, but the light lunch I had a few hours ago has left me feeling pretty hungry.

El is walking up the stairs to her apartment when I pull into the parking lot of her apartment complex. It doesn't take us long to get inside, get our food, and settle onto our separate ends of the couch.

"How's the book?" I ask once we're seated. One of El's New Year's goals was to read more classic literature, and her first pick was *Oliver Twist* by Charles Dickens. Last I heard, she had just started it.

"A bit depressing, but it's an interesting read. It took me a while to get into it, that's for sure." El gives a brief update.

"How far into it are you?"

"I'm maybe half way through. Have you read it before? I don't remember what you said when I asked you."

I shake my head. "Nope, but I've heard enough about it that I have a basic understanding of the story. From what I've heard, it's not a very cheery book."

"That's an understatement if I've ever heard one. I think that's part of why it's been so slow-going to read it: it brings my mood down a bit every time I read some of it."

"You could always give up and start another book." I offer what seems to be the most obvious solution.

"No. I want to read it. I'll just have to push through to the end, even if it's a bit sad."

"So, you're saying it's not as much fun as reading Jane Austen?" I smirk as I ask.

El laughs. "I wish I was reading Jane Austen instead. I like her stories a lot better. For the most part, they're not this depressing."

"I know. By the way, I wanted to let you know how proud I was the other night."

She shoots me a confused look. "What on earth are you talking about?"

"You didn't freak out when Jules said she didn't love *Pride and Prejudice*." I laugh.

"Thanks. I was pretty proud of myself for that too." She says with a giggle.

"But, don't think I didn't notice your eyes almost popping out of your head." I do my best impression of the shocked expression she wore last Saturday.

"Oh stop. I wasn't that bad. At least, I hope I wasn't." El bites her lip for just a second before brushing it off. "Either way, I enjoyed watching the movie, even if Jules didn't."

"I did too." I settle back into the couch.

A relaxed quiet settles around us as we clean our plates. This is one of the things I love most about El, she's okay with silent moments when we hang out. I've always assumed it's a by-product of her being an only child. From what she's told me, she didn't have a ton of friends and no siblings to play with growing up, so she's used to the quiet.

I'm pretty much the opposite. I always had either Henry or my little brothers around, so the calm and quiet tends to get to me before it gets to her.

Sliding even further down on the couch, my eyes close as I feel my body begin to relax even more. I'm almost asleep when movement from El's side of the couch pulls me back. I crack an eye open to see she's taking both our empty plates back to the kitchen.

"I can help." I move to get up, but she waves me off.

"I'm already up and it's almost done. You just sit there and relax. I told you this evening would be low key and I meant it. Feel free to rest while I clean up a few things in here." El disappears into the other room, and I can hear her shuffling around putting the leftovers away and hand washing the few dishes we dirtied.

Part of me feels like I should follow her and insist on helping her clean up, or at the very least, talk to her while she does it. But her couch is really comfortable and I'm tired. So, instead, I pull my bare-feet onto the couch and snag the blanket hanging on the back of the couch to curl up under. For the next fifteen or twenty minutes, I doze on her couch while she's working in the kitchen. When she finishes in the kitchen, I hear her move into her bedroom.

"What are you doing in there?" I call out sleepily.

"Trying to decide if I like the clothes I got this week." That piques my interest. I use all my energy to get up off the couch, with the blanket still wrapped around me, and make my way into her room.

"I love the sweater. I don't love the pants." I offer my opinion of her outfit as I take a seat on the edge of her bed.

She shoots an annoyed look at me.

"What?" I glance down at the bed, just in case I sat on an outfit or something.

"I've had these pants for two years. They're one of my favorite pairs."

Oops. I really should pay more attention. "Oh…sorry. I mean, they're not bad. I just don't love them with that top?" I try to back-pedal the insult I just threw down, but she's not buying it.

"It's fine, Clara. You don't have to love my pants. I love them." She continues to turn back and forth in the mirror, looking at the sweater from different angles.

"You should definitely keep the sweater." I stifle a yawn.

"You think?"

"Yup. What else did you buy?"

El swaps the sweater out for one of the cute dresses she purchased yesterday. She has a couple large bags of clothes sitting on the floor by her closet.

"So, what's with the shopping spree?" I'm a bit surprised she went and bought so much stuff at once. She tends to be much more of a saver than a spender.

"I had an extra check from the library sitting around waiting to be spent. I've been wanting to update my wardrobe for a while now, so I thought it would be a good use of the extra cash. Everything I bought was on sale."

I give an understanding nod. El spends her summers off working part time at the public library. She ended up picking up a couple shifts over the Christmas break because so many employees were either out of town or caught the flu, leaving them short-staffed.

"I'm glad you used the extra money for something fun. That's how it should be." I give her a smile. Glancing around the room, I notice a small, worn out stuffed elephant sitting at the head of her bed that I've never seen before. "Where did this little guy come from?"

A gentle smile crosses her face when she sees where I'm pointing. "That's Peanut."

"He's cute. Where did you get him?" I reach over and grab the elephant.

Sadness flashes across her face for half a second, but then a soft smile appears. "My dad gave him to me when I was maybe ten. It was a birthday present. At least that's what he said when he gave it to me. In reality, it was over two months late. I didn't tell him though. I was just excited he was home. Plus, it was one of the only times I ever got a birthday present from him. He wasn't very good at remembering." El gets quiet for a second. "Anyway, I was going through some boxes last week and found Peanut. I decided he needed some fresh air, so he's been hanging out on my bed."

"Well, he definitely picked a cute one."

"Yeah, he did." She takes Peanut from me and strokes the soft fabric a few times before returning him to his spot by her pillow.

El doesn't talk about her family often, especially her dad, so I'm slightly surprised to hear her talk about him tonight. In the eight months or so we've been friends, I've only learned a few things about her childhood. Like the fact that she never knew her mom and her dad wasn't around much either, so she was raised by her grandma, her dad's mom. I'm not even sure her dad is still alive. She's only mentioned him a few times and always uses the past tense, which makes me think he's not.

I figure she'll tell me about it when she wants to, and until then, I'm trying not to pry too much.

Instead, I go with the flow when she decides to go back to evaluating her clothes. We move past the items she got on her shopping spree and start going through the clothes in her closet. It appears El is taking this wardrobe update seriously and she wants to get rid of anything she doesn't really like or wear. The evening passes as El models various outfits, asking for help making decisions about what to keep in her closet.

The text alert on my phone goes off and once I open the photo from my mom, I turn the phone toward El. "I forgot again."

Upon seeing the photo, she laughs. "Don't worry about it. I'll get it back eventually."

The photo is an empty Christmas platter from when El brought some beautifully decorated, festive cookies to my house when she joined us for Christmas. She left it that night so my brothers could finish all the cookies. The platter has been at my house ever since. My mom occasionally reminds me that I'm supposed to return it to El, but I have yet to remember to do it.

"At least the cookies were a hit with everyone." I offer the compliment with a shrug.

"I'm glad I made a double batch. I knew your brothers could pack food away, but at first, I wasn't sure the cookies were even going to make it through the day the way those two dove into them." She laughs. "Hey, how have things been at work this week? You didn't really say much last night at small group."

I let out a loud sigh and lay back on her bed. "Yeah…that's because it was frustrating and James is making me crazy, but I felt bad complaining about him to everyone since he's friends with a lot of them and wasn't there to defend himself."

"How mature of you." She grabs my hand and pulls me up to a sitting position again. Then takes a seat on the bed next to me. "So, what's he doing to drive you crazy?"

"You know how I told you he decided we're ready to move forward with plans for the new diner?"

"Yes." She nods.

"Okay, so he met with the bank on Tuesday and got a preliminary go-ahead to begin looking for properties."

A look of surprise crosses El's face. "Wow. That's big news."

"It is. Or at least, it would be if he had any intention of letting me be a part of it, but he doesn't. And not only is it frustrating, but I'm starting to question why I'm even there in the first place."

Chapter Six

El raises an eyebrow. "What do you mean?"

"Well…I thought Dean and James brought me on as the Assistant Manager to help James as he opened this new location. I thought we were going to be a team, you know? I thought it was a total God-thing when they offered me the job, but now I'm not so sure…" It's the first time I've verbalized the thoughts running through my head.

"Okay." El pulls her legs up and crosses them underneath her. "Last week, you didn't seem very excited about the new diner and now you're upset you aren't involved, is that right?"

My reaction is immediate and defensive. "I was just surprised last week when he dropped the news. Maybe a little overwhelmed because I wasn't expecting it, but that doesn't mean I don't want to be a part of it. I needed a few days to wrap my head around the idea."

"Alright. Calm down. I was simply asking." She gives me a kind smile that convinces me to take a deep breath and relax a little. "So, did James say he didn't want your help finding a location?"

"Not in so many words. He did, however, ignore all of my attempts to get involved."

El scrunches her nose up. "I'm sorry. That stinks. I can see why you're frustrated, but are you serious when you say you're not sure about working there?"

I throw my hands up in defeat. "I don't know. I really thought working at Jimmy's, with James, was where God wanted me. The whole situation when they offered me the position seemed like it was the right fit. Now, I'm beginning to question that."

"Why?"

"There's no point in me being there if James is going to shut me out. One of the biggest reasons it seemed like a good fit was because I thought James and I would work well together. That hasn't been the case though."

"What are you going to do?" El's question may be a simple one to ask, but I have no idea how to respond.

I lay down again before responding. "I'm not sure yet. If working at Jimmy's isn't right, I have no clue what my next step would be. I literally cringe at the idea of having to get back into the job searching and applying process. I don't have much more of a clue as to what I want to do with my life now than I did last summer. Especially since for the last six months, my focus has been on the diner and learning everything I could about running it."

"Could you apply what you've learned to another job?"

"I don't think I want to stick with working in the food industry if I leave Jimmy's."

"Then I guess we'll just have to pray about it and see what happens."

"I guess so." I cover my face with my hands as another deep sigh escapes me.

She stands and returns to trying on clothes. After a few moments, she says quietly, "Hey, Clara."

I sit part of the way up and uncover my face enough to see her. "Yeah?"

El is wearing an expression of curiosity. "As a kid, what did you want to be when you grew up?"

I drop my head back onto the bed, a laugh bubbling up. "A shortstop for the St. Louis Cardinals."

"Really?" She laughs.

"Yup. That is, until I realized I have almost no athletic ability. Kind of shot that dream in the foot."

"I'll bet. What about after that?" She continues to probe.

"Um...after that..." I have to think for a second before the memory returns. "After realizing I couldn't play for the Cardinals, I decided I would work for them instead."

"Doing what?"

I finally sit up and face El. "Back then, I think the plan was to become the GM because the general manger is responsible for which players are on the team, and I thought that sounded fun."

"Would you still want to work for them?"

"What? Are you kidding?! Of course I would work for the Cardinals! They're my team! I love them." The enthusiastic response spills out of me before the real answer. "But those are the kinds of jobs you have to have connections to get. I'm sure you have to know people to even be able to intern there for a season. It's not a real option."

"Says who?" She challenges.

"Says...anyone who knows anything about how the sports world works."

El shakes her head. "I don't believe it. I mean, your degree was in what? Journalism? Right?"

"Journalism and Mass Communication." I answer, knowing there's no use holding out on her, even if I know what she's proposing will never happen.

"And you worked at a radio station?"

"I did."

"Sports teams have radio announcers..." She starts but stops when the shirt she was trying on gets stuck as she's pulling it off.

I use the wardrobe-related pause to respond before she can keep going. "I *really* can't do that."

Maneuvering out of the shirt, she turns to me. "Obviously. You don't have an annoying, old-man, radio voice. But I'm sure there are people who work with those announcer guys. Plus, an organization that size has to have a bunch of people working in their Communication or Public Relations office. You could totally do that."

"I appreciate the vote of confidence. I still don't think it's going to happen."

"Come on..." El begins to protest, but I hold up a hand to interrupt her.

"However, there are probably other jobs around here in the Communications field that I could look into doing."

With that, El seems pacified that I'll look into some communications jobs in the area, and I manage to divert the conversation to another topic for the next little while. Before too long though, I have to head home. It may be a Friday night, but I have to work in the morning and shouldn't be up super late.

By the time I get home, the emotional strain of questioning my job and wondering about my next steps has caught up with me and all I want to do is crawl in bed. But I haven't done my devos yet, so I slip into pajamas, grab my Bible and notebook, and drop into my comfy reading chair. If I crawl into bed right now, there's a good chance I'll fall right to sleep. My reading chair is still pretty comfortable, but at least I'll be sitting upright.

I crack open my Bible and land at Psalm 16, which is captioned *You Will Not Abandon My Soul.* I was going to continue my New Testament reading plan tonight, but this sounds applicable. The last verse of the chapter captures my attention.

> "You make known to me the path of life;
> in your presence there is fullness of joy; at
> your right hand are pleasures forevermore."

What feels like my millionth sigh of the day passes through my lips, but this one isn't filled with stress and anxiety. It's filled with relief. God will show me the right path. He will bring me to a place of joy if I follow him. My eyes go back up the page to read the last few verses again, and the eighth verse adds some instruction.

> "I have set the Lord always before me;
> because he is at my right hand, I shall not be shaken."

Lately, my certainty about my job has disappeared and my confidence has definitely been shaken, but these verses remind me God has a plan, even if it's not what I expected. Even if it means leaving Jimmy's, the Lord will be with me. All I have to do is pursue him and follow where he leads. Instead of my normal notes or lists, I fill a clean page of my notebook with truths from this passage of scripture.

I will take refuge in God.
I will follow where he leads.
I will live a life of joy.
I will set the Lord before me.
I will not be shaken.

I dog-ear the page in my notebook so I can find it easily. I have a feeling I'll need to remind myself of these statements of faith over the next few weeks as I pray and try to make a decision about my job.

After putting my Bible and notebook away and turning off my light, I crawl into bed expecting to drop off to sleep quickly. Despite feeling more peaceful than I have all week, I spend at least twenty minutes staring at the ceiling trying to fall asleep.

I've tried to push El's words out of my head ever since she said them earlier, but my curiosity gets the better of me. I reach over and grab my phone from where it's charging on my nightstand and open a new page in the internet browser.

It only takes a few minutes to search for and find a list of jobs currently open in the St. Louis Cardinals organization. Not surprisingly, there's nothing of note listed. Just ongoing openings for the summer in their food service and day-of-event areas. Pretty much what I expected. Not quite ready to give up though, I search their website for a list of office personnel and peruse the list of people who currently work in their Communication office, reading the individual bios for jobs that sound like something I could do.

Most of the bios I read include a long list of previous experience, all of which are a little bit different. Returning my phone to its spot charging on the nightstand, I lean back into my pillow and continue staring at the ceiling. Thinking. Wondering if it might be possible for me to get a job working for the St. Louis Cardinals someday. It would be pretty cool if I could. There were definitely employee profiles on the site who have jobs that sound interesting. The key seems to be I need more experience, specifically I need more experience directly related to the communications field.

My intense study of the ceiling continues for a while as I consider what sort of jobs I would have to pursue in order to gain the kind of experience needed to land a job working in the Cardinals Communications office. Henry's friend Trey works for a marketing and advertising company, so maybe a job somewhere like that would help me develop my résumé. Or possibly finding a position with a news company in the area, whether it was with TV or newspaper or radio probably wouldn't matter as long I was working in the field.

The late-night brainstorming session lasts a lot longer than it should and by the time I'm finally drifting off to sleep, I am not looking forward to getting up for work in the morning because I'm going to be so tired. I am, however, looking forward to checking into some of the job ideas I've come up with over the next few days.

Thankfully, Jimmy's was busy Saturday morning during my shift, so the time passed quickly and I didn't have to spend much time in the office with James. I even ended up staying longer than usual just to help the servers keep things running smoothly in the front.

A quick shower followed by a nap are my immediate response when I get home Saturday afternoon. By the time I wake up, it's getting dark outside and the house is pretty quiet. I slip downstairs with Albert at my feet to see what my family is up to this evening.

"Hey, kiddo." Dad gives me a high five when I walk into the kitchen.

I cover my yawn. "Where is everyone?"

"Your brothers are hanging out with a couple of the guys on the basketball team. Your mother stopped at the store for something, but we are going to see a movie once she gets home. You're on your own for the evening."

"Sounds good to me." I give him a big smile.

"Yeah, I thought you might like having the house to yourself." Dad heads down the hall that leads to the office and my parents' bedroom.

I head to the living room and drop onto the couch and start flipping through channels. Mom and dad leave for their movie while I'm watching an episode of *Property Brothers*. When it ends, I flip over to Hallmark to watch their Saturday night movie. It's almost over when my phone starts ringing.

I glance at the screen and see Carter's name pop up.

Ignore.

Carter pocket calls me all the time. He never actually calls me because he prefers texting, so I've learned to ignore his calls since it's always an accident.

A few seconds later, it starts ringing again. And once again, it's Carter.

I sit up a little straighter. It's rare to get two pocket dials in a row, so now I wonder if something is wrong. "Hey, you okay?"

"Can you come get us?" Short and to the point. That's Carter.

"Right now?" I glance at the clock and then to the TV where my movie is paused, waiting to be finished. This is one part of living with my parents I'm not a huge fan of: giving Cam and Carter rides. I can't wait until they turn sixteen and get their licenses in a few months!

"Yeah. I tried mom and dad, but they're not answering." Now he sounds frustrated.

"They went to a movie. I thought you were hanging out with some guys from the basketball team tonight? Why do you need me to pick you up?" Cam and Carter have always been the ones to stay out as late as their curfew allows.

Carter makes a sound that's somewhere between a sigh and a cough. "We're at Ryan's, but…let's just say he invited a few more people than we anticipated."

With that statement, the reason for his call becomes clear. The hang out night at Ryan's has turned into a full-blown party, and my parents have pretty strict rules about parties—and harsh punishments for breaking said rules. No wonder he's calling for a ride home.

"Text me Ryan's address. I'll let you know when I'm close and you guys can meet me outside."

"Deal." The short response is all I get before he hangs up.

I shove the blanket off and shuffle into the kitchen where I slide my feet into a pair of my mom's slippers sitting by the door and grab the spare key to her car. My purse was still sitting on the steps where I dropped it earlier, so I grabbed that on the way into the kitchen.

"Want to come?" My talking-to-my-dog voice is alive and well in the question I pose to Albert, who followed me into the kitchen. He comes over and stands by the door, which I take as a yes.

I let him into the garage, and then wait for him to hop into the back seat before hitting the button to open the garage door. It takes me less than twenty minutes to get to Ryan's place, and the boys are waiting outside, as expected. I'm a bit relieved. I really didn't want to wait long. Especially since this party seems to be growing by the second.

"Thank you for choosing The Evans Family Car Service for your travel needs this evening. We hope you enjoy your ride, and please remember to tip your driver," I say in my best flight attendant voice once they're both settled into the backseat with Al who is licking both their faces.

No response.

"Seriously? Nothing?" I turn back to look at them. "I didn't exactly expect tons of laughter, but no reaction whatsoever? What's the deal?"

"Nothing." Carter is not feeling very chatty tonight.

"Thanks for the ride." At least Cam manages to put together a full sentence.

"Okay, then." I turn back around and turn the radio up as I pull away from the curb.

"Can we stop at Jimmy's? We didn't really eat dinner." Cam asks before I even make it to the end of the street.

I don't typically like going to work when I'm not working, but I'm feeling a little bit proud of them for making the choice to leave once things got crazy at Ryan's. "Sure. We'll have to get it to-go because Albert's with us."

Cam simply nods and continues to pet Al. Carter doesn't respond at all, he simply stares out the window.

When we pull into the parking lot, I glance in the rearview mirror. "Can one of you stay in the car with Al? I need to…"

Carter interrupts me before I have to explain why I want to run inside. "I'll stay."

Two words from Carter isn't much of an improvement, but I'll take it.

"Thanks." I hop out and head in the front doors, with Cam on my heels. I wave to Josh, one of our servers, who is leaning against the back counter. "How's it going tonight?"

"It got pretty quiet about half an hour ago." He pulls his order pad out. "What can I get you guys?"

Cam rattles off a rather long list of food items. Sometimes, I'm still caught off guard at how much food the two of them can eat in one sitting.

"And we need that to-go, please. Thank you." I say as Josh heads into the kitchen. He gives me a short nod and disappears through the door. I turn and head down the hallway to the bathroom, which is the real reason I came inside.

Once that is taken care of, I take a seat on one of the stools at the counter next to Cam. "So, what's with Mr. Grumpy-pants?

He glances out toward the car before answering. "Some of the guys were giving us a hard time about leaving so early."

"Want me to beat them up?" I give him a smile.

Cam cracks a smile. "Maybe some other time."

"Okay. Let me know." This time he simply shakes his head at me. "So, if they were giving both of you a hard time, why aren't you as upset as him?"

Cam shrugs. I keep staring, waiting for him to answer.

"I guess I don't care about their opinions as much as he does." He says a few moments later.

"So, he's upset the guys were giving you a hard time?"

"Yeah." Cam nods, but I can tell that's not all there is to this.

"And he blames mom and dad? Because their rules are the reason he's being made fun of?" I offer my best guess.

Cam looks out toward the parking lot, avoiding eye contact. "Maybe."

"That's understandable." I nod.

I half expect Cam to question me, but Josh appears carrying our food. I pay him and take the smallest of the three bags he brought out. Cam grabs the other two, and we head back out to the car and dump all three in the front seat so Al can't get to them.

The radio is the only sound for the first few minutes of the drive before I think of something I forgot to ask earlier. "Did either of you text mom and dad to let them know I picked you up?"

"I did." Cam nods.

Relieved our parents won't get out of the movie and freak out because they missed a bunch of calls from these two, I move on to my next subject.

"Hey, Carter?" I wait for him to meet my gaze in the rearview mirror. "What do you want to do after high school?"

"What?" His face scrunches up, clearly not expecting that question.

"What do you want to do after you graduate?" I repeat myself.

"Play baseball." He responds in a tone of voice that tells me the answer was obvious.

I'm glad it's too dark in here for him to see my smile in the rearview mirror. I was counting on that being his answer. I follow it up with another question I already know the answer to. "College or Minors?"

"Minors."

I catch Cameron rolling his eye at Carter's answer, but I choose to ignore it and stay on track. "How does that happen?"

"What do you mean?" Carter leans forward, I think I have his attention now.

"You have to be drafted or something, right? How does that happen?"

"Yeah, the goal is to be drafted, which involves scouts and tryouts and stuff to even get a shot at it. Then, you have to prove you're good enough."

Carter keeps talking about the process as I finish the short drive home. With a strategically placed question or two from me, he continues to go on about what it takes and his plans for making it happen even after we get inside.

They both drop onto a stool at the island and dig into their food.

"What it all boils down to is you need to keep playing baseball? As much as you can, right?"

Carter nods, his mouth stuffed with fries.

"So, the opinion of say, some jerk seniors on the basketball team, really won't have any impact on what you want to do with your life, right?"

Carter simply stares at me for a moment. His chewing slows. He's thinking. Maybe trying to come up with an argument to the contrary, but I decide to keep going.

"And mom and dad are probably just looking out for you and your dreams when they set rules to, hopefully, keep you out of trouble. Because if you get in trouble—with either the police or the school—you wouldn't be able to play for the school team, which would hurt your chances."

He swallowed his food, but he still doesn't say anything. Instead, he stares at his burger.

"I'm not saying it doesn't suck that those guys are being jerks. I'm just saying, maybe their opinions shouldn't matter that much. And maybe, the two people who have cheered you on at every single baseball game and completely encouraged your crazy dream might not be the ones you should be mad at. Just a thought."

Carter's attention is focused on his food. I assume he's either mad at me or he agrees with me and doesn't want to admit it. At the very least, he's not arguing with me. I take his silence as an opportunity to slip away to watch the last few minutes of the movie I had started, after messing up his hair a bit on my way past him as a sign of my affection.

My movie is over and I'm lying in bed with a book by the time my parents get home. I consider going down to say hi, but I'm entirely too comfortable. Plus, Al has fallen asleep with his head resting on me and I don't want to disturb him.

Almost half an hour goes by and a knock at my bedroom door wakes Al.

"Come in." I tuck a bookmark in, expecting it to be my mom wanting to ask about my evening.

Instead, Carter's face is the one that peeks around my door.

"What's up?" I wave him in and sit up in bed a little more.

He slowly wanders in and sits on the end of my bed. "Do you think mom and dad are going to punish us?"

"Did you tell them what happened tonight?"

He nods.

"Then I don't think you have anything to worry about."

"Really?" He gives me a hopeful look.

"Yeah. When you found yourself in a not-great situation, you did the right thing."

He lets out a deep sigh of relief. "Good."

"Word of caution though: practice on Monday will probably be pretty rough."

"What? Why? You think dad will say something?" Carter hops up, clearly upset.

"Calm yourself." I wave for him to take a seat again. "Dad won't have to. Parties like that are hard to keep secret, especially if one of Ryan's neighbors ended up calling the cops—and I would bet someone did eventually. I'm sure Coach B will already know. And I've heard he's not a fan of his players acting out. So, the practice afterward can be pretty brutal."

"Great!" The sarcasm is strong in his response.

"You'll be fine." I wave off his annoyance.

He stands and walks over to my comfy chair and with his back to me says, "I guess. Will you be?"

"What?" The confused response slips out before I see what he's doing. I try to move and get my pillow out from under me, but he's faster and the pillow he grabbed off my chair hits me square in the face.

Carter grabs it again and uses the small pillow in his hand to keep up the barrage of hits. I try to fight back with my much larger pillow, but my feet are tangled in my sheets and I can't get them out. I manage to land a few blows. Poor Al is clearly confused about why he was so rudely woken up and shoved off my bed, so he's just standing to the side of Carter barking at both of us.

Amidst my own laughs and shrieks, I hear Cam enter the room, and I double my efforts to untangle my legs. I need to be standing if they're both going to be coming at me.

"Here." Carter tosses a pillow across the room to Cam, who catches it.

I finally manage to slip out of bed, with my pillow in hand, and duck under Cam's first swing. I swing my arm backwards and nail him in the head with my pillow. The three of us keep the pillows flying for a few minutes until another voice sounds.

"Hey!" Dad's voice cuts through all our yells and Al's barking. The boys freeze in place. Cam drops the pillow he's holding. "You know, some of us are trying to relax downstairs."

"They attacked me, daddy." My words come out sounding like a scared six-year-old instead of a capable twenty-three-year-old adult.

Dad smiles and plays along with my pathetic sounding words. "I'm so sorry, honey. Which one started it?"

I point to Carter, who tries to back away, but dad and I both stand between him and the door. Dad takes my pillow from me and throws it in Carter's face, distracting him long enough for dad to wrap Carter in a bear hug, his arms pinned to his side. Carter tries to free himself, but despite all the muscle he's put on in the last few years, he still can't overpower our dad.

Cam appears to be smart enough to not try and intervene. Dad wrestles Carter onto the floor and pins him down. It's rather fun watching Carter squirm and fight to get free.

"Cam! Help me out." Carter waves his one free hand at Cam, trying to tap out.

"I'm good, thanks." Cam laughs.

Carter eventually admits defeat and dad lets him up. The two boys scurry out of the room. Dad is still kneeling on the floor and slowly gets up. "Do me a favor?"

"What?"

"Don't pick any more fights with them tonight. I don't think this old man can take it."

I laugh. "I didn't pick that fight. It was all them. Thanks for being my backup though."

"Anytime." He leans over and kisses the top of my head. "Goodnight, Pumpkin."

"Night, Dad."

I make a point to shut my door behind him, hoping the rest of my evening will be a quiet one. Curling up in my bed, I smile. There are a lot of reasons why I'm looking forward to moving out but having time like this with my family really isn't the worst thing in the world.

Chapter Seven

The rest of the weekend slips by faster than I want it to, as usual. Monday and Tuesday also pass fairly quickly because the diner is busy. It's Wednesday before I have a chance to dive into working on getting a website up and running.

It's little after ten when James comes walking into the office.

"How did it go?" After what El said the other day about how she thought I wasn't interested in the new diner, I've made a point to show James I'm interested and willing to talk about it. Unfortunately, James has remained unwilling to bring me in on what he's doing.

"It was fine. I didn't like either of the properties we went to look at today." He shrugs off his coat and tosses it onto his chair as he walks over to my desk. "What are you working on?"

I slide my sketches with layout ideas over so he can see them. "Ideas for the website."

"Please tell me it's not going to look that bad." He pulls a stool behind my desk to sit next to me.

I choose to ignore his attempt at a joke and move straight into discussing the design and layout—trying to nail down what look we want the website to have. Jimmy's didn't have much as far as advertising material and design style when we first took over, but now that we have a clearer idea about the design style, our goal is to have the website match any and all promotional material we create.

We're only beginning to get an idea of the direction we want to go when James' phone starts to ring.

An odd look crosses his face when he checks the caller-id. "My dad is video calling me."

"Answer it. I want to say hi!" I make a move to grab his phone, but he holds it away from me and swipes the screen to accept the call. A second later, both Dean and Sharon appear on the phone screen.

"Hey, guys. What's going on?" James props the phone in front of us on my desk, so we both show up on the screen.

"Hi, Clara. How are you?" Sharon asks with her face a little too close to the screen.

"I love how she completely ignored me. I'm her son." James whispers to me, shaking his head.

I wave off his comment, my eyes fixed on the screen. "I'm good. How are you guys? How's Arizona?"

"Warm." Dean's answer is short and to the point.

Sharon nods. "It is much warmer here in the winter than back home, but I love it. We're having so much fun. But we want to hear how things are there. James, how was the meeting this morning?"

"Took you long enough to realize I'm here." He jokes before actually answering his mother. He goes into more detail this time than when I asked, probably because his dad asks a ton of questions about the properties and everything that will need to happen with the new location.

"What's your timeline?" Dean leans in a little closer to the camera.

"Well, a lot depends on how long it takes us to find the right location. I would love to be open by the end of May, sooner if possible."

"Wow. That's not too far away." Surprise is written on Sharon's face.

"It's not, but I think we can do it. It's not like we're starting completely from scratch. We have the systems set up. We already have our food distributer. We have the menu in place. We already have one successful business, now the goal is simply to implement what we do here in another location."

"You really think this is going to be simple?" I'm legitimately curious about how he's feeling about this, and while he hasn't been much of a sharer lately, I have a feeling he'll answer with his parents in the conversation too.

"I'm not saying it's going to be easy, but I think it will be less difficult than if we were opening a new restaurant with absolutely nothing else to model it after." He counters.

"I think you're right, Jamie." Dean nods slowly, "The fact that you already run one diner will be helpful, but it will still be challenging. Set your expectations accordingly."

"Of course, Dad." James gives an understanding nod, and I have the distinct feeling I'm on the outside of some secret communication between the two of them. I don't get a chance to ask about it though because James continues. "Did you tell Glo about our plans?"

"Glo? As in…" I begin to ask for clarification, but James cuts me off with a quick nod. He's asking about his dad's mom, who was married to the original Jimmy and helped open and run Jimmy's Diner in the beginning.

"Yes." The brief look of concern on Dean's face disappears and is replaced with a smile. "We told her when we went to see her last week. She was excited. I'm actually a little surprised she hasn't called you. She kept saying she was going to."

"Maybe I'll give her a call this weekend." James smiles.

Sharon jumps into the conversation. "We can't wait to see the location you end up picking. We really are excited you're doing this."

"Thanks, Mom. Now, those of us who are still employed should probably get back to work." He leans forward to grab the phone.

I block him from reaching it. "What if I wanted to hear more about Arizona?"

"I'll give you call sometime, Clara. Can't have your boss getting upset with you." Sharon laughs and sends me a wink.

"You want to say that again, Mom? The part about me being the boss? I think she needs reminding sometimes." James joins in on the fun.

I try to elbow him, with limited success.

"Clara, don't let his head get too big. We'll see you kids later." Dean waves as James ends the call.

"What did your dad mean?"

"About my head being too big?" He smiles and drops his phone onto his desk. "I think that was a joke."

"No, I know he meant it's my job to keep you humble. I was asking about earlier when he was talking about your expectations for the new diner. I felt like I was missing something."

"Oh…" James stands and moves the stool back to its spot in the corner of the office. Keeping his back to me, he makes his way over to his desk. "Dad knows I can get a little...uh…frustrated when things don't go as planned. It was his way of telling me not to get worked up if it takes longer than I think it should to open the new diner."

It feels like he's being evasive, but since I can't see his face to be sure, I decide to let it go. "Hmmm. Okay. Well, back to work we go."

Once again, I turn my attention to sketching out the website design. I'm getting dinner with Leah tomorrow before small group to talk to her about helping us, but I want to have some ideas in place already.

Almost two hours later, a weird noise from the other side of the office pulls my attention away from my work. I grab the closest small object—which happens to be an eraser—

and chuck it at James. The tiny projectile hits him in the shoulder and he instinctively sits back and pulls his headphones out.

"What's up?" He's clearly oblivious to the noise I'm hearing, which amazes me.

"Did you eat breakfast today?" The question comes out with more of an accusatory tone than I intended.

He makes a face. "Why do you care?"

I make sure to lighten my tone before I go on. "Because your stomach is doing a really great impression of a whale. It's obnoxious."

"What are you talking about?" Now he just looks confused.

"How do you not hear how loud your stomach is being? I can hear it from way over here at my desk." I stare him down. "You haven't eaten anything today, have you?"

It looks like he's going to argue, but then he pauses, and I can see his brain trying to remember. "I may have forgotten to grab something before I met with Mr. Simmons this morning."

I shake my head. He does this all the time. I for one will never understand how a person could forget to eat. That's a completely foreign concept to me. "It's past noon. You should probably eat something.

"They're busy with the lunch rush. I can wait." He shrugs.

"No, you can't. Your body is literally yelling at you that it needs food, and I'm sick of listening to it." I make my way over to the door and open the door. "Danny. James forgot to eat again. Can you make him something?"

Momentarily, I feel bad for asking because I can see he has a full docket of orders to be made and it looks like he and his assistant, Wendell, are pretty busy. But Danny responds almost immediately. "Sure thing. What's he want?"

I shoot a raised eyebrow to James, waiting for a response to the question I know he heard Danny ask.

James seems hesitant to even answer, but I think he knows I'll order something for him whether he answers or not. "I guess I'll have a burger. But I can wait."

"He'll have a sunrise burger and fries. I'll have the same thing." I relay the information to Danny.

"Okay. I'll have them ready for you soon." Danny calls over his shoulder as he continues to work.

"Thanks, Danny. You're my hero."

I close the door behind me when I step back into the office.

"I want a sunrise burger, huh?" It's James' turn to raise an eyebrow.

"I figure the extra protein would be good for you. Plus, it sounded good." I shrug and head to my desk, anxiously awaiting my burger. "I'm glad your parents called. It was fun to get to talk to them. It's cool your grandma likes the idea of expanding."

James leans back in his chair. "Yeah, I honestly wasn't sure how she would feel about it. I'm definitely glad she's okay with it."

"I wonder what it was like for your grandparents when they first started the diner. Obviously, they weren't stressing about social media posts and websites, but I wonder what the process was like…" I trail off for a second, trying to imagine what it was like for them sixty years ago. Suddenly, I sit up straight. "I just had the best idea."

James' only response is a hesitant glance my direction.

"We should interview your grandma." I say it excitedly, my mind spinning a mile a minute at the possibilities.

"What?"

"Seriously. It would be a fun promo. We could make a video of you interviewing your grandma all about what it was like when they started Jimmy's and then use the videos to promote the new location!" The more I think about it this idea, the more I like it. Now, I'll just have to get James on board.

"I'm not sure she would go for that."

"Oh, come on! You have to at least ask. I'm sure she would love getting to talk to her grandson all about her life. We could insert some photos from the early days into the video. It would be so cool."

James considers this for a moment. "How about we run the idea past my dad. See what he thinks?"

"Deal." I'm just happy he didn't completely shoot me down. Turning back to my computer, I open a new document and start typing out ideas and potential questions for this video interview, praying I can convince both Dean and James it's a good idea.

ꟷꟷꟷ

I leave work a little early the next day because I have my small group tonight. When James and I first started working together, there were a few times when I ended up getting stuck at work late on small group night and I had to show up to my group smelling like burgers and Danny's famous chili. It's terrible. Each time it happened, I tried to sit far away from people because I felt super self-conscious, and I ended up being in a rush to leave as soon as it was over.

The last time it happened, I showed up to work the next morning and made James promise I wouldn't get stuck at work late on small group nights. I told him I have no problem staying late any other night of the week, but I cannot do it on small group night. Lucky for me, he understood and promised to let me leave early since he doesn't come to my small group and can stick around as long as he needs to.

That was one of the decisions we made early on. We work together, we go to church together, and we have a lot of the same friends since we grew up in church together. We agreed we didn't need to be in the same small group. Last time we talked about it, he was checking out some of the other young adult small groups at church to find one he likes.

Leaving early gives me time to go home, shower and change, and get dinner before my group. Then I feel good enough to hang out for a while afterward.

Today, I hurry through my post-work shower and outfit change, so I won't be late to meet Leah for dinner. When I get to Langhorne's, I realize I must have beaten her here. I've been craving their fries all week, which is weird since I work in a diner that serves fries, but the ones here are so good.

Standing just inside the door, I take a look around trying to decide where to sit. Large windows take up most of the front wall of the old brick building and let in a lot of light, contrasting with the rest of the dimly lit room. The large, u-shaped bar is about halfway back and takes up the middle of the room with stools all around it. Small, square tables with chairs fill the rest of the space in the main room. To the left, a large opening in the brick wall leads to the second room, which is also filled with tables and chairs. It also includes a small stage in the back corner, where locals, like El's friend, can perform on the weekends.

The high ceilings in the main room help the narrow space feel larger than it is. The walls are covered with old photos and newspaper clippings of famous or infamous Missourians—that particular addition to the décor was Henry's doing. Personally, I think it was a nice touch. It gives the place a unique feel.

Choosing to enjoy the small amount of sunlight left today, I take a seat at the table closest to the front door and begin to look over the menu. I've decided what I want to eat and finished a glass of water by the time Leah comes rushing into the building.

"Sorry. I hit traffic and then I couldn't find parking." She lowers herself into the chair across from me, looking flustered.

"Don't worry about it." I wave it off. "Although I do need to use the bathroom. So, I'm glad you're here."

I leave Leah at the table perusing the menu to take care of business. Focused on adjusting my shirt as I exit the bathroom and head back to the table, I hear my name come from behind me.

I turn to find Henry staring at me, brows furrowed. "Hey, Henry."

"Uh…hey. Did I know you were coming?" He pulls his phone out like he's checking to see if he missed a text.

"No. I'm not here to see you." I nod for him to walk with me. "Leah and I are grabbing dinner before group tonight. I needed to talk to her about something."

He raises an eyebrow. "Everything okay?"

"Yeah. Just work stuff." I shrug.

"By work stuff, are you referring to your boss?" Henry stops walking and stares me down. Based on the handful of interactions between the two of them at Jimmy's, Henry's made it clear he doesn't like James. Probably because James acts like Henry is a pariah every time they're around each other.

"Stop." I meet his stare. "I don't know what your issue is with James, but I don't want to hear it."

"He started…"

I cut Henry off with a wave of my hand. "Not interested. Besides, that's not what I want to talk to her about. I need Leah's help designing the website we've decided to set up."

"Oh. I didn't know she did that sort of thing." He stops at the bar.

"Now you do. She's a freelance graphic designer."

"Cool." He turns his attention back to the papers in his hand.

"Well, it looks like you're busy, and I'm hungry. I'm going to head back."

"Yeah. Sorry. I need to take care of this. I'll try to stop by and say hi before you go."

Leah raises an eyebrow as soon as I sit down.

"What?"

"I know you get sick of me saying this, but you and Henry look so good…" She trails off at the sudden appearance of our waitress, Belle.

"You guys ready?" Belle delivers the question with a disapproving glance and a disinterested tone. Ever since the first time I showed up at Langhorne's, Belle has disliked me. She got it in her head that Henry and I were a couple and has since continued to blame me ruining her chances with him. Every time I think her cool demeanor toward me is beginning to thaw, something seems to happen to remind her how much she dislikes me.

"Hey, Belle. How are you?" I am determined to win her over. I'm not even sure why it's so important she likes me, but it is.

She looks me over suspiciously. "Fine. What do you guys want?"

Leah picks up on the tension and hurries to place her order. I follow suit and Belle walks off in a huff.

"What was that about?" Leah whispers once Belle is gone.

"You know she's never liked me. Plus, I'm sure she heard what you said about Henry."

Thinking back over her words to me before Belle walked up, a look of realization comes over Leah's face. "Oh…right. Sorry."

I give Leah an ornery smile. "I don't know if you remember me saying I didn't want to deal with people thinking Henry and I were together…"

"I know. You asked me not to say anything. And then I did." She interrupts me.

"Yes, you did." I watch Belle as she chats with the guy working the bar and wonder how I'll ever manage to get through to her.

"I'm sorry. It's just…"

Turning my attention back to Leah, who seems hesitant to say what she's thinking. "It's just what?"

"It's just…how can you be sure he's not the guy for you?" The sincere look on Leah's face tells me this isn't some random, teasing question. She's being serious.

I pause to think about it for a second, wanting to give her a serious answer and not a flippant one.

"For one, he's not a Christian." Not only is this a reason I think Leah will understand, it's also my number one rule for anyone I consider dating. And I don't just mean it has to be a guy who goes to church and knows the right things to say. I mean someone who is actively and whole-heartedly seeking after God.

"Yet. He's not a Christian yet, but that could change at any time. Stephen and the guys have all had some great conversations with him about God and faith and everything. It's going to happen." She says this definitively.

"Good! I pray every day that Henry will give his life to Christ, but that won't change how I feel. I care about Henry, a lot. But he'll always be like a brother to me. There's never been anything romantic between us, and I don't think there ever will be."

Leah looks a little dejected.

"Sorry to burst your bubble, but I think he'll always be the annoying brother I didn't really want but maybe needed."

"I guess I can live with that." She pauses for a moment as Belle returns with our food, which she drops on the table unceremoniously before disappearing. "Maybe we could set him up with someone else."

"Leah!" I laugh and shake my head.

She smiles. "Don't worry, I'll find someone for you too!"

I simply roll my eyes at Leah and say a quick prayer so we can dive into both the food and the subject I wanted to discuss with her. We spend the next twenty minutes going over the ideas I have for the website and Leah has a lot of good feedback about both the appearance of the page and how to set it up. It doesn't take me long to realize we will need a lot more time together to get this website figured out.

"Do you have time on Monday or Tuesday to work on this?" Leah poses the question before I have a chance.

"Definitely. I can make any day work." I'm so relieved she's willing to help me that I will make a point to be available whenever she is.

"Sounds good. Let's plan on me coming by Tuesday morning." She pulls her phone out and opens her calendar app. "That will give me enough time to put together some ideas based on what we talked about today. Does that work for you?"

I nod as I follow her lead and enter the meeting into my calendar, so I don't forget about it. Before we leave, I answer a number of questions Leah has about our goals for the website and what we hope to accomplish with it to give her a better idea about how to design it.

After paying and leaving Belle a generous tip, we make our way to our cars. I end up following Leah out of downtown in the direction of the house where our small group is held.

By the time we get to the house our small group leaders, Adam and Sam, rent with two other guys, quite a few other vehicles are already lining both sides of the street in front of their house meaning we'll have a good-sized group tonight. We typically have at least eight people, but it's often more than that. It really depends on people's schedules.

As soon as I step into the house, I get hit in the face with something soft.

"Score!" Sam pumps a fist into the air at his success from his spot on the living room couch.

"Thanks a lot." I roll my eyes as I slip my shoes off in the spacious entry way, which is littered with everyone's shoes. I'm honestly not sure why we all take our shoes off. I've never heard either of the guys tells us to do it. Maybe one of their roommates is a stickler about it or maybe it's one of those things someone did once and everyone else simply follows suit.

Either way, my shoes join the pile. As do Leah's before she disappears into the kitchen to the left of the entryway. Probably looking for her husband since his car is out front, but I don't see him in the living room in front of me.

Leaving my shoes behind, I snatch up the crocheted mini-flying disc that hit me in the face. As per their usual, my small group friends are casually seated around the living and dining room areas of the house, and this small flying disc is providing them with something entertaining to do while they chat. In the summer, we hang out in the backyard and use an actual Frisbee, but we use the small, crocheted version when we're indoors so we don't break anything.

I make my way into the living room and use my left hand to poorly fling the cloth disc into the dining room, which is off to the left of the living room. I was aiming for my friend Dana, but the small disc goes sailing past her to nail Sam and Adam's roommate Alex in the arm. A surprised look crosses his face because he was definitely paying more attention to his conversation with the guy sitting across the table from him than he was to the location of the disc.

"Oops. Clearly I need to work on my aim." I point at my original target.

Dana laughs and sits back so Alex can toss the disc back into the living room, where Adam, Sam, and Jules are all sitting. I choose to duck into the kitchen to grab something to drink.

Sure enough, Leah and Stephen are standing on the opposite side of the kitchen, near the door that leads to the entryway. The only other person in the room is El, who is staring at her phone.

"Hey what are you up to?" I grab a cup from the counter and move to the fridge to get some water.

El lowers her phone and gives me a forced smile. "Finally!"

"I didn't realize I was late."

She glances at her watch and her voice drops to a whisper. "Technically, you're not. I was just beginning to feel like a third wheel here. Especially now."

I glance over to where Leah and Stephen are still talking quietly amongst themselves. "Leah got here like two seconds ago with me. Any chance you're being a little dramatic?"

"Maybe. But have you noticed everyone else in this group is in a relationship. Other than us." She points back and forth between herself and me, looking increasingly more concerned.

I shrug. "I mean…I hadn't really noticed, but I suppose that's true."

"Doesn't it bother you?" She's still whispering.

"Not really." I give her an apologetic look and catch a flash of fear in her eyes. "This is really bothering you, isn't it?"

"Yes. No." She shakes her head. "I don't know."

I gently put a hand on her arm, trying to coax her to meet my look. "Talk to me. What are you thinking?"

El chews on her lip for a minute. I wait for her to say something, feeling grateful when I see Leah and Stephen head out to the living room.

"Sometimes, when I see Stephen and Leah, Adam and Dana, and Sam and Jules all looking so happy, I get tired of being on my own. I've been on my own for a long time. Even before my grandma passed away, she was sick for a while, so I was basically raising myself. I'm tired of it, and somedays it's hard." She crosses her arms as she leans against the counter.

"I'm sorry." I want to say something more. Something profound and helpful. Something that will make her feel better. But I don't have any idea what to say. Instead, I pull her into a hug.

She accepts the hug, arms still crossed, but pulls away quickly "I don't know why I'm being so dramatic today…"

"You're not being dramatic. It's okay to struggle with things. That's normal. I may not be struggling with the same issue, but I've got my problems too. You know I do."

El nods gently. "I know. How are things with James this week?"

"Eh…things are pretty much the same."

"Well, I'm praying for you. And him. And the whole situation." She offers with a small smile.

"Thanks. I'll be praying for you too. Either you meet the man of your dreams soon or God will give you patience and peace about it."

"Thank you." El hesitates for just a second. "And if you don't mind, don't mention it to anyone. I don't really want to get into it with everyone else."

"I won't say anything, but you might want to consider talking to the rest of the girls about it. They might have more advice than I do."

"Maybe. Or they'll just try to set me up with every available guy they know." She shakes her head. That doesn't interest her.

I start to protest, then I recall my conversation with Leah at dinner and smile. "You may be onto something."

El gives me her first real smile of the evening. "Right?!"

A loud, elephant-like noise comes from the living room. I shoot an amused look at El. "I think that might be Sam letting us know he's ready to get started. The two of us shake our heads at how strange our friends are as we head into the living room to get this evening's discussion started.

Chapter Eight

"How many of you can recite James 1:2?" Adam asks once we've all settled into the living room.

I glance around to see almost everyone has raised their hand, including me. While it's not necessarily a verse I set out to memorize, I've heard it referenced enough to be able to quote it.

"I figured as much. Just because it sounds fun, I want to hear it." He gives all of us a coaxing wave.

Seeing no way out of it, we oblige and collectively recite the verse from the NIV. "Consider it pure joy, my brothers and sisters, whenever you face trials of many kinds…"

"Very good." Adam gives us a golf clap when we finish. "Sam, buddy, can you read the next couple verses?"

"Yes, I can. I learned how to read in Kindergarten." Sam replies matter-of-factly with a look of pride.

Adam rolls his eyes at his best friend. "*Will you* read the next couple verses out loud for us?"

"Of course." Sam smiles and begins to read the next couple verses.

We sit in silence for a bit once Sam finishes before Adam addresses us again. "Thoughts?"

Jules is the first one to respond. She's staring down at the Bible in her hands as she talks. "The summer I was fifteen, a friend from school invited me to go to church camp with her. Now, I had never gone to church, but I said I would go, mostly to get away from my parents who were almost constantly fighting at that point. James 1:2 was the theme verse for the week and I thought it was the most ridiculous thing I'd ever heard.

"I didn't think it made sense. Being happy when bad things happened to you. So, I mostly ignored the sermons and tried to have fun for the week. My friend kept inviting me to stuff at her church though, and eventually I started attending youth group because it was better than being at home. The leader who had been our counselor at camp eventually started meeting me for coffee once a month. It was during one of those coffee dates that the verse came up again.

"I was really struggling with my parents' divorce by that time and she kept talking about choosing joy. Once again, I thought it was ridiculous. She helped me understand God and faith and how choosing joy in the midst of hard times is an act of faith. Over the years, James 1:2 has become a life verse for me, so much so, I wanted a reminder."

She holds up her right wrist and pulls her sleeve down a little. From across the room, I can't really see what she's showing. Luckily, I've seen the small tattoo that says "Pure Joy" in cursive before. I always liked it, even though I didn't know the story behind it. If I had to describe Jules in one word, it would be joyful, so it's pretty cool to hear how God brought that about in her life.

"That's awesome"

"Nice."

"I like it." The chorus of responses come quickly.

Jules pulls the sleeve down and drops her hands back into her lap, "All that to say, this verse is a reminder I have a choice no matter what is going on in my life to choose to trust God and believe he has a plan."

"Thanks for sharing, Jules." Adam nods to her. "Who else has thoughts on this passage?"

Alex's friend is the next one to share a response to the passage. Unfortunately, he talks so long and in such a condescending manner, I lose track of what he's saying. My mind wanders to the list of tasks I need to get done tomorrow before the weekend.

It's close to ten minutes later when the guy takes a long enough breath for Sam to slip in and cut him off, drawing my attention back to the discussion.

Whether in an attempt to keep long-winded guy from starting again or simply to continue into the passage, Sam dives into the passage. "One of the things this passage talks about is wisdom. Reading it quickly, it can seem like it jumps from one subject to a totally different one. The reality is the two are deeply connected. Wisdom—Biblical wisdom—gives us insight on how to walk with God. Wisdom teaches us to persevere through the trials."

Sam passes the lesson back to Adam with a short nod.

"The best part about spiritual wisdom is it's free to anyone who asks for it. This passage clearly states that. And look at Solomon. Given the opportunity to ask for anything, Solomon requested wisdom to lead his people well. Eventually, he became known for being the wisest king Israel ever had. That's a pretty cool way to be known."

"Of course, at the end his life, his legacy is not so great." Alex's friend interjects, as if he's trying to prove Adam wrong.

Adam doesn't flinch. He actually looks a little more excited. "Right? King Solomon's life ended in disarray because he began to rely on his own strength and didn't seek after God the way he did in his early years. His life is a perfect example of how wisdom comes from being close to and knowing God. And that wisdom and relationship can see us through anything."

Dana leans forward from her spot on the couch. "Can you imagine how different the world would look if we all lived life like this chapter tells us to: being joyful in hard times, seeking God's wisdom in everything we do, and living faithfully?"

Her question and a comfortable silence settles over the room—even Mr. Know-it-all appears to be thinking about that possibility. Stephen and Alex both chime in with some possible outcomes for applying this scripture to their personal lives, and their suggestions get me thinking.

Ten minutes of continued group discussion later, Adam begins to wrap up. "Before we leave tonight, I think it's important we spend some time in individual prayer. I'm going to put on some worship music for a few minutes and everyone can spend some time talking to God about the scripture we discussed tonight and how it will apply to each of our lives."

With that, instrumental worship music fills the room and everyone gets quiet. I look down at my notebook, where I've been jotting down notes as we've talked tonight and add a couple questions to the bottom of the page.

Trials = Joy
Perseverance – Wisdom – Humility
These all come from God
Be in close relationship with God
How do I choose joy in the midst of hardships?
What situations do I need to apply this to?

As I listen to the worship music playing, the one situation that comes to mind is working with James. Of late, trying to connect with James at work has been the only real trial in my life. Our study tonight made one thing abundantly clear: trials can be overcome only through God.

Lord, I am so confused right now. I could really use some of that spiritual wisdom we were talking about tonight when it comes to working with James. I don't know what the problem is, but it seems like the two of us don't work together well. Please give me wisdom and guidance about what to do. Part of me wants to find another job and fast. The other part of me doesn't want to lose James as a friend, and I think I would if I quit. But most of all, I'm tired of feeling so uncertain.

I sit silently for another couple minutes waiting to see if God will speak to me and give me some guidance. Unfortunately, the only voice I hear is Sam's saying a quick prayer of dismissal. After which, everyone hops up from their spots on the floor to return glasses and coffee cups to the kitchen.

"That was awfully applicable." El says from her spot on the floor next to me.

I laugh. "I know, right? I'm not sure if I love it or hate it when that happens."

She scrunches her face up, thinking. "Maybe a little of both?"

"Hey what are you doing this weekend?" I change the subject because I'm tired of thinking about James and work.

"I need to clean my apartment and do some grading, but other than that, I don't have anything planned. Why? What are you thinking?"

"I don't know. I just know my family will be gone for a basketball tournament all weekend, so I have the house to myself and no plans."

"Do you want to do a movie night?" El stands up and begins to make her way to the kitchen as I follow.

"Not really. I'm a little sick of watching movies. I want to go out and do something."

"So dinner?" She offers with a hopeful glance.

"I guess." I shrug. "Just getting dinner seems boring. We could get dinner first and then do something fun after?"

"Any suggestions?"

I shake my head. "Not at the moment. I'll think on it for a bit and let you know what I come up with tomorrow."

ᘏᘏᘏ

Work on Friday passes without any major issues coming up, which is a bit of a relief. I really didn't have the emotional energy for anything crazy. Even without any real craziness, the last hour of the day dragged on like it would never end.

I get home to find my dog is apparently starved for attention because Albert is at my feet the moment I walk through the door. I almost trip over him at least four times as I make my way into the house and up to my room. Giving in to his pleas for attention, I decide to take him for a walk. It's officially February now, but it hasn't warmed up much yet, so I try to make these walks fairly quick.

Al and I are making our way to the sidewalk at the same time a car pulls up in front of the McKinley's house. I let Al direct me over to where Hannah is exiting her car and do my best to keep him from plowing into her.

"Hey, Clara. How's it going?" She calmly pushes Al down and squats down to pet him.

I offer her a smile. "Today was pretty decent. How about you? How's your last semester of high school treating you?"

"Busy. Lots of homework." She gives a half-hearted shrug as she stands up.

"I remember that about my senior year."

Hannah nods, still focusing her attention on Albert. At first it seemed friendly, now it feels like she's avoiding my eye contact.

"So, I haven't seen you at any basketball games recently." The game I went to earlier this week was the third game in the last few weeks where I didn't see her. I know Mom said she's been staying home more because of her dad, but I'm curious if that's the only reason.

"Yeah…" She adjusts her backpack her shoulder, shoves her hands into her pockets, and shuffles her feet a bit—looking exactly like her older brother does when he's talking about something uncomfortable. "I'm not really friends with most of those people anymore, so I probably won't be going to many basketball games."

"I'm sorry. What happened?" Whatever it was, losing your friends when you're already going through a hard time sounds pretty terrible. My heart breaks a little for her.

Hannah shakes her head a few times. "It's not important. It, uh…it does make me glad I'm almost done though."

"I bet." I try to give her an encouraging smile. "You can always join us if you want to go to a game. Mom and I are usually there. You always seemed to enjoy going. It would be a shame to give it up totally just because you aren't going with the people you used to go with."

"Thanks, Clara. I appreciate the offer." She doesn't seem all that interested in my suggestion.

"You know, Henry comes sometimes. You could come with him."

"Maybe." She nods before turning to head inside.

"Hannah." I pause, waiting for her to make eye contact. When she finally does, I continue slowly, hoping to find the right words. "I remember, when I was your age, how everyone always talked about how high school was the best years of their life and how life in high school is as good as it gets."

A look of recognition flashes in her eyes.

"I wanted to tell you it's not true. For most people, high school is simply a blip on their timeline. Once you're done with high school, you have a lot more choice in who you hang out with and how you spend your time. So, hang in there. You'll be done soon. You'll go to college. Or you'll get a job. You'll build your own life. It will get better."

For the first time since we started talking, traces of a grin sneak onto her face. It's small, but it's there. "Thanks, Clara."

"Of course." I nod toward Al, who has lost interest in Hannah and is now trying to pull me in the opposite direction. "I should probably get going before this guy pulls my arm off. I'll see you around."

She waves as I take off at a slow jog in the direction Al is pulling. We make our way to the neighborhood park a few blocks away and find it completely deserted due to the cold weather. I pull a tennis ball out of my coat pocket, unclip Al's leash, and throw the ball as far as I can. Al lopes along after the ball with a lot less speed than he used to and I'm reminded how old he's getting. I find a bench to sit on while he retrieves the ball and makes his way over to me. The two of us repeat this process a number of times before Al loses interest and refuses to chase the ball down anymore. Instead, he's wandering around the park sniffing every tree he can find.

Catching up to him, I clip the leash back onto his collar and lead him over to where the ball is waiting. On the way home, my attention focuses on Al walking beside me. His age is beginning to show. He went gray around the mouth at some point while I was in college, giving him a distinguished look. Now, he's starting to slow down a bit. He still wants to play and take walks most days, so I'm not too worried about him. It does make me sad though, knowing he's in his later years. For the first time, I notice he's gained some weight lately.

We've had issues with this before, but it's been a while. When the boys were in elementary school, they would feed him extra after I had already taken care of him. Since there are two of them, Al ended up getting quite a bit of food every day for a while. Once he started putting on weight, my mom figured out what was happening and moved his food so the boys couldn't reach it and told them they weren't allowed to help feed him until they got older.

I doubt Cam and Carter are sneaking him extra food again, so I may need to check into feeding Al a little less. The vet is always reminding me the extra weight will only make things more difficult for him as he gets older.

"We don't want that, now do we?" I ask Al out loud, even though he has no idea what I'm talking about. He simply stares at me for a moment before turning his attention to investigating the ground in front of him.

Once we get back to the house, Al heads straight for his water bowl and then flops down on his dog bed on the floor under the stairs. I follow suit and grab a glass of water.

The house is quiet. The boys' tournament started tonight at a school on the southwest side of St. Louis. Since dad's parents live in the area, my mom went down tonight to stay with them so she could be there for the full duration tomorrow.

Grabbing some food for dinner, I settle into my favorite spot on the couch to relax for the evening. A while later, my ringing phone interrupts the cheesy movie I'm watching.

I pause the TV and answer the phone. "Hey, Kenz."

"What's the name of that one movie?" She doesn't bother wasting time on pleasantries.

"I might need a little more to go on." I laugh. I should be more taken aback at her random outburst, but these kinds of phone calls are fairly normal for Kenzie. She can never remember the name of movies, even if it's one she really loves.

"The one with the girl from *Sisterhood of the Traveling Pants*." She says definitively, as if she's just given me a super helpful clue.

"Alexis Bledel?" I offer the name and pause to think, hoping to come up with what Alexis Bledel movie Kenzie might be talking about.

"She's the one in *Gilmore Girls*, right?"

"Yeah."

"Not her. One of the other girls." Kenzie almost sounds frustrated at my failed guess, which annoys me a little because she's given me basically nothing to go on.

Thankfully, she continues to ramble about the one she's talking about. "It's kind of an odd movie, but it was good. She like travels through time or something…"

Somehow, the nonsense she's spewing actually helps my brain click. "*Age of Adaline*? With Blake Lively?"

"Yes!" She shouts into my ear. "That's it! That's the one I was trying to think of!"

"She doesn't time travel." I state matter-of-factly. "Her character has an accident that keeps her from aging, so she lives through multiple time periods."

"Well, that's kind of the same thing." I can picture Kenzie waving off my objection like a fly that's bothering her.

"Not really, but I'll let it slide. Why do you want to know anyway?"

"I'm looking for something to watch on Netflix." This is the calmest Kenzie has sounded for the entire phone call.

"Are you off this weekend?" A bolt of excitement runs through me. I have this weekend off, so I could potentially drive over to Kansas City to hang out.

"Just tonight. I work tomorrow, Sunday, and Tuesday."

With that, my excitement, much like my newly-developed plans, crashes and burns. "Stink."

"Shoot. It's not here." Kenzie says, completely ignoring my disappointment.

"What?"

"The movie. *Age of Adaline*. I can't find it on Netflix. I wonder what else I could watch…it's suggesting *Woman in Gold*. Have you seen it?"

"I think so. It's a little slow, but it's interesting. It might be based on a true story. I'm not sure."

"It looks good. Plus, Ryan Reynolds is in it. He's cute." At this point, Kenzie isn't really looking for response, she's pretty much talking to herself, out-loud. I can tell because her sentences become more like mumbling by the second.

I opt to get out of listening to her monologue. "Sounds like you found something, so I'm going to let you go."

"Yeah. Bye." She's definitely distracted. Most likely, she already hit play on the movie.

I hang up the phone and return my attention to the Hallmark movie I'm watching. The movie ends and another one is about to begin when I hear someone knock on the front door. Surprisingly, Al doesn't bark, but he does run to the door.

I look through the window as I flip the porch light on and see Henry standing on the porch.

"Hey." I open the door far enough for him to come in, but he stays on the porch. "What's up?"

"I was sent on an ice cream run for my parents." He holds up a paper bag from a local creamery. "I thought you might like to join us since you're on your own tonight."

"You know I never say no to ice cream. Let me grab some shoes." I slip into a pair of mom's shoes by the garage door. Al tries to follow me out, but I signal for him to sit just inside the door. "Sorry, buddy you can't come."

"Sure he can. Dad loves him." Henry whistles and waves him out.

"Your mom doesn't." It's not that Mrs. M doesn't like Albert. She has no problem petting or playing with him when he's outside, but she doesn't like having animals in her house.

"Trust me, it's okay."

I pull the front door shut behind me and wish I had grabbed a coat even though I'm only walking next door. "Shouldn't you be working tonight?"

"I took the night off to help Mom out."

His explanation concerns me. "Is everything alright?"

"Yeah. Dad had a little bit of a fall this morning. Don't worry, he's fine." Henry waves off my worry before I can express it. "He went to the hospital and got checked out. It's all good. His balance just isn't what it was before the surgery. I think Mom was more shaken than he was hurt."

"That's good I guess."

He opens the front door of his parents' house and his voice drops to a whisper as we enter. "Yeah. I figured I would hang out here for the night to keep her from worrying too much. I even convinced Hannah to join us for a movie, so all in all, it's been a good evening."

"Good, I'm glad." I whisper my response and follow him into the kitchen where his parents are sitting at the table and Hannah is on a stool at the island. Al rushed into the room ahead of us and makes a beeline for Mr. McKinley.

"Hey, there pal." He leans over to play with a very happy Albert.

"Hi, Clara." Henry's mom looks tired as she greets me. Suddenly I feel a little bad about intruding, especially since I brought Al with me.

I carefully lower myself onto the stool next to Hannah. "Thanks for letting me crash your ice cream party."

"You didn't crash it. You were invited." Henry calls from the other side of the island, where he's getting out bowls and spoons.

"As long as there's plenty of ice cream, I don't mind." Hannah winks at me with a smile.

"Don't worry, I got enough for everyone."

I chat casually with the McKinley family as Henry dishes up and passes out bowls of ice cream, with our preferred toppings. By the time we all finish our treat, Mr. M is starting to look pretty tired as well, despite the fact that it's barely nine o'clock.

"I think I'm about ready for bed, kids." He grabs a cane I didn't notice earlier from its spot against the wall. He waves goodnight to us with his free hand as he makes his way out of the kitchen toward the stairs with his wife following right behind him.

Hannah hops up and takes her bowl over to the sink. Henry blocks her path to the stairs.

"Get out of my way." She tries to push him, but since she's half his size it doesn't work out too well for her.

"You have to give me a hug first."

Hannah rolls her eyes. "Why are you so annoying?"

"That's no way to talk to your only brother." He smirks and blocks her attempts to get around him. I can't help but think if Leah could see this interaction right now, she would totally agree Henry treats me like he does Hannah.

"Fine." She gives up and tolerates a hug from him. Finally getting past him, she waves to me. "See you later, Clara."

I wave to the disappearing Hannah and turn to Henry. "That was fun, thanks for inviting me."

"Of course. Plus, having a guest, even if it's only you, forces my mom to relax and leave dad alone at least a little bit."

I opt to take the 'even if it's only you' comment as a compliment—like I'm not really a guest because I'm part of the family—instead of as a way to say I'm not important. "Given what she's been through the last few months, I can understand why she would be worried. Don't be too hard on her."

"I'm trying not to be. I'm trying to understand her, but I actually understand how dad's feeling."

"What do you mean?"

He studies me for a second, like he's trying to decide if I'm kidding or not. "Come with me."

I follow him down the hallway toward the front door, Albert at my feet, but Henry stops at the French doors that open into the home office. He walks in and turns the light on. Maneuvering around the desk, he faces the back wall, which is covered with family pictures, pictures of Henry in his various football uniforms, and Hannah on the cheerleading team.

He points to a specific picture toward the middle. It's an action shot of Henry in his scarlet and gray college football uniform; he's flying through the air, his arm stretched out to catch the football a few inches above his fingers with two defenders coming at him.

"It was one of the best plays of my career. I managed to come down with the ball in the end zone after a thirty-five yard pass for a touchdown." There's a passion in his voice that tells me he's reliving every detail of the play as he tells me about it.

"Pretty impressive."

"It was amazing. We took the lead with that touchdown, in the fourth quarter, against our rivals. I was pumped." He seems lost in thought, so I wait for him to continue even though I'm confused as to where this conversation is going. "On our next possession, it was third and six. I went for a deep post route, which means I ran 20 yards and cut to the center of the field. When I looked back to catch the ball, the defender blindsided me. It knocked me out. I woke up in the hospital the next morning to find out I would never play again.

"It was a cervical spine injury. I had to have surgery. Do tons of rehab to restore mobility and motor function. I never lost the ability to walk, but re-learning other simple tasks was incredibly frustrating. So, on that level, I understand what my dad is going through." He makes eye contact for the first time since he started talking about the game.

"I vaguely remember Mom telling me you got hurt, but I never realized how bad it was." Or maybe she told me and I didn't care. I wasn't very interested in hearing about Henry then. I was in college having a great time with my new friends. I didn't want a reminder of the friend I lost.

"It was rough for a bit. I was really angry for months—I had been so sure I would end up with a career in the NFL—but eventually I had to let go of the dream and move on. I turned my attention to school and graduated earlier than planned. And now I'm here."

"So, what now? Is there a new dream?"

He shrugs and stares down at his feet. "I'm still working on that. For now, I'm trying to enjoy life."

"Okay." I nod. Still feeling a bit shocked at how bad his injury was.

"What about you? How are your goals for the year going?"

We make our way out of the office and head back outside. "Um…I guess I've been a little sidetracked with work. It's been busy."

"Come on, it's February already. Have you even talked to your friends about that trip you want to go on?"

"No." I sound guilty.

"You should get on it. Even if you don't actually go until November, start planning now. Make sure it happens."

"I will." I walk up onto my front porch.

"Promise?"

"I'll do you one better." I hold out my right hand, pinky extended. Just like we use to do.

Henry laughs and wraps his pinky around mine, accepting the pinky promise. "Deal."

I'm halfway through the door when I stop and turn around.

"In case you're looking for suggestions for a new dream…" I pause trying to gauge his response. Unfortunately, he's standing just past the reach of the porch light, so I can't really see him. "…I personally think you would make a great football coach."

"Oh?" His response is less enthusiastic than I was expecting, almost like he doesn't care.

"Mom agrees with me. And she would know. She's been married to a pretty great coach for like a quarter of a century."

"That makes her sound really old." Henry ignores my suggestion again.

"I'm serious."

My eyes are adjusting to the darkness, so I can vaguely see the outline of his head nodding. At least now I know he actually paid attention.

"Goodnight, Clara."

"Night." I toss another wave over my shoulder and follow Al into the house, locking the door and turning off the porch light. It's not even ten, but I'm wiped. I trudge upstairs and get ready for bed. Pulling the blankets tight around me to warm me up, I say an extra prayer for Henry tonight. A prayer that he will find God and find direction for his life because I have a feeling that despite his confident exterior, he's as unsettled about his life plans as I am about my job. Seems like we could both use some wisdom right about now.

Chapter Nine

My conversation with Henry is still on my mind when I wake up Saturday morning. After getting some breakfast, I drag my laptop to the couch downstairs and pull up some apartment search sites. After two hours of flipping through pictures and reading about various apartments and condos, I'm beginning to feel discouraged.

I have some pretty solid conditions that will have to be met before I will even consider looking at an apartment. First of all, I need a place that allows large pets because after leaving Albert at home the entire time I was in college, I'm determined to bring him with me this time when I move out. Second, I have a very specific price range I need to stick with to stay within budget. Especially if I end up looking for another job and have to survive a few extra weeks in between paychecks. I'm also hoping to find a place on this side of town or even in midtown. Not that there's anything wrong with living on the south end of town, but the northside is what I know. It's where I grew up. I like this area. Lastly, since I'm a young female living alone, I need to make sure wherever I end up is a decent neighborhood, and I know there are a couple areas I would do well to avoid.

It's mid-morning when my phone goes off, letting me know El is calling.

"Hey." My voice sounds dejected even to me.

"What's wrong? Still having trouble coming up with ideas for what to do today?"

Her question catches me off guard. I've been so focused on Henry's instructions to get moving with my New Year's goals, I totally spaced off my plans to hang out today.

"Um…well…uh…" I hem and haw, trying to come up with something on the spot.

"Nothing, huh?" She laughs, sounding more like her usual self than she did the other night.

"No. Not really. Sorry. I got distracted."

"With what? Are you doing something fun without me?"

I let out a sigh. "I'm doing something super frustrating. Does that count?"

"Definitely not. What are you up to?"

"Looking for a place to live."

"Ah…your parents finally give you the old heave-ho?"

I know she's kidding, but the comment rubs me the wrong way. My response is short and terse. "No."

"O-kay. Obviously, you're not in a joking mood. So, you're not having much luck?"

"Basically. Everything is either too expensive. Or too small. Or doesn't allow pets. It's super frustrating."

"I'm sorry. It sounds frustrating. Anything I can do to help?"

"I don't know. Can you magically make the perfect apartment appear?"

"Unfortunately, no. I would be happy to come lend moral support, though. If you want."

I close the open tabs on my computer. "Sure. I think I need to take a little break from looking, but you should definitely come over."

"Okay. I'll be over in a little bit."

Almost half an hour later, Al hops up from his spot next to me on the couch and makes a beeline for the front door where he stands and proceeds to bark, warning me someone is outside. I wait for El to come in, since I texted her that the door would be open and I am refusing to come let her in because I want her to let herself in.

However, a few minutes pass, Al quiets down but remains at the door, and I'm confused. If Al had been barking at a passing car or someone walking by, he would've returned to the couch as soon as the person was gone. Instead, he stands at the door, vigilantly waiting for something to happen.

I head to the front door and look out the window to see why he keeps standing here, and what I see surprises me. El's car is in my driveway, as expected. But she hasn't made it inside yet because she's standing next to her vehicle talking to Henry, who appears to have stayed at his parents last night.

I momentarily consider going out to join them, but I'm still in my lightweight pajamas and it's cold out there. Instead, I get a glass down from the cupboard and fill it up with water, watching and waiting for El to make her way inside. Since he doesn't like James, I'm a bit relieved to see Henry is at least getting along with El.

It's not long before Henry heads to his car and El makes her way to our front door. I'm sitting at the island when she actually lets herself in. It looks like she came bearing gifts.

"Is that what I think it is?" I point to the bag in her right hand that appears to have a small box inside of it.

"You sounded like you needed a little pick-me-up." She holds the bag up for me to see it better. "So, I stopped and picked up a special treat."

"Yay!" I hop down and do a quick happy dance. She brought donuts. But not just any donuts. Donuts from Crystal's Bakery. It's a little hole-in-the-wall in downtown Rockton that makes the best donuts in the entire state, maybe the entire country. I love them so much. "Thanks, friend!"

"You're welcome." El gives me a smile and the donuts as she leans over to give Al the attention he's demanding.

I grab a small plate for each of us because it feels more civilized and hold the box open so she can pick which kind she wants.

A minute later, we've settled onto stools at the island with our donuts and a glass of milk when she pulls her large, stylish purse over to her and removes her iPad. She sets it up in front of us and a few swipes later, she has a rental site pulled up and is entering my preferred search parameters. She's using a different site than the one I was on earlier, and the first results look promising.

The two of us snack on some donuts while we scroll through various listings, marking the ones that initially look interesting so we can come back to them in a bit. By the time we're done looking over them closely, we've found three fairly decent options.

"Want to see if we can look at them today?" El's enthusiasm is almost overwhelming.

"Do think that's possible?"

"Maybe. Only one way to find out." She clicks on the link for our top pick and pulls out her cell phone.

"If we're going to look at these places, I need to change." I point at my pajamas and she dismisses me with a wave of her hand to go change. I scurry up the stairs and try to find something that makes me look responsible and trustworthy. By the time I settle on an outfit, El has arranged for us to view two of the places today. She couldn't get ahold of the third one, which is actually a small house not too far from Jimmy's, but we'll probably still drive by it to check out the neighborhood.

El offers to drive for our excursion since her car will warm up quicker than mine because she's driven it more recently.

"So, what did Henry have to say this morning?" I ask when we're halfway to the first apartment complex.

"Oh, he was just asking what we were up to today. When I told him the plan was to help you find a place, he said I could probably blame him."

I nod and point for her to take the next left. "You probably can. He was bugging me about my goals for the year last night, so I was feeling particularly desperate to move out this morning when I woke up."

"What goals?"

"Oh, my New Year's goals. Things I want to accomplish this year." I point left for her to turn onto the road the apartment complex is on.

"Interesting."

I shoot her a suspicious look. "What?"

"It's interesting that despite all your arguments about not being interested in Henry, he's the one you shared your New Year's goals with." She's fishing.

"Only because he happened to ask. It wasn't a big deal."

"Okay. Then what was on your list? Besides moving out?"

I'm about to answer when a large facility on the left side of the street distracts me. "What is that?"

"I don't know, some kind of factory?" El shrugs and turns her attention back to me, clearly waiting for a response to her question.

"Take the next right and we're there." I point just past the factory on the opposite side of the road where she needs to turn.

Once we pull into the visitor parking at the front of the lot, I look back down the street. I don't know why I'm so curious about the large plant, other than the fact that I've never seen it before, and I don't see a sign with a name anywhere to satisfy my curiosity.

El is quiet as we get out of the car and head toward the office door. We're halfway up the walkway when a strange scent causes us both to come to a stop.

"Do you…" I start to question.

"What is that smell?" She says at the same time, a bewildered look on her face.

I sniff the air a few times slowly. "It almost smells good, but…"

"Really gross at the same time?" She offers.

"Yeah. So weird. I wonder what that's about."

El nods toward the office door. "Whatever it is, let's get inside so we don't have to smell it anymore."

I hurry to follow her into the office.

"Hello, ladies." A petite, and annoyingly perky brunette stands up behind a desk. "How can I help you?"

I assume this is the leasing agent El talked to on the phone.

"I'm Eleanor. This is my friend Clara. We called about getting to check out one of your apartments." El reaches out and shakes her hand. I almost feel like I'm the one along for the ride, not the one who is actually looking for a place.

The woman has me fill out a form with some contact information, and then she leads us back outside. She takes us through the building next to the office that houses the workout room, the laundry facilities, and the media center/clubhouse that can all be used by residents.

Walking behind her as we head to the next building past the office, I notice the smell again. One glance at El and I can tell she notices it too. But our tour guide doesn't say anything about it, which makes me wonder if the two of us are losing our minds.

We're shown into what seems like a fairly spacious one-bedroom apartment on the ground floor. El and I take our time wandering around the apartment, looking over every nook and cranny, including the cupboards, closets, and ceilings. The whole place seems nice. It almost seems a little too good to be true because the price is lower than a lot of similar apartments in the area.

"What's your rule about pets? Online it looked like there wasn't a limit as far as size. Is that accurate?"

"Yes." Her perfect curls bounce as she nods. "We welcome renters with pets. We even have a dog park on the south end of the property. Then just beyond the dog park there's a walking trail that leads to the city park that backs our property, so there's plenty of opportunities to get those pets out for exercise."

"That's pretty cool." I nod, once again looking over the pricing pamphlet she gave me when we first got here.

We take a few more minutes to look around and ask a few more questions before we're ready to head out.

"Actually, do you mind if we walk down and check out the dog park and the trails?" I ask as soon as we're outside.

The leasing agent glances at her watch. "I have another showing in a few minutes, but if you want to walk over there, that's fine with me. You'll head down between buildings C and D, and the dog park will be on your left."

"Perfect. Thank you so much." El leads the way as we walk in the opposite direction as the leasing agent.

The funky smell lessens a little as we walk toward the dog park, or maybe I'm just getting used to it. Either way, I'm grateful for the reprieve.

"What do you think it is?" El points and directs me around the outside of the dog park, toward the trail leading to the city park.

"I have no idea. It smells familiar, but not. It kind of smells like food, but it also smells a bit like chemicals. I can't put my finger on it." I take a few more intentional sniffs to see if I can identify it.

A voice sounds behind us. "It's chips."

I spin around to see a girl about my age holding a Chihuahua entering the dog park.

"What?"

"You're talking about the smell, right?" She waves her free hand back and forth in front of her nose proving El and I didn't imagine the smell. We nod and she continues. "It's chips being made at the manufacturer across the street."

"Chips, huh? What kind of chips?" Another whiff identifies the potato smell.

The girl lets her dog down to play on the various doggie toys around the area. "They make potato chips."

"Interesting. Does it always smell like this?" My nose scrunches voluntarily. I'm not sure I can live near this smell all the time.

"It depends on the day. As long the wind is blowing north, you can't really smell it. But if there's a westward wind or no wind at all, it can get pretty bad."

"Does it bother you? Or do you get used to it?" El seems to have caught the smell again because she's holding her fingers under her nose.

"You sort of get used to it. Unless we have like a week where the winds are blowing north, then when the wind shifts west or south, it's pretty noticeable."

"Was it this bad when you came to look at the apartment?" I think this smell might be enough to convince me not to live here.

"I actually signed the lease sight—and smell—unseen. I was moving here from out of state for a job and needed something fast. It looked good online and the price was right, so I went for it." She turns to check on her Chihuahua.

"If you knew about the smell then, do you think you still would've moved in?" I'm really feeling a bit wary of this option. That too-good-to-be-true feeling has settled into my stomach something fierce.

"Honestly, probably. But only because I was desperate. I had been looking for a few weeks before I found this option and I needed something quick. So, if you're desperate, you'll learn to live with it. If you're not, maybe give yourself some time to find another place."

"Okay. Thanks. I really appreciate it." I wave to the girl as we turn and head back to the car.

Once we're halfway to the next apartment complex, El puts the front two windows down as we drive.

"What are you doing? It's cold!" I whine as I dive for the button on my door to at least get my window up.

El grabs me with her right hand. "Wait."

"For what? Frostbite to set in?" I'm being dramatic. It's not super cold out, but I was just warming up after our outdoor walking tour.

"Breathe." She releases my arm and waves her hand toward her face then away from her face in rhythm with her breathing. "I've never realized how important clean air is before in my life! I will never take it for granted again!"

Her declaration makes me laugh, but I do take in a few deep breaths of the crisp, clean winter air. "Okay, now can I put the window up? I'm cold."

"Fine." El laughs and puts her window up as well. "But seriously, it was weird."

"It was."

"Please tell me you're not going to move there. I don't think I would ever be able to come over."

"Yeah…I'm thinking it's going to be a no."

"What a relief." She turns into the parking lot of the next complex. It's not as nice as the last one, but according to the website, they allow dogs and are within my budget.

Stepping into the office, I begin to think checking this one out might be a mistake. The leasing agent is a large, balding guy in his fifties who apparently doesn't know how to buy clothes that fit or shower.

I shoot a hesitant look at El, but she looks determined.

"You here to see the apartment?" His gruff voice and his backwoods accent match his appearance.

"Um…yes?" I give El another inquisitive look. Not sure I really want to do this.

"Alright. This way." He heaves himself up from behind the desk and ambles out the door. We follow a few steps behind as he takes us to the second building down from the office and slowly makes his way up the stairs. Once he's at the top, he unlocks the door, pushes it open, and waves for us to enter. "Here you go. Lock it up when you're done. I'll be in the office if you have any questions or want to fill out an application."

With that, he begins his slow decent down the stairs.

Surprised, and a little relieved, by his departure, I slowly step through the open door into the living room. It's smaller than the last one and the carpet is older, but it's not bad. The kitchen seems dark, even with every light in the front area turned on. Once again, the bedroom is smaller than the stinky chip apartment, but not altogether bad. The bathroom is pretty rough though. It's dark like the kitchen and looks like there's a bit of a mold problem, and I get the feeling this place is not super quick to handle maintenance issues.

We walk back to the door, locking it behind us, and head down the stairs.

"I feel like I need to take a shower." El says, making a beeline for her car.

"I agree. It's not that it was super disgusting, but it wasn't very clean looking either. This place looked so much better in the pictures."

"I assume this one is a no?" She gives me an expectant look.

"Duh."

"Sorry, I feel bad both places ended up being a letdown."

"It's okay. I still want to drive by the other house, but we should hit a drive through or something first because that one is on the way back to my house."

We settle on going to an Italian fast-food place that's not too far away, and then El heads toward the small one-bedroom house we saw online. As we get closer, I take in the houses on my side of the street: some of the other houses look nice and some look old and dilapidated. Glancing around, I see a couple guys standing in the driveway of a house on El's side of the car. And then I look down at the GPS.

"Um…El, you just missed the turn. You were supposed to turn right down that street and it was going to be on the left.

She doesn't respond. She's staring straight ahead.

"El? Hello?" I wave a hand in front of her face. "You missed the turn. We need to turn around."

"Nope." She starts shaking her head, a look of determination on her face.

"I'm positive. Look, we're that little dot. The house was back there." I point to my screen and then in the direction we were supposed to turn. She's almost to the next major intersection.

"You are not living in that neighborhood." She says definitively with another shake of her head.

"What are you talking about? It looked nice. Why are you being so weird?"

"Nice? You think having drug dealers for neighbors sounds nice?!"

"Drug dealers? What are you talking about?" I shift in my seat so I can see her better.

"Didn't you see those guys in that driveway back there?" She shoots me an exasperated look and makes a left turn onto one of Rockton's main roads.

"Yeah, I saw them. You think those guys were drug dealers?" They looked super normal to me.

"They were dealing drugs. I'm positive." She glances in her rearview mirror suspiciously, like she expects one of them to follow us. I roll my eyes. It seems it's her turn to be over-dramatic.

"You know this because of all the drug deals you've been a part of, huh?" My response is a sarcastic one because I'm really annoyed she wouldn't turn around.

Silence.

I look over and El is staring straight in front of us. She's tense, nervous. All of a sudden, I wonder if I've crossed a line with my comment. The idea of us driving by a drug deal seems so ludicrous to me, but based on the look on El's face, I'm going to guess the possibility doesn't seem as crazy to her.

"El…" I want to apologize, but she interrupts me.

"I've lived in neighborhoods like that before. Trust me when I say something shady was going down. It's not the kind of neighborhood you want to be in, okay?" Her statement is quiet but forceful.

"Okay. I trust you." My response is equally quiet, and now the car has fallen into an awkward silence. I look around for something to talk about since El doesn't offer up any more details about the drug deals she's apparently seen. Not that I would know what to say if she did. So, I say the first thing that comes to mind. "Gosh…I'm so hungry."

"Yeah, me too." Her voice is still quiet, but it doesn't sound as defensive as before.

We pull up in front of my house a few minutes later to see Henry is shooting hoops by himself in my driveway.

"Hey, if it's okay with you, I think I'm going to head home. I feel super tired all of a sudden." El sounds convincingly tired, but she's also glancing at the driveway when she says it, which makes me think she maybe isn't up for socializing with Henry right now.

"Uh…yeah. That's fine. Let me just grab my food really quick." I hop out of the car, pull my purse over my head and open the back door to get my food. "See you tomorrow?"

Normally, that's a given, but the way she's acting right now, I'm actually not sure I'll see her at church in the morning.

"Yeah. And, I'm sorry we didn't find you a new place today."

"No worries. Like that girl was saying, I'm not exactly desperate. I have a good place to live until I find something I love." I shrug and give her a smile. I know it's small, but I need her to know I'm okay with the way today turned out.

"Sounds like a plan." She offers a halfhearted smile.

"Thanks for coming with me. The whole experience would've been way worse if I had been on my own."

She smiles again. "Of course. See you later, Clara."

I watch as she pulls away, my hands full of food containers. I ordered some extra so I would have something to eat for dinner either tonight or tomorrow night. Once she turns off my street, I head toward my house.

"Hey, Henry." I give him a chin nod as I pass where he's standing in the driveway.

"Are you okay?" He sounds legitimately concerned, which surprises me.

"Yeah. I'm fine. Why?"

He dribbles the basketball back and forth between his hands and stares at me. "For starters, you look upset. Second, you said 'Hey, Henry', not 'What are you doing here?' or 'Who said you can be on my property, punk?' or any number of…"

I cut him off before he can continue. "You're complaining that I wasn't mean to you?"

"No. It's a little unexpected is all." He's still staring at me, like if he stares hard enough, he'll be able to read my mind.

"Well," I hold up the food in my hands. "I'm going to head in. I'm pretty hungry."

"How did the apartment search go today?" He calls behind me.

I stop on the front porch and turn around. "I didn't find anything, but I'm glad we looked."

"Everything with you and El okay? She took off pretty quickly."

Part of me wants to tell him what happened in the last neighborhood and what El said, but a bigger part of me feels like I should respect her privacy. She doesn't open up about her past often, so it seems like a bad idea to share it with someone else.

"Things are fine. She had somewhere to be." I feel guilty about the lie as soon as I say it, but I just want him to leave the subject alone.

He nods his head. He doesn't believe me, but he's going to leave it alone. "Hey, Hannah is helping Uncle Bryan out today. I was going to go over and say hi. Maybe play a few games. Want to join?"

"I'll pass. Thanks for the offer though." I wave and head inside.

The next hour passes lazily as I eat my lunch and channel surf with Al hanging out at my feet. After finding a spot for my leftovers in the back of the fridge where my brothers won't see them, I'm feeling restless. I was pretty excited to have the house to myself today, but right now I'm bored and wish I had someone to hang out with instead of being alone.

Remembering Henry's offer, I decide hanging out at Uncle Bryan's bowling alley and playing a few games would be better than sitting at my house doing nothing, so I grab my jacket and head out to my car.

Chapter Ten

Mid-afternoon on a cold Saturday in February appears to be the best time to go bowling, based on the number of people inside. It doesn't take long for me to spot Hannah behind the counter. Last I heard, she quit her job at the mall last fall after Mr. McKinley had surgery because of everything going on with her dad. I'm guessing she's been helping Uncle Bryan out at his bowling alley when he needs her.

She's got a couple people lined up in front of her collecting their shoes, but she smiles and nods toward one end of the building when she spots me. I follow the direction she's pointed me in to see Henry at the furthest lane. My quick pace slows a bit when I realize his friend Trey is with him. Even though I know Henry invited me, I'm not sure if I should join them or not since he clearly found someone else to hang out with after I shot him down.

"Hey, Clara." Trey spots me before I can make up my mind.

Henry turns around, surprise written on his face. "Hey. I didn't think you were coming."

"I got bored." I shrug and drop my phone and keys onto one of the unused chairs behind their lane.

He nods toward the scoreboard. "We're almost done with this game, but we could add you to the next one."

"Sounds good." I take a seat and watch as Trey takes his turn. He knocks three pins down with his first throw and only one with his second.

"I hope you're okay with losing." Trey huffs as he trudges back to the chair next to me and drops himself into it.

I glance up to the scoreboard to see he has just over half as many points as Henry, which would be frustrating. "It is a bit annoying how often he wins."

Trey leans forward, getting closer to me. "Maybe you and I should kick him out and play just the two of us."

I smile sweetly. "You think we should?"

Henry turns his attention from the lane where he just rolled another strike. "Don't let her smile fool you. She'll kick your butt too."

"Oh, really?" Trey glances back and forth between Henry and me.

"Yeah. She's *almost* as good as I am."

"Whoa! I am so much better than you!" I defend myself as Trey heads up for his next frame, which goes a little better than the last one.

Henry and I bicker back and forth about which of us is better while the two of them finish up their game. I'm excited when they get done and add my name to the lineup. It's been at least a month since I was here last, and I have to keep myself sharp if I have any hope of beating Henry. Because despite my trash-talking, I know he really is a little bit better than me.

"So, how's work?" I ask Trey as Henry kicks off the next game.

"It's been pretty busy lately." Trey is a videographer for a large marketing and advertising company in town. "I have a couple projects that are almost finished and a few more we're in the beginning stages of right now. Bouncing around between the projects and contacts and trying to keep up with everything can get crazy."

Trey hops up and takes his turn, once again not doing as well as Henry did on his turn. After I play my round, I take my seat next to Trey again.

"How's work going for you? Is the restaurant biz all you thought it would be?" His question is lighthearted but hits a nerve for me.

"Yes and no. I really like the social media part of my job. I also don't mind scheduling and working with our employees. It's just sometimes…" Our conversation is once again interrupted by the need to bowl another frame, but when we're both back to our seats I continue. "Sometimes, I wonder if it's the right fit for me. I was pretty excited about it when I started, but now I'm not so sure. I guess not all of us can get our dream jobs right out of college."

My last remark came out with a little more attitude than I meant it to, so I try to temper it with a friendly smile.

Trey holds his hands up in defense. "Easy there. I did not get my dream job right out of college, so don't be using that accusatory tone with me."

"Really?" I was under the impression T3 was his first job, so I'm a little surprised to hear him say this. Of course, I have to wait until we've both played our round and Henry is up again before I get a response.

"Yup. I worked at my dad's tire shop for a bit and did freelance work before I was hired full-time at T3. Plus, it's a great job and all, but it's not necessarily my dream gig. It's a good stepping stone though. Maybe the diner job is a stepping stone for you until you find something else you like better."

I think about what he said while I make my throws. I get nine pins down on this frame, which keeps my score close to Henry's.

"You know, we might have some positions open at T3 you would be interested in, if you want to stick with the social media and marketing work. You should check it out." Trey says as he heads up to make his fifth attempt.

"That's not a bad idea." Henry, who has been silently observing my conversation with Trey so far, sits next to me while his friend is up making his throws.

"You think?" I don't know how I feel about the idea of working at T3, but it could be a good option now that I'm thinking about it.

"I do. Plus, Trey would totally put in a good word for you, wouldn't you?"

"Definitely." Trey echoes behind me as I make my way up for my shot. "It's a great company. You should really look into it."

Satisfied with my score on this frame, I turn back to face the guys. "Maybe I will."

By the time we finish our game, I'm convinced I should check out the T3 job postings online when I get home later. The fact that Henry beat me by five points almost doesn't bother me because I'm distracted with the thought of a new job lead. I try not to argue too much because I still beat Trey by almost thirty points, and I don't want to be obnoxious.

Trey disappears pretty quickly, which I would guess is due to Henry's annoying tendency to brag. Henry and I make our way back to the counter where Hannah is now spraying and sorting stacks of returned bowling shoes.

"You hanging in there, kid?" Henry asks as we approach the counter.

"I think so." She gives a smile. "For the most part, it's been pretty fun, as long as I ignore the occasional rude customer."

"I'm glad. I didn't realize you were working here until Henry said something earlier." I brush a few stray strands of hair out of my face.

"I don't really." She rolls her eyes. "Only when Uncle B is short staffed. He's family. I feel like I can't say no when he asks for help."

I laugh. "Well, at least you get a little extra money."

"This is true." She nods and then moves to the other end of the counter to help a family who just walked in.

Henry and I wave a silent goodbye and head out the door.

"What are you up to now?"

He glances at his phone to check the time. "I should be heading to work pretty soon. What about you?"

"No real plans. I'll probably head home and read or watch a Hallmark movie or something."

He makes a face at my Hallmark movie option. "Seriously? That sounds so boring."

"I think it sounds relaxing." I argue and stick my tongue out at him.

He begins backing toward his truck, which is parked on the opposite end of the parking lot as my car.

"Whatever. I'll see you sometime this week?" The statement sounds more like question.

"You would see me tomorrow morning if you came to church. We could even get lunch after."

Henry doesn't really respond to my invitation. Instead, he simply waves and gets in his truck. I try not to feel too disappointed. The last time I saw Sam, he told me he's had a couple really good conversations with Henry lately, so I'm hopeful.

Once I get home and pull up the website, I feel pretty good about the idea of applying for a job at T3. They have a number of openings, some of which I know I'm not qualified for, but there are two I think I could do. I might need to update my resume this weekend.

I should probably also make sure I'm 100% positive about leaving before I actually send out applications.

⁂

I'm still wrestling with the idea of leaving Jimmy's when I enter the young adult Sunday school class the next morning right as Stephen is taking his place at the front of the room to get the class started and prompts us to find seats. I sit through Stephen's entire lesson going back and forth between paying attention and staring at the back of James' head, trying to decide if I should leave Jimmy's or not.

"Before you all leave, I would like to remind you to check out the tables in the lobby. Our bi-annual Volunteer Fair is happening today and you should stop by. We have a table set up for each ministry opportunity and the people at each table can answer your questions about getting involved. In a church this size, even when you're a part of a Sunday school class like this one, it's easy to feel a little lost. Volunteering helps you truly connect with other people in the church on a regular basis. That's all I've got. Have a great day guys." Stephen waves us off to the lobby and, eventually, to the main service.

I mill around in the multi-purpose room talking to people who don't attend our small group. As much as I love my group, I feel like it's important to get to know the other people who are a part of the young adult ministry. Most of my friends have exited the room by the time I finish chatting with one of the newer ladies I've noticed here the last few weeks.

When I get out to the lobby, it's pretty empty and the music in the sanctuary is playing, so I've managed to miss the beginning of service yet again. It's not the end of the world. I tend to talk too long after Sunday school with either my fellow young adults or other people in the church lobby. It's one of the hazards of growing up in this church—I know a lot of people, especially the older crowd who always want to talk.

"Looks like you're a little late to the party, Clara."

I turn to see Pastor Drew, the youth pastor, walking toward me. I smile and accept the side hug he's offering. "Yeah, I was busy talking."

"Sounds about right." Drew came on as the youth pastor here when I was in eighth grade, so he knew me all throughout my high school years. "Since you're already running late. How about we chat for a second?"

I shrug and lean against the Welcome Center in the middle of the lobby. "Sure, what's up?"

"I think you should be a youth leader."

Part of me wants to laugh, but it looks like he's serious. "What? Why?"

"We can always use more leaders. You're good with teenagers, so I think you should give it a shot."

"I'm not sure." I shake my head slowly. I have been wanting to get more involved in church, but my first reaction is that helping with the youth group isn't the right fit for me.

"Come on. You have no idea how much fun it is." He gives me an encouraging smile before continuing. "How about this? You come to youth group this week, check it out, and remind yourself how awesome it is. Then, we can talk more about it. How's that sound?"

Honestly, I'm not thrilled by the thought of being a youth leader, but I have no clue why I feel so against the idea. Maybe I should check it out this week.

"Fine. I'll see you Wednesday."

"Awesome!" Drew gives me a high-five. "Now, you should probably get into service. Can't have my youth leaders setting a bad example."

Before I can protest and point out that I haven't actually agreed to do it yet, Drew takes off toward the other side of the lobby. Wondering what I just got myself into, I slip into the sanctuary and find a seat on the end of a row next to my friends.

Now, I'm not only wondering about work, but I'm also wondering about this volunteering opportunity. I go back and forth on the matter all morning on Monday since the office is pretty quiet. Mostly because James hasn't been in much. He left a little after nine to meet Mr. Simmons to check out a couple more properties, and we haven't seen him since. Part of me is relieved.

It would be a bit difficult to work across from him all day when I'm mentally updating my resume. Although I'll have to get used to the idea if I decide to move forward and start applying for other jobs, and the idea of moving on to a new job is getting more appealing by the day.

"Hey, do you think you could help us out for a bit? We're a lot busier than normal." The question interrupts my work a little after eleven.

I look up to see Scout standing in the doorway looking at me expectantly.

"Uh…yeah. Of course. What kind of help do you need?" I get up to head out to the front of the restaurant.

A look of relief comes over Scout's face. "I think we will be okay serving if you can help with the ancillary stuff."

"Will do." I offer her what I hope is a calming smile and follow her out the kitchen door.

A quick glance around the room tells me Scout isn't wrong. We are busier today than we normally are on Mondays for lunch, but I suppose more business is always a good thing.

It's a good thing I don't mind working the front. I especially don't mind when I don't have to worry about orders. Not that I dislike waiting tables, but it can be stressful. I prefer the lower stress "ancillary stuff" as Scout called it—refilling drinks, delivering food, clearing tables, taking payments. Doing those tasks means I get to flit from table to table and chat with all the customers instead of being super focused on only a few tables I'm supposed to be covering.

An hour slips by quickly and I notice the dirty dish side of the dish pit is pretty packed when I'm dropping a stack of plates and utensils I just cleared. Since it looks like Danny and Wendell are busy prepping food, I decide I'll get some of them started to keep it from getting too bad back here.

Thankfully, I remember to slip on a plastic apron before I start, ensuring the cute sweater I'm wearing won't get soaked while I spray the dishes. I've accidentally soaked myself with the industrial sprayer once or twice when I forget to put an apron on to protect myself.

Due to years of practice, I'm able to expertly stack the plates, bowls, and cups in the dish racks and send them through the dish washing conveyor belt pretty quickly. It's maybe ten minutes before I fill up the plastic drying shelves with the racks of clean dishes.

Undoing the apron, I head back out front. A little after one, I see Wendell stick his head out of the side entrance to the kitchen and flag me down.

"What's up?"

He holds the cordless phone from the kitchen out to me. "I've got someone who wants to talk to the manager."

"Can you ask James to take it?" I've got a rag in one hand and a table's bill and credit card in the other.

"He's not here." Wendell shakes his head and holds the phone out to me again.

"What? Where is he?" I mutter the second question more to myself than anyone else, but Wendell shrugs in response. Giving up, I swap him the rag for the phone and turn to take care of the bill in my right hand. I also brace myself for whatever complaint I'm about to get while trying to sound positive at the same time. "Jimmy's Diner this is Clara."

I'm grateful when the person on the phone turns out to be one of our food suppliers with a question about one of our recent payments. I don't know much about that part of the business because James takes care of it, but I'm happy as a clam that it's not an angry customer. I hurry to get the credit card and receipt back to our customer, putting the call on hold while I return it, and head into the office.

As Wendell said, James' chair sits empty behind his desk. It's been over four hours since he left. Part of me, a very small part, is almost worried about him since he's been gone a lot longer than he said he would be. Most of me is simply annoyed.

I try to focus on finding the information the woman on the phone needs. It takes me a little bit to locate the right file on James' desk, give the information to our sales rep, and get off the phone. I put the file away, return the phone to its stand in the kitchen, and head back out front. It's emptied out enough in the last few minutes that I can head back to the office to work on some social media posts for Valentine's Day next week.

When James finally comes walking into the office, he's on the phone so I can't even bust him for disappearing for over half the day. I wait, not very patiently, and employ my eavesdropping skills to determine he's on the phone with his dad. It was a toss-up between the bank or his father, but then he shot me an eye-roll he would only use on family.

"Guess what?" He grins at me as soon as he hangs up.

"What?" I'm too annoyed to play guessing games right now. I know nothing went horribly wrong today while he was gone, but the fact that he was gone for so long and didn't bother to check in here irks me.

His excitement drops a little. "You're not even going to guess? Who are you and what have you done with Clara?"

I give him a blank stare in response. The more he pushes this, the less I care about whatever he has to say. It's probably just something about his parents' latest adventure anyway. While it has been interesting to hear about what they've been up to, I would much rather talk to Sharon to find out. Which reminds me, I never got to talk to her the other day after our video chat.

"O-kay. Well…I found it!" His eyes are wide with expectation when he says this, but the significance is lost on me.

"Found what?" I don't remember him saying he lost anything.

"The new location. I found where I'm going to open the second Jimmy's Diner." Once again, anticipation and excitement are written all over his face.

"Wait? What? Seriously?" I try to look excited too, but I kind of feel like I got punched in the stomach.

He nods vigorously. "Yeah. I'm so pumped. It's the perfect location. The building is great, and it looks like it will fit within our budget."

"Wow. That's…big."

"I know. I just talked to my dad, and he agrees it could work."

"That's great."

"It is. This property is in the exact area I wanted to end up in, which is awesome. I can't believe how great it is."

"Good, good. So, what's the next step?" I'm trying to get myself to focus on what he's saying, but I'm having a hard time.

"Well, after we went to look at the property, Mr. Simmons and I went back to his office to talk over some of the details needed for the business plan. The official one. I know I already discussed the general idea with them, but that was before I found a place. Now I have details about the location and cost, so I need to put together a detailed plan."

"Gotcha. Is that what you're working on right now?"

"No. I got most of done when I was at home."

"When did you go home?" If I didn't know he has an apartment, I would think that he lives here because he spends so much time here. It's really strange he went home in the middle of the day instead of coming back to work.

"After meeting with Mr. Simmons. I wanted to get the proposal together as quickly as possible, and I figured there would be too many interruptions if I was here." James moves stacks of papers around his desk, clearly looking for something.

I try not to take what he said personally. I know the servers and kitchen staff pop in with questions most days, but the way he said it makes me feel like I'm a bother to him.

"Did you move my stuff?" There's a hint of accusation in his question.

"Yeah I was looking for an invoice. What's-her-name, our food rep, called with a question. *Since you weren't here...*" I emphasize the fact that he wasn't here, just in case he's about to actually get mad at me for touching his desk. "...I had to do a bit of hunting around to find it."

"Oh. Okay." He neatly arranges the piles I apparently didn't put back correctly. "Anyway, I was able to get a lot done with the business proposal. I was also able to make a few phone calls I needed to make to help move this thing forward."

"Like your dad?"

"I actually had a few others to talk to first. I needed information from them to answer the questions I knew he was bound to ask, especially since this property I'm interested in means we'll be buying the property not leasing."

"So, you decided to buy? I thought Dean said leasing, with an option to buy, would be a better plan."

"He didn't say better. He said it might be safer, but this property is too good of an opportunity to pass up."

"Okay. Is there like a link or something? Where I could see some pictures...get an idea of what we're doing."

James looks up at me suddenly, almost like he's surprised by my request. "I'm sure there is. I don't have it. Mr. Simmons gave me this spec sheet, but I haven't looked at it online."

I accept the sheets of paper he's handing over to me. It's got one somewhat crappy picture on top and two and half pages of random information about the property. "Is this square footage right? That sounds way too big."

"Well, that sheet is for both buildings the company is selling. One was their warehouse, which is why the number is so high. It's a massive warehouse. The second building has been their main office, but they've outgrown both the office and the warehouse. They've been trying to sell it for a while. They built a brand-new facility that's over twice the size and moved into it six months ago. While they initially wanted to sell both buildings together, they're at the point where they want to be rid of it, which means they're open to selling them as two separate properties. If you look at the last page, it should have all the details about the office building."

"Okay." I flip through to the last page and find the info he mentioned. The size does look right and the price range James wrote in the margin sounds like it's in the ballpark. "Do you think we can get it renovated and get all the equipment we need and stick to your budget?"

"Obviously. If I didn't think we could, I wouldn't be looking into buying it." He sounds offended I would even ask.

"Of course."

"One of the things Mr. Simmons and I talked about was that it will need to be re-zoned if we're going to open a restaurant there."

"What's that mean?"

"Pull up a map of the city." He nods toward my computer, makes his way around his desk to mine, and waits for me to pull up the location address. "The whole city is broken up into different zones, and the zone determines what type of buildings can be in an area. That property is currently designated for Industrial use. For a restaurant, it will need to be zoned for commercial business use. Now, all the other corners of this intersection are zoned for commercial business, so Mr. Simmons doesn't think it will be difficult to get it rezoned. Other than securing the finances, I think the rezoning will be the biggest hurdle to get over. Our lawyer will make it a condition of the sale. He said…"

"We have a lawyer?" I interrupt him.

"We need one. Buying commercial property is a tricky, complicated business. I would be an idiot if I didn't have a team of people going over everything to make sure I'm on the right track."

"What team of people?"

"In this case, Mr. Simmons, obviously. Mike, over at the bank. Our lawyer and an accountant to make sure everything will work out for us. And then, obviously, my dad."

Once again, it sounds like I'm not a part of the whole opening-a-new-location thing. This conversation was beginning to make me feel like I'm in the loop, but it appears I'm not a part of the team.

James goes on a while longer about rezoning, lawyers, and buying property, but I don't really hear much of it. The thought of leaving Jimmy's and finding another job is taking hold in my heart again. I want a job where my opinion matters, where my boss doesn't treat me as if I'm not here.

The rest of the day ticks by slowly as I have to listen to James on one phone call after another with his special team of people as they begin the process of making an offer on this property. At one point, my attitude about my job is so bad all I can think about is finding a different job.

I work hard to stay focused on writing social media posts for the rest of the afternoon, but my mind keeps drifting off to other job possibilities and daydreaming about what it would be like to work elsewhere.

By the time I'm ready to leave for the day, I can hardly think of anything other than finding a new job and getting away from James. It's pretty disappointing because I was so excited when I first started. Now I can't wait to be done working with James. I slip out while James is on yet another phone call with someone on his "team."

As I pull out of the parking lot, I grab my phone and call Kenzie, hoping she's not at work so I can talk to her.

"Hey, Clara." She sounds cheery.

"I'm going to quit my job."

Chapter Eleven

"Oh really?" There's laughter in her voice now. She's not taking me seriously.

"Yes." I say definitively.

Her voice sobers. "Okay. What's going on?"

"I can't work with James anymore. It's too hard. And disappointing. Not to mention discouraging. I can't work that closely with someone who doesn't value me or my opinions." Especially someone who is supposed to be my friend.

Kenzie is quiet for a few seconds before responding. "I get it, Clara. It's really hard working with people who don't treat you with respect. I understand it probably better than most. Are you sure quitting is the right solution?"

My response is sharp and loud. "It's the only solution."

I was expecting Kenz to be more supportive, so having her question my decision is frustrating.

"Okay." Kenzie's calm demeanor is irritating. "I get why it would seem that way…"

"It doesn't *seem* that way! It *is* that way!" My exasperation comes out loud and clear.

"Alright. Clara, if you're set on leaving and finding a different job, that's fine, I guess. I just have one question."

Feeling defeated instead of victorious at her statement, I respond half-heartedly. "What?"

"You took this job because you knew God was telling you it was right, and don't try to play that down—you and I both know God directed you to take it. So, are you leaving because God's taking you in a new direction or because you're unhappy with how things are right now?"

"I…uh…I…" I don't have an answer for her. "I guess…I don't really know."

"Have you prayed about it?"

Thinking over it, most of my prayers about work and things with James have been complaint and emotion-fueled brain dumps. Not that I haven't sincerely prayed for direction at times because I have. But in this moment, with Kenzie waiting for a response, I'm not sure I can say my desire to leave my job at Jimmy's Diner is from God. So, I don't say anything.

Kenzie's tone is an understanding one when she continues. "I get it, Clara. I really do. I can't tell you how many times I've almost quit in the last nine months. But every time, God has made it clear this is where I'm supposed to be right now. If you pray about it and still feel strongly that leaving Jimmy's is what you should do, I will support you one hundred percent."

"Okay."

Kenzie changes the subject and continues to chat for almost a half hour before getting off the phone, by which time I have made it home and curled up in my comfy chair. Despite my desire to ignore it, the advice Kenzie gave me feels like a huge weight on my shoulders and forces me to think it over.

Giving in, I slip into some non-diner scented clothes and plop back into the chair with my Bible and notebook in hand. I casually page through my Bible, once again unsure of where to read. I don't even really know if I should be reading. Maybe I should be praying. Honestly though, I'm not in the mood to pray at this exact moment, even if I know I should.

I end up flipping to a page that has a bookmark covered in scripture references, one of many small items stuck in my Bible to hold my place in case I eventually remember to come back to it, which rarely happens. Surprisingly, this is one I placed recently. The only reason I know that is because it's the chapter we started discussing last week at small group. Since I have no idea what I should be reading or even what I should be praying right now, I figure I might as well read what Sam and Adam asked us to read for this week.

I start by re-reading the section we covered last time and then continue to read the rest of the chapter and the next and the next, until I finish the book of James. It's only five chapters, taking up a couple of pages, so it's not a long read. By the end, I notice the weight on my shoulders feels a little lighter, even though I haven't figured anything out. None of my questions about life have been answered. My problems with James haven't been miraculously resolved. But I can feel a sense of calm coming over me anyway.

Grateful for the reprieve, I decide to read the first chapter again, slower this time, looking for anything that speaks to me specifically. And verse twelve practically jumps off the page and smacks me in the face.

"Blessed is the man who remains steadfast under trial, for when he has stood the test he will receive the crown of life, which God has promised to those who love him."

Remain steadfast.

Remain steadfast.

Remain steadfast.

The two words seem to be on repeat in my soul when I read the verse again. So much so that I open my little notebook and flip to the next blank page in it and scrawl them in large letters across the page.

Steadfast. It's not a commonly used word, which makes me wonder what the word truly means. Thanks to a quick

Google search and Dictionary.com, it only takes me a few second to find out it means:

1. fixed in direction; steadily directed
2. firm in purpose, resolution, faith, attachment, etc., as a person
3. unwavering, as resolution, faith, adherence, etc.

Firm in purpose. I jot the words much smaller underneath the two-word phrase I just wrote down, but it's not enough. I decide to dig deeper and start hunting through various Bible study websites for the deeper meaning of the original Greek word that's translated as steadfast in this verse. What I find are phrases like "to persevere," "to endure bravely, with trust," "to remain," and "to stay and not leave." All of which I list in my notebook, carrying over to the next page.

Whether I like it or not, I think I've found the answer to Kenzie's question. If I decide to leave Jimmy's now, it will be because it's what I want, not because it's what God is calling me to do.

This truth settles in fast and hard. And I don't like it. I don't want to stay. I don't want to persevere or endure. I want to leave. I want change.

I slam my Bible shut and toss it and my notebook onto my bed. I snatch my purse up from where I dropped it on the floor when I got home and make a beeline for the front door, barely pausing to answer my mom's question about where I'm going.

It doesn't take me long to drive to the movie theater, get a ticket for a movie that looks mildly interesting, and buy some snacks since I haven't eaten anything for dinner yet. As I sit staring at the screen, munching on popcorn, I do my best to push everything I learned during my devo time out of my head.

ᘎᘎᘎ

I'm still trying to ignore it Wednesday as I drive to youth group, which is something else I wish I could ignore. However, I promised Pastor Drew I would be here, so I have to go.

I ate a quick dinner after work so I could get over to the church early. Pastor Drew emailed me and asked me to come half an hour early to join the youth leaders meeting taking place before the service starts.

I make my way into the same room that hosts my Sunday school class because the youth group uses the multi-purpose room on Wednesday nights for their service. I find quite a few people milling around waiting for the leaders' meeting to start.

"Glad you could make it, Clara." Drew says as he walks by me on his way to the front. I take a seat toward the back as all the leaders in the room notice Drew up by the stage and find their seats. I would guess there are at least fifty people in here. I wasn't really expecting so many people, but I suppose it makes sense given that the youth group at my church is as big as some entire churches.

"Welcome, everyone!" Drew calls from his spot at the front of the room. "It's good to see you guys. To any newcomers, I'm especially excited for you to join us. I know some of you are simply here to check things out, but I'm praying you all stick with us. We need all the help we can get."

A ripple of laughter makes its way through the group.

"To give you an idea of what all we do, I'm going to have a couple people who are already leaders come up and give you the low-down on everything."

The first guy Drew calls up talks all about the Wednesday night services and how they aim to help students dig into the scripture and understand how it applies to their lives. The goal being to give them a good foundation for their faith.

The second person Drew brings to the front is a woman who looks a little younger than my mom and she talks about the Sunday night small groups that take place all over town.

"Being a teenager is rough and we want to offer as much support and encouragement to them as we can. Part of the way we do that is by offering them a community where they are encouraged to ask questions and think critically about their faith. We can always use more leaders in these groups to help us facilitate the discussions."

I have fond memories of the small groups I was a part of in high school. At my request, my parents had nothing to do with the youth group, but some of my friends' parents were leaders, including Dean and Sharon. They actually hosted a small group at their house for a couple years, which I attended. Other than parents, we had a lot of college students as leaders over the years. They were a little less consistent because they were gone during breaks, but it always made us feel really cool to get to hang out with people in college. I smile to myself at that thought. Looking back now, my friends and I were so silly, but I suppose that's how most people feel when they think about their high school days.

The meeting doesn't last very long. Probably because after about twenty minutes, a few students begin to show up to set up the stage for the service. Pastor Drew wraps up the meeting with prayer, and his heart and enthusiasm for reaching teenagers is evident. Hearing him pray makes me reconsider my hesitations about being a youth leader. I mill around the back of the multi-purpose room, chatting with some of the leaders and students as they arrive.

Time passes quickly and before I know it, we all find seats as the worship team begins to play. One of the things that hasn't changed since I was in youth group is the worship team is almost better than the main church worship team that leads during Sunday service. The energy is different—probably on account of the fact that they're still in their teens and have more energy—but it's a great time of worship. It's really cool to see how passionate they are about praising God.

Pastor Drew is in the beginning of a series about following God's plans and dreams for life. "As you guys know, for a while last month a lot of people were thinking and talking about what they want to do differently this year. I'm not here to tell you that's wrong, but I am going to challenge you guys to ask a different question. Instead of saying, 'what do I want my life to look like this year?' try asking, 'what does God want my life to look like this year?'

"So many of us, myself included, get too wrapped up in our own plans and goals for the New Year. We forget or ignore the fact that as believers, we should constantly be asking God what our lives should look like. We're only a month into the new year, and already people are slacking on their goals. Not only do we need to pursue what God wants for us first, we also need to be consistent and follow through on his directions."

Drew's message, which hits so close to home that it's a little obnoxious, lasts about half an hour before he calls the worship team back up to the stage. I watch as a number of leaders make their way to the front and face the audience as Drew invites the students to use the next little while to pray—alone or with a leader—about what God has planned for them. I'm honestly surprised at the number of students who go forward and find a spot to pray as the worship team continues to provide a reverent atmosphere.

Pastor Drew quietly prays a prayer of dismissal and tells those who want to stay to pray and worship can, and those who are ready to leave can do so as well. A little over half the group quietly exits the room—or at least it's quiet for a group of almost one hundred teenagers.

I follow some of them out and end up talking to a group of girls and one leader. The woman explains she leads a small group for mostly junior and senior girls, a few of which are huddled around us right now. As I listen to the conversation, I see Cam and Carter out of the corner of my eye slip out of the multi-purpose room and head into the church gym with some of their friends.

"Where do you guys go to school?" I turn my attention back to the girls and throw out the first question that comes to mind. One of them goes to Rockton. The rest of them either go to the other high school in town or are homeschooled.

"Hey, Clara. What are you doing here?" The question comes from behind me before I can continue the conversation any further.

Turning around, I see one of our servers, Sophie, approaching to hug a girl in the circle around me. "Hey. Pastor Drew asked me to come by, so here I am."

"Cool." She nods in a way that gives the impression that my presence here is more weird than cool.

"Yeah. How's your day going?"

"Pretty good. I had a test in Bio, but I think I did okay on it."

"That's good." I nod. "I was never very good at science. I always preferred my art and English classes."

"Ick…I hate art. It's like a special form of torture. At least the way Mrs. Peterson does it."

I try not to visibly react to Sophie's comment. Mrs. Peterson was one of my favorite teachers when I was in high school. As a matter of fact, she was one of the teachers who wrote letters of recommendation for me when I was applying to colleges. Swallowing my opinion, I change the subject and the two of us continue to chat awkwardly for another few minutes, but I feel more uncomfortable by the second. Eventually, some of Sophie's friends drag her off to talk to a cute guy. Feeling relieved and desperate not to have to make awkward conversation with her again, I make up an excuse and start toward the door.

A hand on my arm stops me, and I turn to see Peyton has now materialized next to me.

"Hey Clara, you one of the new leaders Drew was talking about?"

"What are you doing here?" The question comes out with more of a bite than I mean it to, but it doesn't seem to faze Peyton.

"I became a youth leader this past year after I graduated. I thought you knew that."

I shake my head slowly. "I did not. Listen, I…uh…have to go. I'll see you later."

"See ya tomorrow." Peyton waves and turns back to the guys he had been talking to before he stopped me.

I pull out of the parking lot quickly, but I don't head straight home. I need to talk about what just happened. So instead, I find myself a few minutes later knocking on an apartment door and doing an it's-too-cold-to-be-outside dance on the doormat.

"Hey. Are you okay?" El's brow is furrowed as she opens the door to let me in.

"Sure…I guess. I don't know. I'm…ugh!" I make my way into her living room and plop down on the couch.

"Okay. How about you try again and see if you can manage a coherent sentence this time?" El slips into her teacher voice as she takes a seat next to me.

"I went to youth group tonight."

"Oh right. The youth pastor wants you to be a leader. I take it that didn't exactly go well?"

"I mean, the actual youth service was great. I always loved Pastor Drew when I was a part of the youth group, and he's still an awesome teacher. But I finally figured out why I felt weird about it."

"Was it because it makes you realize how old you are?" El smirks.

"No. Although now that you mention it, I do feel old. It was more because I saw my brothers and some of my employees. I think my problem is I spend all day working with and supervising kids either in high school or just out of high school. I don't really want to spend my free time with high schoolers."

"That seems fair. I've never volunteered in kids' church for the same reason. I would much rather help Leah and Stephen in the young adult group and get to talk to grownups. So, I don't think it's bad that you don't want to work with the youth group. It's good you tried though."

I continue, not really paying attention to what El said. "Plus, I think it's weird to be there and act like I'm friends with them when I'm also their boss and we're not close. And I never wanted my parents involved in the youth group, so I can't image Cam and Carter would be thrilled to suddenly have me around for everything."

"Clara, I'm not disagreeing with you."

"What?" I turn to look at El.

"I don't disagree. If it doesn't seem like the right fit, then you don't have to do it."

"I don't have to do it." I stare at the black TV screen in front of me and let her words settle into my mind. It seems silly that El saying that would affect me like this, but I feel so relieved. Ever since Drew asked me to help, I've had this uncomfortable knot hanging out in my stomach. I knew I didn't really want to help with the youth group, but I didn't exactly feel like I could say no.

"No. You don't. Just tell Pastor what's-his-name it's not for you. It's okay."

"Is it?"

She laughs. "Of course. Why wouldn't it be okay?"

"I don't know. I should be serving at church, right? I always have in the past."

El shrugs. "Sure. If you want to volunteer, then volunteer. I think there are a lot of positives to helping at church, but the youth group isn't the only ministry that needs volunteers."

"True." I lean back into the couch to think.

"Take some time to pray about it, maybe ask people for suggestions. Figure out what your gifts are and see how you can use them to serve the church. You might be surprised what you end up doing."

"You think?"

"I was."

"What do you mean?" As far as I know, El only helps with the young adult group—planning events, setting up before and after events, etc. She's good at it, but I don't know why that would be a surprise. She's a teacher, which has made her a master planner.

"Sometime last year Stephen connected me with one of the little-known ministries at the church. A group of women take baked goods to a girls' home once a month to give them a special treat and let the girls know they are loved. I don't go because I don't really feel like that's my specialty, but I do help bake the treats they take."

"Wait, seriously?" I have been a part of this church my whole life and I've never heard about this ministry before.

El nods. "Yup. And I'm really glad there is because it's a cool way to get to use something I really enjoy doing to minister to people who are often ignored by society and at times the church."

"That's really cool…" I absentmindedly chew the inside of my lip trying to figure out an area where I could serve and actually enjoy it.

El watches me for a few seconds. "You don't have to figure it out tonight you know."

"I guess. I just wish I could."

"Take some time. Pray about it. Seek God's direction. Ask Him to show you what your strengths are so you can use them for Him."

I nod, even though I don't particularly want to ask God about this right now. With my luck, he would tell me I have to work with the youth group. I don't really want to get into that now though, so I try to maneuver out of this conversation. "So, what were you doing before I showed up and crashed your evening?"

"I was reading." She nods toward her coffee table, where a large book is sitting.

Picking it up, I scan the front cover. "*The Complete Sherlock Holmes, Volume 1*. Wow! How many volumes are there?"

"This printing was split into two volumes."

"Does this mean you finished *Oliver Twist*?"

"Yes. Finally!" She laughs and takes the book from me. "It took me forever. I like that this one is actually a collection of stories."

"Are the stories long?"

"Not terribly, which makes it easier to feel like I'm making progress. They're interesting though. They keep my brain working hard to figure out what's going on."

"Hmmm…sounds fascinating."

A laugh spills out of El. "You probably wouldn't like his writing, but feel free to borrow it when I'm done."

"I think I'll pass." I smile. We chat for a few more minutes, but I get the impression El would love to get back to her book so I decide to head home and leave her to her reading.

ቦቦቦ

My conversation with El last night has been stuck in my head most of this morning while I'm at work. The more I think about it, and I even prayed about it briefly, the more confident I am in my decision to not be a youth leader, even if the rest of my life is still a mess. Now all I have to do is let Pastor Drew know it's not going to happen. I've contemplated shooting him a text message a couple times today, but I feel like this is a conversation I would rather have in person.

Which is why when it comes time for me to take my lunch break, I decide to make the short drive over to church.

"What are you doing?" James asks as I collect my purse from the bottom drawer of my desk and slip into my coat.

"Last time I checked, you're legally required to let me take a lunch break." My response is a bit snippy, which is pretty normal for me this week.

He holds his hands up in surrender. "Well, obviously. You normally spend it at your desk on Facebook, so I was surprised to see you leaving. That's all."

I scrunch my face at his response. "That is a sad commentary on my life. I need to get out more. Anyway, if you must know, I'm running over to church."

James waves at me as I leave the office. "Tell your mom I said hi."

Even though seeing my mother isn't my reason for going over to the church, it's inevitable I will see her, so I don't bother correcting him.

The church secretary assumes the same thing and waves me through to the back office when I walk in. I make my way through the door separating the reception area from the maze of offices and head toward Drew's office.

"Knock, knock." I step into Drew's office doorway to see he's seated behind his computer.

"Hey, Clara. Come on in!" He waves me in and moves a few stacks of paper off to the side of his desk. "Sorry I didn't get a chance to talk to you last night after service. What did you think?"

Lowering myself into one of the seats in front of his desk, I respond honestly. "The service was amazing. It was a great message."

He nods his appreciation. "Does that mean you're up for joining us as a youth leader?"

"It does not." I bite my lip as soon as the words come out of my mouth. As sure as I am about this decision, I still feel like I'm letting him down. "I just…it's not the right fit for me. As much as I love you and Amanda and would love to get to hang out with you both, I really don't think being a youth leader is a good fit right now."

"Okay. I totally understand. Youth ministry isn't for everyone, and I definitely wouldn't want you to do it because you felt like you had to. I prefer having leaders who feel like it's their calling."

I let out the breath I didn't realize I was holding. I'm so thankful he's not upset about it.

Drew's not done though. "I want to say, even though I understand, it doesn't mean I'm not bummed. Mandy and I were both excited at the possibility of you joining the team. We thought you were a natural leader when you were a student and would make a great leader now too. But like I said, I don't want you to do it because you want to make us happy or because you think it will make you happy. Do you remember what my motto was when you were a student?"

I smile as the words I've heard him say a thousand times flood back into my mind. "You always said if we wanted to be truly satisfied in life, we need to pursue Jesus, not happiness."

"Exactly. My hope for you now is no different. Keep pursuing Jesus."

Unable to agree to that particular directive at this exact point in my life, I stand up to leave. "I think right now, I'm going to go pursue some lunch before I have to get back to work."

"Have a great lunch. I'm glad you stopped by."

Chapter Twelve

I skipped small group Thursday night. I texted El and told her I was tired from a long week and wouldn't be there. Part of me wanted to believe that was the real reason I didn't go. But when I skip Sunday school and end up barely making it to the main service Sunday morning, I finally have to acknowledge, at least to myself, that I might be avoiding church-related activities because I'm so frustrated with God right now.

I sit through the service and try to look like I'm paying attention, but my mind keeps wandering to the thought of staying at Jimmy's. Despite my best attempts to ignore what I know God was speaking to me the other day, it keeps coming up and I can't ever really push it out of my mind. Even looking for jobs has become less enjoyable because I feel like I'm doing something wrong. I try making a pro-con list about leaving during service but it's a half-hearted attempt. I know I'm trying to justify doing something God is telling me not to do, which takes all the fun out of it.

When service ends, I beg out of going to lunch with the young adults by saying I'm going out with my family. El and Leah both look like they don't quite believe me, but they don't push it. Not wanting to be a total liar, I wander through the lobby searching for either my parents or my brothers. By the time I've found my parents, they've made plans with another couple because the boys are hanging out with some friends from the youth group this afternoon.

A quick lunch from a fast-food drive-thru is followed by a nap. Or at least me attempting to take a nap. Just as I'm about to fall asleep, my phone starts to ring.

Kenzie.

For the third time since our conversation Monday, I silence the ringer and ignore the call. She's calling to check up on me, and I'm not interested in having that conversation right now.

Eventually, I hear Mom and Dad get home, but it sounds like they're both settling in for their Sunday afternoon naps because it's quiet downstairs. I continue to lay in bed with Albert. Unfortunately, Al won't chill enough for me to get to sleep. He keeps hopping up to adjust his position right as I'm almost asleep. Instead, I sit up and pull him up into my lap, slightly against his will. But the way I see it, if he's not going to let me sleep, I'm not going to let him sleep.

I'm still in bed playing with Al half an hour later when I hear the doorbell ring. Knowing Mom and Dad are home, I don't bother getting up to answer it. But a few seconds later, Al goes running to the door of my room and barks twice. The door cracks open, and I'm surprised to see El's face poke into my room.

"You awake?" She asks softly before spotting me.

I unbury myself from my bedding to stand. "Yeah. What's up?"

"Funny. That's what I was going to ask you." El proceeds to enter my room, shut the door behind her, and take a seat on my comfy chair by the window.

"What do you mean?" I nervously tuck my disheveled hair behind my ears. I really do need a haircut.

"I brought snacks." She ignores my question and holds out the tote bag she's carrying.

I take the bag from her and gently sit on the edge of my bed closest to where she's sitting. Looking into it, I see a bag of already popped popcorn and a plastic container full of cookies.

"I wasn't sure if you would be in the mood for salty or sweet, so I brought both. They're chocolate with white chocolate chips. You said you liked those, right?" El asks nonchalantly, as if she doesn't know they're my favorite kind of cookie.

I smile despite myself. "Yes. I do. These look great."

I pop the container open and take a cookie out, offering one to her as well. She takes one and closes the lid on the container without saying anything.

"So, what's with the snacks?" I slide back onto my bed a little further and tuck my legs underneath me.

"You know how I feel about showing up at someone's house unannounced. I figure bringing food makes up for it."

I nod remembering our chat about this a few weeks ago. "So, why did you show up unannounced?"

"Come on, Clara. You cannot just sit there and pretend you're okay. I'm your friend. I can tell when something is wrong. So, what's going on?"

"I don't know…" I'm not really sure what to say. If I tell her what's going on, I'm going to sound like a horrible person. If I don't, I have a feeling she might just sit there and stare at me for the rest of the day.

"Okay. Does this have something to do with being a youth leader? I thought you talked to the pastor and explained why you don't want to do it."

"I did. He totally understood. It's not that." I wave off her suggestion about what's bothering me.

"So, are you frustrated you haven't found your own place yet? Because you will. I know it's been a little challenging, but you'll find something." She shoots me an encouraging smile.

"No. I mean, yes, I want to move out. No, it's not really been a bothering me."

"Alright, so what? Is it work? Are things not going well with James?" El hits the nail on the head with her third guess.

Now I have to decide. Either I lie to her outright and say everything is fine or I tell her the truth. I don't particularly want to explain what's going on, but I definitely don't want to straight up lie to her. I chew on my lip for a minute, trying to figure out what to say. "On Monday, James came in and announced he found the property he wants for the new diner."

"Okay…and?"

"He was going on and on about how great it would be and about the team of people helping him figure it out. The realtor guy, the accountant, the lawyer, his dad…" I trail off.

"And he didn't mention you?" El's question is quiet.

My response isn't. "Of course he didn't! I'm not a part of the team. I'm not involved in this new endeavor. I don't get to be a part of it. And I'm so sick of it!"

"Yeah, that would be hard. I get that. Are you thinking about leaving? Is that what's upsetting you?"

"I was. I was so ready to do it. To find another job and leave." I break off, we're getting to the part I don't feel so good about.

"Was? So, you don't want to leave now?" She's confused. I can see it on her face.

"It's just…I called Kenzie on Monday, all ready to pull the trigger on leaving." I hop up off my bed and start pacing. "Then she asks me if I'm leaving because I want to or because God is telling me I should."

"Sounds like a good question." El is watching me closely.

"Yeah. It made sense, so I spent some time reading my Bible and thinking about it. And I got a pretty clear answer."

A look of understanding comes across El's face. "Ah…let me guess, it wasn't the answer you were hoping for?"

"No. It wasn't." I release an exasperated sigh. "The desire to leave is definitely only from me…not from God."

"You don't want to stay though, do you?"

"No." My response is more of a whimper than an actual word.

El is quiet for a few seconds, but I can imagine the speech she's preparing. All about how I should want what God wants for my life and how I should be grateful for the direction and go along with it. I can hear her speech so well that I begin to mentally prep my response.

"You know I didn't grow up in church. Not even close. I didn't become a Christian until my senior year of college." Her words are so completely not what I was expecting, I have no response, so I simply nod. While I don't know much about her growing up years, I did know the few facts she just shared already.

"I was dating someone at the time. My boyfriend and I had been living together for at least a year and a half." The words come out slowly, like she's considering each one before she says it.

"Anyway, it wasn't long after I got saved that I started to see the way we were living wasn't right. The more I went to church and read my Bible, the more convicted I was about the fact that we were living together. But, he was the first guy who had ever really made me feel like I mattered. He treated me well, he cared about my opinions, he pushed me to chase my dreams. He was a good guy. He just wasn't a Christian, so he didn't see why living together was an issue. Weeks turned into months, and I was wrestling with it more and more. Finally, it got to the point where going to church, which was something I had grown to really love, became almost painful because I knew I was disobeying God."

I glance down at my hands. That's pretty much exactly how I feel about life right now.

"There was a woman at the church, Donna, who had taken me under her wing from almost my first day there.

Acted as the mother I never had. She and I talked that subject to death. I was always trying to find a way to make it okay that I was doing my own thing, but she was quick to point out that I was actually being disobedient. She wasn't mean or nasty about it. She simply spoke truth into my situation.

"Doing my student teaching in Rockton when he and I still lived in St. Louis was already creating extra strain in our relationship. Then, I was wrestling with this knowledge that the life I was choosing wasn't God's best for me. It all came to a head about a month after I graduated. My boyfriend was frustrated with me because I was 'shoving my religion down his throat' and I was miserable because I knew I was choosing sin. We got into a huge fight one night, and I knew what I had to do. So, the next day we broke up and I moved out. I stayed with Donna and her husband Greg for a little over a month until I got the job in Rockton and officially moved out here."

El smiles for the first time since she started telling me this story. "All that to say, you're not alone. You're not the first person to struggle against the direction God is leading, nor will you be the last."

"Thanks." I stop chewing my lip long enough to give her a small smile. "You don't happen to have any advice for how to stop feeling like this do you? Because I hate this. I hate feeling so conflicted."

"I would say…pray. Which I know sounds super cliché." She holds up a hand to stop me from brushing off what she's saying. "More specifically, pray God will make his will something you want. Because right now you're wrestling between His will for your life and your will for your life. You and I both know he knows far better than you or I do about what's best for us, even if what's best doesn't feel great at the time.

"Breaking up with my boyfriend was horrible—in the moment. We had been together for over three years by the time I actually ended things. I was pretty miserable for a while, but if I hadn't broken up with him, I never would've considered applying for jobs outside of St. Louis. Moving here brought so much good into my life. I can't imagine what life would be like, or what I would be like, if it hadn't happened. Keep praying. It probably won't happen overnight, but the more time you spend with God, the more you will want what he wants."

"Thanks, El." I say quietly, knowing she's right, but still struggling to give in.

"Also, not to beat a dead horse, but I would also suggest praying for James." She gives me a knowing smile. "And not the kind of praying that is the equivalent of complaining about James. I'm talking about a heart-felt prayer."

I laugh at how on point that particular instruction is. "Fine. I'll try to actually pray for him."

"Good."

I pull another cookie—my fourth, I think—out of the container. "These are delicious, by the way."

"Thank you." El reaches over and takes another one.

The two of us hang out for at least an hour, talking about everything from the weather to the plans for our upcoming young adult event before she announces she needs to go clean her apartment. While I don't believe it's as messy as she makes it sound, I know her well enough to know she won't be able to really unwind after work this week until she's cleaned, so I don't argue with her. I do however, keep the container of cookies—with no intention of sharing them with Cam and Carter.

ꟷ ꟷ ꟷ

Monday arrives and it's officially the week of Valentine's Day, which has zero personal significance to me since I'm single, but we do have different promotions running each day this week.

The promo we're doing today is for the kid-sized heart-shaped pancakes that Danny came up with. So, I'm not surprised when we're busier than normal Monday morning with more moms and young kids. One of the moms I spot in the middle of the craziness is Grace Harper, who is married to James' oldest brother Allen.

"Hey, Grace. Hi, kids." I walk up to their table and offer both kids a high-five. Ava, their four-year-old, gives me a hearty slap on the hand, while Asher, their two-and-a-half-year-old, glares at me and crosses his arms in front of him as much as his little arms will let him. I squat down next to the table. "Come on, buddy. Can I please have a high-five?"

Asher shakes his head and maintains his resolve.

"Asher, can you say hi to Miss Clara?" Grace reaches over and brushes his light brown hair out of his face.

"No." He keeps up his grumpy stance.

"Sorry. I guess he's not up for socializing this morning." Grace gives me an apologetic smile. "How are plans for the new diner coming? I heard Jamie found a location."

"Yeah, he did." I try my hardest to sound upbeat and supportive. "James is probably more equipped to answer your questions about how all that is going. It's all a little over my head. Actually, I'm going to run back and let him know you guys are here."

Grace tried really hard to listen to my response to her question, but halfway through, Asher tried to empty the contents of the salt shaker onto the table, so she had to turn her attention back to him and is now trying to wrestle the shaker away from him. "Thanks, Clara."

I head back to the office as Grace does her best to move all the items on the table out of Asher's reach. I slip into the kitchen and poke my head in the office door to see James staring at his computer screen.

"Hey."

He pulls his attention away from the screen slowly. "What's up?"

"Grace and the kids are here. And you didn't hear it from me, but I think Asher could use some extra attention from his Uncle Jamie."

"Okay, thanks." James smiles and stands to follow me outside. No matter how much he drives me crazy at work, I have to say, I've always been a little impressed with his willingness to drop everything for his niece and nephew.

I head back to the front to continue making rounds and chatting with customers. Out of the corner of my eye, I see the grumpy-as-could-be Asher transform into the happiest kid in the world when he spots his uncle coming toward him. Asher is sitting on the inside part of the booth with his mom on the outside, but he slips down under the table and squat-walks out from under the table to wrap himself around James' legs. It's pretty adorable.

A minute later, Scout returns to their table with a tray full of food for them and James slides in next to Ava with Asher on his lap. While he joins them for breakfast, I do my best to keep things running smoothly despite the fact that having more kids in here than normal means there are more messes. But for the most part, the fun factor of having kids around is more enjoyable than troublesome.

It doesn't take long for the morning crowd of moms to give way to a mostly empty diner, which means I can head back to the office.

"Our numbers for the day look good so far." James informs me as soon as I enter the office.

"Good, I'm glad. How was breakfast with the kiddos?"

"Messy. I feel like I need to change my clothes after Asher ended up getting more of his pancakes on me than in his mouth."

I take a closer look at the shirt he's wearing and notice a few spots look like they've been wiped off. "Eh…you're fine. I can hardly tell."

"Thanks. At least I don't have any meetings at the bank today or anything. I don't mind wearing this if I'm going to be holed up back here all day."

"Were you able to fill Grace in on what's happening with the new diner?"

He nods briefly. "Yeah we talked about that some. She's excited to see it."

"I am too." I agree with the sentiment hoping he'll hear my interest in the project.

"You've already seen the property."

"I've seen some pictures." I did eventually get the link to see the property photos from the realtor sometime last week. "I meant I can't wait to see it in person. And I'm excited to see it once it's renovated. It's a great space, and I'm looking forward to it being transformed into a diner."

"I agree. I'm excited to see it finished. Speaking of which, I want to put together some sort of announcement to go on the website and Facebook page."

I reach for the legal pad I use to brainstorm and make notes while I'm at work. It's the much larger, work-related equivalent of the notebook I carry around in my everyday life. "Okay, what are you thinking?"

"Nothing crazy. At this point, I simply want to get the news out that we are working on a second location, including an estimated time for it's opening."

"When will that be?" I ask more out of personal curiosity than to fulfill my work duties.

He leans back in his chair and looks at the calendar hanging on the wall. "Well, I would like to close on the property by the end of this month or the beginning of March. Then, planning a few months for renovation and setup, ideally, would put us at the end of May."

"Okay, cool. So, when do you want to make the initial announcement online?"

"Let's shoot for the first week of March, once we've finalized the purchase."

"Sounds good. I will make sure to get a post together."

James' phone starts ringing before he has a chance to respond, and just like that, our conversation, which was going fairly well, is over. He's back to discussing the new property. Based on the side of the conversation I'm hearing, this particular call is about a meeting to get the rezoning approved.

I turn my attention back to preparing the schedule for the next two weeks, but I also use this time to take El's advice and say a prayer for James. I'm still not thrilled about staying, but talking to El about it yesterday helped me feel less upset about the whole situation.

When I get home, I drop my purse on the steps so I remember to grab it when I go upstairs and call out to see if anyone is home. There's no response, which I take to mean Dad and the boys are still at basketball practice. In the kitchen I find a note from my mom on top of a stack of large, glass serving dishes informing me she will be working late today to help get ready for an event they're having at church tomorrow evening. The note also asks me to take the serving dishes next door for Mrs. McKinley.

Albert whines when I leave him behind to head next door with the stack of dishes in my hands. I use my elbow to knock on the McKinley's door before stepping back to wait. I forgot to put my coat back on before I walked out of my house, so I don't wait very long before knocking again, a little louder this time. Finally, I hear the lock being undone.

"Hey, Clara. What's up?" Hannah opens the door a little further to let me in once she sees it's me.

"I come bearing gifts." I step in and hold the dishes up a little higher, even though my arms are getting tired.

Hannah closes the front door and leads me down the hallway to the kitchen. "Are those for the party?"

"Uh…maybe? All I know is I'm supposed to bring them over for your mom."

We step into the kitchen, where Mrs. M has clearly been cooking up a storm. "Wowza."

"Yeah…it's been crazy here today. She just left a few minutes ago to make her third store run of the day—not including the stop I made on my way home from school." Hannah laughs as she works to clear off a corner of the counter for me to set this stuff down.

"What kind of party are you guys having?" I ignore the aching in my arms.

"It's some Valentine's dinner with some of dad's co-workers. They've done it for years. I just know I don't want to be here Wednesday night."

"Is he back to working full-time?"

"Not quite, but it seems like he's working a little more each week. Or at least he's able to be there for longer stretches of time each day."

Hannah's finally gotten enough stuff moved so I can set these glass plates down. "Good. I'm glad. How are you doing with everything? I imagine it's been a bit rough."

"Yeah…" She nods and pushes her hair back from her face. "I'm glad he's doing better now. It was hard to see him feeling so sick all the time."

"I bet. If you ever need someone to talk to, I'm here to listen."

"Thanks." Hannah smiles.

I start to the door. "I'll see you…"

"Actually…" Hannah's voice from behind me stops me from heading down the hallway. I turn toward her and wait to see what she has to say. "…can I ask you a question?"

"Always." I step back into the kitchen and take a seat at the table.

Hannah lowers herself into one of the chairs across from me. "Do you…well…I don't know…how did you decide what college to go to?"

"It's a pretty intimidating decision, huh?" I give her what I hope is an encouraging smile. "Uh, well, location was a big thing for me. I knew I wanted to be close enough I could drive home on the weekend if I wanted to, which helped me narrow it down a bit. Then I looked into what programs and activities were offered. And then I prayed a lot and eventually felt like UMKC was the right choice for me."

Hannah nods in acknowledgement of my story but doesn't say anything. I give her a few seconds to respond before continuing.

"Do you have any idea where you want to go? Or what you want to study?"

She lets out a heavy sigh. "I don't know. I…I had a plan. Sort of. But now, after everything with dad…I just…I don't really know anymore."

"Are you saying you don't want to go away for college?" According to Henry, most of her prospective schools were out of state. On the East Coast I think.

Her eyes are focused on her hands, following along as she draws invisible lines on the table. "Maybe."

"It's okay to stay in Rockton if that's what you really want to do. But, Hannah, you don't *have* to stay because of your dad either."

She looks up at me for the first time since we sat down. "What do you mean?"

"If you're going to stay close by because it's what you really want, that's cool. But if you're sticking around because you feel guilty leaving when your dad isn't 100%, it's probably not going to be the best choice for you in the long run. Does that make sense?"

"Yeah." She nods. "I don't think it's guilt. I just…I don't really want to be far away right now."

"I get it. This year has been crazy for you guys. So, staying here and doing classes at the community college could be a good thing for you. You would save some money and get to stay at home for a little longer. Have you talked this over with your parents?"

"Not really. I've been trying to figure out what I want first. Plus, they have a lot on their plate right now."

"They do, but that doesn't mean they don't care or don't have advice to offer about this. Choosing a college and figuring out your next steps after high school is a big deal and they want to be involved."

"You think?" She seems so hesitant.

"I do." Seeing her look so uncertain and timid breaks my heart a little because Hannah was always a super outgoing, confident kid. I wish there was more I could do to help her out right now.

"Okay. Thanks, Clara."

"Of course." An idea pops into my head. "Hey, what are your plans for getting out of the house Wednesday?"

"I haven't really decided yet. I just know I don't want to be here."

"Why don't you come over? My family is normally out of the house Wednesdays, and being that it's also Valentine's Day, it could be fun to have some girl time."

"Really?" She looks more excited by the offer than I expected.

"Yeah, absolutely. I'll probably invite my friend Eleanor too, if you don't mind."

Hannah shakes her head. "No, that sounds like fun."

"I'm not sure what time your parents' party is starting, but I'll probably be home by five. You can come over any time after that."

"I don't think their party starts until like seven, but I'm sure Mom will be getting things ready all afternoon. I'll come over whenever I can slip away from helping her."

"Okay, perfect." I stand and give her a hug before I go. "I will see you on Wednesday."

Chapter Thirteen

Reasons I hate doing promotions:

1. So many people!!!
2. So many grumpy people!!!
3. So much food. Bleh. It gets old fast. I don't know how Danny does it, making the same things all day!
4. The clean-up is constant
5. I end up working longer because we're so busy.

But, it's nice to see my marketing efforts are making a difference. I'm accomplishing something. It's a good feeling.

Despite all the complaints I wrote in my notebook earlier today, I do actually like doing promotions. Even if it means we have a few crazy days like Tuesday and Wednesday have been.

The real issue is today has been full of people trying to take advantage or argue about the deal like their lives depend on it. Outside of being a tiring thing to deal with, it also takes time away from the work I actually have to get done, which means I'm late leaving work.

I'm not too worried about it though because I don't have to do much for the dinner I planned for our girls' night. Mostly due to the fact that I ended up delegating.

El, Jules, and Dana all accepted the invite and offered to bring something to add to our menu for the evening. I wasn't planning to invite Jules and Dana since I figured they would have date nights planned, but El insisted I ask just in case. Lucky for us, Sam has to work and Adam has class so they are doing their Valentines celebrations later this week. The only bummer is Leah couldn't come because she and Stephen had already committed to dinner with another couple.

I didn't eat much for lunch because we were so busy, so I'm looking forward to enjoying the spread we have planned for tonight. El is making her favorite chicken dish with some sort of sauce, Dana is bringing cheesy-potatoes, Jules is bringing vegetables and sparkling cider, and I'm providing the bread and dessert. If I had to make either of the items I'm providing, I would be scrambling right now, but I volunteered for those two foods because I knew I could get them cheap from work and it would be super easy.

As soon as I get home, I drop the food on the counter and run upstairs to take a quick shower. Standing in my closet, I decide to wear leggings and a loose-fitting, long-sleeved tunic shirt. This outfit is cuter than what I would normally wear to hang around the house, but it's just as comfortable. I try to blow-dry my hair quickly, but I give up. It's too long right now and takes forever to get totally dry. My crazy mane will just be a bit damp tonight.

I'm almost done setting the table with my mom's china dishes when I hear a knock at the door. I shout for whoever it is to come in and I'm happy to see Hannah coming through the door. She told me she would come, but I was still half expecting her to change her mind. Al gives her a hearty greeting as she walks into the dining room.

"This looks great." She looks over the table setting, which looks pretty good with mom's fancy napkin holders and candles in the middle of it. “Although, I’m beginning to feel a bit underdressed.”

Hannah shoots a hesitant glance down at her outfit, which is her standard jeans and cute top. She dresses so much nicer than I did when I was in high school.

“Don’t worry. You look great. This is not a formal thing. I just thought it would be fun to get all this stuff out. It doesn’t get used nearly enough.”

She nods. “It looks like you added a few more people.”

I bite my lip. I debated telling her Jules and Dana would be joining us, but I was worried it would scare her off. “Oh…right. Well, I told you I was going to invite El, and she ended up insisting on a few others. Don’t worry though, they’re great. You’ll love them.”

“Okay.” She gives a nervous nod and wanders into the living room, Albert at her feet.

I move into the kitchen to pull out some of the serving utensils I anticipate we will need this evening. I’m about to move on to my next task when my phone starts ringing. A quick glance tells me it’s Kenzie again. She’s called and texted me a few times in the last couple days, but I’ve dodged all her communication. So, even though I don’t have much time until my friends start to get here and a few more things I want to accomplish, I go ahead and answer the call.

“Hey, friend.”

“Don’t you ‘Hey, friend.’ me! You’re ignoring me.” Her tone is sharp, but not angry.

I wince, knowing I deserve it. “I know. I know. I’m sorry. Forgive me?”

“Maybe.” Now she’s just messing with me. I can hear it in her voice. “Only if you tell me what’s going on.”

“The short version, because some friends are about to come over. Basically, you were right. I was wrong. You happy now?”

Kenzie laughs. “I’m always happy to be right. Care to elaborate?”

I shoot a glance across the room to where Hannah is sitting on the living room floor playing with Albert. "I seriously have people about to show up any minute. Hannah is already here. Can we maybe talk this weekend?"

"Yeah that's fine. I work Friday, but I'm off on Saturday."

"Saturday it is, then."

"Thanks for finally answering your phone." Kenzie practically sings her response.

I roll my eyes at her even if she can't see me. "Whatever. Bye."

As I return my phone to its place on the counter, I feel a weight lift off of me. I don't like it when Kenzie and I aren't talking. Or when I'm dodging her calls.

"What was that about?" Hannah has materialized on the other side of the kitchen island.

"Oh. Uh…it was my best friend Kenzie. We haven't talked in a few days. I was…or we um…" I pause trying to figure out how to explain the situation but decide it's more complicated than I want to get into right now. "Anyway, I wanted to let her know we could talk this weekend."

"So you guys got in a fight?"

"Not really. She gave me some advice last week—good advice—that I wasn't exactly ready to hear. And we haven't been able to talk since, so she wanted to check in."

"Gotcha." Hannah looks like she's about to say something else, but a knock on the front door interrupts her.

I open the door to let El, and her pan of delicious smelling chicken, into the house. "Hey, for once, you're not the first one to arrive. This is Hannah. Hannah this is my friend Eleanor."

"It's nice to meet you." Hannah stands up a little straighter and gives El a big smile.

El hurries to set the still-warm pan on the counter and pulls Hannah into a tight hug. "It's so great to finally meet you. I've heard so many good things about you. And please call me El, everyone does."

Hannah shoots me an amused look over El's shoulder, but returns the hug nonetheless.

"Sorry, Hannah. I should've warned you she's a hugger." I laugh as I grab the platter I'm planning to use for the chicken El brought.

"It's totally fine." Hannah waves off my comment.

"Here, let me do that." El comes over, clearly intent on taking charge of her food. "So, Hannah, you're a senior in high school, right?"

I leave the two of them together in the kitchen, chatting as if they're old friends. El has that effect on people. Another knock on the door pulls me from adjusting and arranging the settings on the table.

"Come on in." I wave Dana into the house.

She throws the arm that's not loaded with stuff around my neck. "Thanks for the invite. I was feeling a little bummed Adam had class tonight, so I'm super excited to hang with my favorite girls tonight."

"Do you need a hand?" I point to the bags hanging from her arm. The same arm that's balancing her dish of cheesy potatoes, which smell amazing.

"No, I've got it." She slides the pan onto the counter and lifts her purse and the tote bag up to the counter as well.

"What's in the bag?" I try to get close enough to look, but she holds the top of it closed and moves it away from me.

She gives me a mischievous smile. "Nothing you need to see right now."

With a laugh, I give up my attempt and introduce her to Hannah.

"You're Henry's sister? That's so great. Adam, my fiancé, has been hanging out with him quite a bit lately. He thinks Henry is the best." Dana is all smiles tonight, especially when she mentions her *fiancé*.

Hannah hides a smile at Dana's admiration for Henry. "Yeah…he's pretty alright. Most days."

Al is in his happy place having so many visitors in the house who will pet him and play with him. He gets even more excited when Jules comes rushing in the front door. Albert loves Jules. I'm not entirely sure why he gets so excited, but he practically tackles her every time she comes over. It's hilarious. Tonight, he comes running over to greet her and starts running around her legs in a circle.

Jules quickly hands her bag with the food and drinks over to El and sits on the floor to play with Albert.

Everyone hangs out around the island as El and I finish getting all the food set out on the table. Once it is, the five of us take our seats around the table. I'm at the head of the table with Dana and Jules on my left and Hannah on my right with El next to her.

"I'll pray before we get started." El offers and reaches her hands out. We quickly join hands around the table, and El offers up a prayer of thanksgiving for the food and for friendship.

As soon as she says 'amen,' we start scooping food onto our plates and passing the serving dishes around the table.

"How are the wedding plans coming, Dana?" El asks as soon as everyone has some food.

Dana lets out a deep sigh, but smiles. "I can't remember what I've told to who, but we were able to nail down the where and when. We are getting married May 18th on my parents' farm not far from where he proposed. I know it's a little bit of a trip, but I hope you all will be able to come."

All of us assure her we will be there, but despite my positive response, I'm a little worried about being able to go since James is set on opening the diner by the end of May. Even if I have to drive out the morning of the wedding and leave immediately after, I'm going to do everything I can to be there for it.

"I was able to find my dress last weekend when my mom and sisters came to visit, and no, I will not show you guys. I want it to be a surprise for everyone because it's so perfect. You guys are going to love it." Dana's smile stretches across her entire face as she says this. "We also picked out the bridesmaid dresses for my sisters and cousins last week. And I have a pretty good idea of what the groomsmen will be wearing."

"Nice. Do you know what you're doing for decorations?" I ask between bites of amazingly delicious food.

Dana nods and tries to swallow the bite she snuck in. "Decorations will mostly be fresh flowers and strings of lights. I want it to be pretty simple. The plan is to start right before sunset, so it gets dark while we're doing the ceremony. Then have the twinkle lights lighting the area for the reception. I think it will be really pretty."

"Have you decided on the hairstyle? I know you showed me a few ideas last time." Jules chimes in.

Dana nods again and brushes her short, dark hair back from her face. "At first, I wanted to try to grow my hair out a bit so there would be more of it to work with, but it drives me crazy when it gets past my shoulders, so I'm thinking some simple beach waves. I haven't totally decided if I'm going to do a traditional veil, a halo veil, or even a tiara-type situation. I'm trying to decide what I like best."

El grins. "You know, if you showed us the dress, we could probably help you decide."

"No!" Dana laughs. "Although I appreciate the offer to help."

"It was worth a try." El shrugs.

"Anyway, the plans are coming along. I'm so grateful my mom and sisters and my aunts and cousins are all so willing to help. They've done most of the hard work. It's one of the upsides to having a big family. Honestly, I'm more worried about Adam trying to find a new job and us finding a place to live after we're married."

"He's looking for a pastoral position, right?"

"Yes. He's looking for an associate pastor position. Obviously, he can keep working for his father until he finds something, but he is really hoping to get into a good church."

Something clicks in my brain and I drop my fork. "Wait. That means you guys are going to leave. Is that what you're saying?"

A sad smile crossed Dana's lips. "Pretty much. Unless God opens up something unexpected at our church, getting a job as a pastor will most likely force us to move to a new church."

"Wow. I really hadn't thought about that. I definitely don't want to lose you guys." Sadness is written all over El's face.

"Even if we end up at another church in the area, my hope is we will still be able to come to small group on occasion, and I will definitely still need our girls' nights."

"Here, here!" Jules holds her glass up in the air, and after a little coaxing, we all clink glasses in agreement. "We better still have our girls' nights. I need them to keep me sane."

"I didn't realize you were ever sane." My quip elicits laughter from everyone except Jules.

Jules tilts her head, as if weighing the validity of my statement. "True. But I used to be slightly more sane. Sam is making me crazy right now."

"Uh oh. What's going on?" El's brow furrows and she's clearly concerned. She has been a huge fan of Jules and Sam as a couple since before they were actually dating. I'm pretty sure she secretly has their wedding all planned out for them.

"I'm just frustrated." She makes a face, as if she's trying to figure out what to say. "I don't want this to come out wrong or sound like I'm not happy to be having dinner with you guys, but I kind of thought our first Valentine's Day as a couple would be spent…um, I don't know, together."

"Didn't Sam have to work tonight?" I'm confused as to why she's upset. I get that it's a bummer, but sometimes that's how it goes.

"No, I said he's working tonight. The difference being he actually *volunteered* to work tonight."

"He did not!" El is aghast.

"What?" Dana seems wary.

"Seriously?" My response slips out before I can stop myself.

The only one who doesn't say anything is Hannah, but I assume that's because she doesn't really know Jules very well.

"He did! I was so mad when I found out. I know it shouldn't be a big deal, it's just a greeting card holiday, after all. There's no real significance to it, but it still feels like a slap in the face."

"Did you ask him about it?" Dana, always the sensible one, chimes in.

El interrupts before Jules can answer. "Oh, she doesn't need to. I'm going to give him a little talking-to when I see him next!"

Jules cracks a smile. "Thanks for the offer, but I did ask him. He didn't really have an answer, which made it even more annoying."

"Well, I can definitely understand why you're upset about it, but I for one am glad you were able to join us tonight." I reach over and give her arm a little squeeze.

"Thank you. I'm glad we could get together too. Now, I don't want to talk about this anymore." She waves her hand in the air as if she's shooing all her negative thoughts about Sam out of the room. Then her gaze lands on Hannah, who's sitting directly across from her. "How about you? Tell me a little about yourself."

Hannah, who has been sitting quietly by my side taking in the conversations going on around her, looks surprised to suddenly be addressed so directly. "Oh…um…what do you want to know?"

"Let's start with something easy. What's your school situation?"

"I'm a senior at Rockton High School. I can't wait to be done, even though I have no idea what I want to do with my life once I finish."

"Don't worry, I didn't have a clue what I wanted to do with my life when I finished high school. You'll figure it out." Jules offers some words of encouragement.

"What did you end up doing?"

Jules takes a drink before responding. "Well, I worked a few crappy jobs for very little money. I took a few gen ed classes at a community college and figured out that I hated classes in college as much as I did in high school. Eventually, a friend suggested I look into cosmetology. I had always loved doing hair and makeup for my friends, and I loved trying different styles on my own hair. So, I went for it and ended up absolutely loving it. I'm convinced I have the best job in the world."

"That's really cool." Hannah says quietly.

"You were supposed to be telling me about yourself. Don't be distracting me with good questions." Jules jokingly wags a finger at her.

Hannah laughs and pushes her empty plate away toward the middle of the table. "My apologies. What do you want to know next?"

I sit back and for the next fifteen or so minutes watch my amazing friends show interest in and encourage my sweet, young neighbor, and once again, I feel so grateful for these ladies. The extra attention and care they are pouring on her have an immediate effect. I can see glimpses of the more confident and outgoing version of her coming out.

Eventually, we all get up and clear our dinner plates, put the food back into its containers, and grab some dessert, which we take into the much more comfortable seats in the living room. I notice Dana is trying to discreetly bring her tote bag with her into the other room. Choosing to respect her desire to keep what's in the bag to herself, I try to focus on the conversations happening around me.

We enjoy our desserts before Dana pulls the bag onto her lap.

"Do we get to know what's in the mystery bag now?" I ask excitedly.

"You're so dramatic." Dana chuckles as she looks into the bag and reaches in to rearrange something inside. "It's not really a mystery. It's just little gift bags I put together for you lovely ladies."

"That's so sweet." El exclaims.

While Jules, El, and I anxiously await our gifts, I notice Hannah get up and start collecting the dishes we used for dessert. A pang of guilt hits me. I would bet anything she's clearing so she doesn't have to feel left out of the gift giving. For a second, I almost hop up and join her, but I have a feeling that would make it worse.

"Here you go." Dana hands a little pink and red gift bag covered in hearts to Jules, then passes one to El and I before she notices Hannah isn't sitting with us anymore. I expect to see a look of panic when she realizes she doesn't have one for Hannah, but instead, Dana simply sticks her hand back in the tote and pulls out another small gift bag with Hannah's name on it. "Hannah, I'll put yours by your seat here for when you're done."

Hannah turns around, dishes still in her hand, shock written all over her face. "Oh…okay. Thank you."

I haven't even opened my gift yet, but I can't help but lean over and give Dana the best hug I can manage while we're both seated.

"Thank you." I whisper just loud enough for her to hear, and based on the look on her face, she knows I'm thanking her for including Hannah.

Jules and El miss the exchange because they're poking around the pink and white tissue paper to see what's inside. As soon as she's finished offering her thanks for the gift, Jules stands up and announces she needs to head home.

It is getting late and I bet my family will return soon, so I'm not opposed to our party wrapping up.

Jules, with her gift bag and empty potato dish in hand, is the first to leave. Dana is right behind her, but not before I spot her getting a hug from Hannah. El and Hannah chat for another few minutes while I start to hand wash the dishes we used, at least the larger ones my mom doesn't like putting in the dish washer.

The two of them make their way over to the kitchen just as Hannah is getting ready to head out. "I should probably go finish up some homework. Thanks, Clara, for inviting me over. I had a lot of fun tonight."

I dry my hands off after washing the last dish. "I'm really glad you could come."

Hannah gives me a surprisingly strong hug for her tiny frame and walks out the door, gift bag clutched tightly in her hand.

El wanders over to the dining room table and helps me finish cleaning everything up.

"Thank you for tonight." She says when we've finished. "I know that you know I've been struggling lately being single, so I wasn't really looking forward to this particular holiday. But I had a great time tonight."

"Good." I pull her into a hug. "And thank you for being so nice to Hannah. She's had a rough go of it the last few months, and I think this was exactly what she needed."

"She's a pretty easy person to be nice to. She's such a sweet girl."

"I know. With Henry as an older brother, I'm not sure how that happened."

"Ha-ha. Very funny." El gives me a disapproving look, but she's stifling a laugh so I can tell she's not actually annoyed.

"What can I say, I'm hilarious." I give a low, flourished bow.

"Annnnd, on that slightly delusional note, I think I'm going to call it a night." She laughs.

I stick my tongue out at her. "Thanks a lot."

"Anytime." She gives me one more hug, collects all of her stuff, and heads out the door.

I take another minute to wipe down the counters one last time, and then make my way upstairs to change into pajamas and do my devo time.

Once I'm settled into my comfy chair, I also grab my gift from Dana to look through it. The first item I pull out is a purse-sized bottle of my favorite lotion, followed by a container of bath bombs of the same scent. I pop the top of the lotion bottle open and breathe in the scent. I love this smell. I can't believe Dana knew.

Next out of the bag is a cardboard container about the size of my hand with pink and red hearts all over it. I shake it to see if I can tell what's inside, but all I hear is a few muffled thumps. I pull the top open and smile. Chocolate. It takes me about two seconds to open one of the mini-chocolate pieces and pop it in my mouth, despite the fact that I already had plenty of dessert tonight.

The last, and heaviest item in the bag, turns out to be a scented candle. I immediately pull the lid off and inhale the scent, which makes me cough. While the smell is really nice, it's also much stronger than the lotion, so the deep whiff of it was a little much.

Standing, I put the candle, lotion, bath bombs, and chocolate on my desk and run downstairs to find a lighter. I want to try my new candle tonight before I go to bed. Kenzie used to have scented candles in our apartment all the time, and I loved it.

Mom never used them in the house growing up. Probably because she was worried about Cam and Carter sticking their hands in the flame or catching something on fire and burning the house down, but I absolutely love lighting candles to make a room smell better.

I hurry downstairs and start rooting around in the junk drawers in the kitchen. It takes a minute of digging, but I eventually find the lighter my dad uses to start the grill and head back upstairs. The candle smells great once it's lit and I can't wait for the smell to fill my room.

Before I settle back into my chair with my Bible, I decide to go put the gift bag from Dana in the hall closet with mom's collection of gift bags and tissue paper to be reused later. Taking the tissue paper out of the bag, I notice a card tucked inside that I didn't see before, so I slip it into my pocket and finish putting the gift-wrapping materials away.

I pull the card out of my pocket and take a seat in my chair. Reading the note inside puts a smile on my face.

> Clara!
>
> I love you so much, girl! You are so sweet and always have a smile for me. I love your sense of humor too. God's love is so evident in you.
>
> I'm so appreciative of the invite tonight. Having this group of girlfriends makes me feel like I can do anything. You all mean the world to me.
>
> Love, D – Zeph. 3:17

Grabbing my Bible from the arm of the chair, I flip through the Old Testament trying to find Zephaniah. I turn to the end of the Old Testament and basically go through page by page since the Minor Prophets are so short they're easy to miss.

Finally, I land on the correct page and read the verse Dana wrote down for me.

"The Lord your God is in your midst, a mighty one who will save; he will rejoice over you with gladness; he will quiet you by his love; he will exult over you with loud singing."

I'm not sure how she found this verse, but I love it. So much so, I copy it down in my handy, little notebook. I also grab a notecard from my desk and write it out to put on the mirror in my bathroom as a reminder of how God sees me. Instead of continuing on to my normal Bible reading for the evening, I simply sit and think over this verse and what it means for me, and I go to bed feeling so incredibly loved and valued.

Chapter Fourteen

I make a point to find Dana as soon as I get to our small group Thursday night. She's sitting in the living room when I walk in the front door, with a nod of my head, I silently ask her to join me in the kitchen.

"What's up?" She asks with a smile when she walks into the kitchen.

I wrap my arms around her in a tight hug. "I wanted to say thank you for the present last night. I didn't get a chance to open it until after you left, and I wanted to make sure you know I appreciated it."

"Oh good. I'm glad you liked it." Dana keeps an arm around my waist. "I had such a great time. I'm so happy we were able to get together."

"Me too. And thank you for having a gift bag for Hannah too. I know you hadn't met her before, so that was amazing."

"Of course. I'm just glad you mentioned she would be there in your text, otherwise I wouldn't have had one ready."

"Out of curiosity, and you don't have to answer this if you don't want to, did her bag also include a card?"

Dana smiles. "It did. I wasn't really sure what to write at first, but I prayed about it and felt like I should simply offer words of encouragement and hope. So that's what I did. I said I was glad she could join us and used a couple scriptures to let her know how much God loves her."

"Well, I haven't talked to her today, but I know she was surprised and so grateful to be included."

"Good. She's such a sweetheart."

Sam starts walking into kitchen but stops when he sees us in the corner. "Oh, sorry. Am I interrupting your girl time?"

I wave off his fake concern. "It's all good. We had plenty of girl time last night. You know, when you were too busy working to take your girlfriend out for Valentine's Day."

"I'll…come back later." He says before slowly backing out of the kitchen.

Dana swats my arm. "Clara, I thought Jules said not to say anything!"

"It sort of slipped out." I shrug.

She laughs and rolls her eyes as we head through the entry way and into the living room.

"No, I think it was Q." Adam is mid-conversation with Sam, who is doing a good job of avoiding eye contact with me, and one of their friends.

"Talking about the imaginary roommate again, I see." I interrupt before they can continue their conversation. Adam, Sam, and Alex supposedly share their spacious house with another guy named Quinton. In the nine or so months I've been attending this small group, I've never actually seen this Quinton character. I'm not convinced he's real, and I've told the guys this a few times, referring to the mysterious Quinton as their imaginary roommate.

Both Sam and Adam shoot me annoyed looks before Adam responds. "How many times do we have to tell you he's not imaginary? He lives right upstairs."

"So, you say…but I've never seen him." I shrug and offer a mischievous grin.

"I showed you a picture." Adam argues.

"No, you showed me a picture of a random guy whose name you say is Quinton. It means nothing."

"One of these days, Clara, he's going to come to our group or some other hang out night, and you'll see how real he is."

"I doubt it." I stick to my nonsensical opinion on the subject and walk away.

"Why do you insist on arguing with them about Quin?" Dana asks as I take a seat next to her on the couch.

I laugh and wave off her concern. "Oh, I'm just having a little fun with them. Plus, I do think it's weird he's never once been around for small group in the last nine months. We've even switched what night we meet on, and he's still never been around."

"Whatever." She shakes her head at me. "As long as you know he really does exist. I actually know him."

"Sure you do. I see you've crossed over to the dark side." I stick my tongue out at her.

Leah joins us and the subject of the imaginary roommate is put aside for the time being. Another twenty minutes or so go by before Adam and Sam indicate they're ready for us to get started, and everyone moves sit down in a misshaped circle.

"Alright, guys. Why don't you all open your Bibles to the book of James." Sam says as he flips through his own, very worn Bible.

With Dana on one side of me and Leah on the other, I sit and listen as the group discusses the second chapter of the book of James. For the most part, I don't chime in tonight. I may be here, signaling I've progressed a bit since last week when I was so frustrated with God, I didn't even come, but I'm still not one hundred percent on board with the whole staying at Jimmy's thing. I know I should be. All the scripture I've read this week has only served to confirm God is telling me to stay and I'm trying to be okay with it, but sometimes working with James makes me so crazy that everything I've read flies out the window, or at least out of my head.

So, instead of jumping into the discussion, I simply listen, take notes, and doodle in my notebook. When I flip open my notebook, it opens to a page I dog-eared a few weeks ago. The words pack a powerful punch.

I will take refuge in God.
I will follow where he leads.
I will live a life of joy.
I will set the Lord before me.
I will not be shaken.

I wrote this thinking God would lead me to leave Jimmy's, and I would need to follow and trust him in that. But he's been telling me to stay, and I definitely haven't been very willing to follow that direction and I sure haven't been living a life a joy. This realization hits me hard. I need to let go of this negative attitude I've developed about my job and about James.

"Guys, listen to this. This is from the Message." Sam catches my attention as he reads the last two verses from the section they've been discussing. "'Talk and act like a person expecting to be judged by the Rule that sets us free. For if you refuse to act kindly, you can hardly expect to be treated kindly. Kind mercy wins over harsh judgment every time.' Mercy wins over judgement. What a powerful statement."

A few people respond, but all I can think about is that I haven't exactly been acting kindly, or with mercy, when it comes to James.

Basically, all the scripture from tonight is convicting me about how I've been acting. So, after jotting down some highlights from this chapter, I begin writing out a truly heart-felt prayer on the next page, blocking out all of the conversation happening around me.

Lord, I'm sorry. I'm sorry for the attitude I've been carrying around the last few weeks. I know you have what's best for me in mind. I'm sorry I *haven't submitted to You. I've felt hurt and frustrated at the way James is shutting me out of the decisions he's making, so I've reacted by caring less about him and I've become less willing to help out when he needs it. I also haven't been very willing to offer grace or mercy to him. Show me how to live out these principles. I really do want to live the life you have for me. Help me love the way you love. Help me show mercy the way you do. Give me grace to deal with things at work the way you want me to.*

My silent prayer lifts my soul more than I could've imagined. I didn't realize how much I had let the frustration and anger affect me the last few weeks. Do I still feel bummed I'm not going to have as much say or be as involved with the new diner as I had initially hoped? A little. But suddenly, it seems a lot less important than it did before. It definitely doesn't seem like a big enough deal to ruin my friendship with James, which is what's been happening whether he realizes it or not.

I look up from my notebook and notice the discussion has moved on to other parts of the chapter and no one seems to have a clue about the monumental realization I've just had. And I'm okay with that. For now, I'm okay if this change is just between me and God.

I listen passively for the rest of the Bible study time, mostly because my mind is more focused on figuring out how to move forward at work.

Leah turns to me as soon as Sam closes in prayer to discuss some of the design options we've been needing to go over for the website. For the first time in a while, I truly enjoy discussing something that has to do with the new diner and I'm so grateful. Now, the key will be to carry that over into the next few days at work. If I can remember what happened tonight, I think I will be able to move forward, even if James is being frustrating and difficult.

ꕥꕥꕥ

"I just got a text from Henry." I hold my phone up where Mom can see it as I follow her out the garage door Monday evening. A few days into my plan of offering more kindness and mercy to James and I haven't really noticed a difference yet. I have noticed that dealing with my issues, at least on a personal level, has helped me to enjoy life a little more, which is great.

She squints in the direction of my phone before giving up. "I can't read it. I assume it's about the game?"

"Yeah, he said he is off tonight and will be there, so we should save him a seat."

"That's easy enough." Mom says as she slides into her SUV. I hop in the passenger seat and we head to the school for tonight's basketball game against our local rivals, the Hawthorn High Tigers.

We're over half an hour early and the place is already pretty full, but that's fairly common for a Rockton vs. Hawthorn game. Mom and I make our way to our favorite spot and make sure to save plenty of space for the two of us plus Henry. As per her usual, mom wanders around the section chatting with other parents. I do my best to keep anyone from sitting in the seats we have saved.

The time before the game passes quickly, and Henry slips in right as the game is starting. We spend most of the first two quarters locked in on the extremely close game. Our boys are up by ten at half-time. As soon as the buzzer sounds, Mom, and half the gym, get up and make a beeline for the bathroom. Since I took my bathroom break ten minutes ago, I stay in my seat and people watch.

"It's nice to see some traditions never die." Henry leans towards me to be heard.

I turn my attention to him. "What do you mean?"

"The student section. That is what you were looking at, right?" He points across the gym.

"Yeah. I was trying to read all the signs they came up with for tonight."

"Well, I was saying it's nice to see they still go all out. We used to have such a great time getting ready for games."

"I'm sure you did." I have absolutely no clue what that was like. Henry and I were definitely in different friend groups in high school.

Henry turns to me with an intense look on his face. "Did you come to a lot of games in high school?"

For half a second, the question makes me sad. It's a glaring reminder of just how separate our lives were when we were in high school. I shake the feeling off. It's a bummer we weren't friends then, but he's been a pretty great friend since we re-connected last summer.

"Yeah. We were at most games. I didn't sit in the student section very often because Mom liked having my help with the boys. They were in elementary school and difficult to keep track of. Most of the time, I would sit up here with them. Sometimes a couple of my friends would join us. I often saw you down there causing a ruckus though. It always looked like you guys were having fun."

"We did have a lot of fun." He runs his hand along the back of his neck. "Hey, Clara. I'm really sorry…I wish we would've been friends then."

"You don't have to apologize. *Again.* I told you before: you and me, we're good. You don't need to keep apologizing." I give him a pointed look.

He laughs. "Okay. Fine. That's the last apology you're ever going to hear from me."

"Whoa." I hold up my hands. "I didn't mean you couldn't apologize for other stuff. Just not for that. I'm sure there are plenty of other things you should be apologizing for."

"Oh yeah?" Henry starts to challenge me, but changes the subject instead. "Actually, I think I should be thanking you."

Surprised by his statement, I give him a quizzical look.

"I talked to Hannah yesterday. Heard all about your little dinner party last week."

"Oh. Did she have fun? I was hoping it wouldn't be too weird for her, since she didn't know anyone else."

He laughs. "Are you kidding? She kept going on and on about how great it was. I guess she had an amazing conversation with El all about books, which made her day. Then, she said something about a present from Dana, maybe?"

I nod in answer to the implied question.

"Well, I really appreciate it. I haven't seen her in that good of a mood since before Dad's surgery. Thank you, Clara. I mean it." This is probably the most serious I've ever seen Henry, except for the night he told me his dad had a brain tumor.

"Of course. I'm glad she enjoyed herself. Is she here tonight? I haven't spotted her anywhere?"

He shakes his head at me. "She was planning to stay home and watch a movie with dad tonight. It appears not even a super fun night with you guys has convinced her he's going to be okay."

"Well, think about what it's been like for her. Your dad has always been the epitome of the strong, silent type. Nothing ever fazed him. He was always so stoic. Someone you could always count on, you know?"

Henry gives a short nod of understanding, but he still looks like he's worrying about her.

I put my hand on his arm to make sure I have his attention. "Henry, it was hard for me to see your dad in that hospital bed and then needing help to get around the house. I can only imagine how hard it's been for Hannah to watch someone she's always had as an immovable rock in her life suddenly need help walking to the bathroom. That would be difficult for anyone, much less someone trying to navigate her senior year and make decisions about her future. She's got a lot on her plate and it probably seems overwhelming at times."

"So, how do I help her?" His brow is furrowed, and he's looking at me intently.

I pause before responding. I want to give him a helpful answer, but I want to do it in a way that maintains the confidence Hannah had in me when she opened up to me last week.

"Keep being there for her. Listen when she needs to talk. Talk to her about how you feel." I catch his skeptical look. "I know it freaked you out when your dad got sick. Let her hear how you're coping. How you're processing."

Henry doesn't respond. At least not verbally. He simply stares out at the basketball court for a few minutes before turning back to me and calmly saying, "I think you're right."

I give him my best imitation of his classic smirk. "I knew you would come to recognize my brilliance eventually. Hannah will be okay."

"Not about Hannah." He shakes his head, like he's confused. "I mean, you're probably right about that too, but that's not what I meant. I meant, I think you're right about God."

For half a second, I feel like all the oxygen has been sucked out of the room because I can't breathe. I've been praying for him to come to that conclusion for a long time, and after everything that happened with his dad, I was beginning to think it would never happen. He seemed so interested last summer when he was coming to my small group on occasion, but then his dad got sick and helping his family became his first priority.

My small group friends kept praying for him and I know Adam, Sam, and Stephen have all made a point to reach out to him. While I think he enjoys their friendship, he no longer seemed interested in hearing about matters of faith. It was like he would shut me out anytime I talked about church or

God. So, his sudden declaration catches me completely off guard.

"What?"

"I think you're right. You, Sam, Adam, your parents. All of you. You told me to talk to Hannah about how I've been since dad's surgery, but mostly I felt frustrated and discouraged and scared. Except for when I'm with you guys. It's like…like everything seems more possible. Like there might be a light at the end of the tunnel. Like there's…hope or something. And I want that."

"Oh." I'm doing my best not to cry right now, sitting in the middle of the bleachers that are starting to fill up with people again. I feel like I should have some wise words for him, or at least offer some instructions about how to give his life to Christ. But I have no words.

"What do I have to do? I'm supposed to pray or something right? Sam explained it to me a few times, but I don't really remember…" He trails off, looking slightly insecure, which is rare for him.

I scramble to get my thoughts in order. "Uh…yeah. You just…tell God what you're thinking. That you believe and want to surrender your life to him."

"Do I need to…close my eyes and say it out loud?" He gives a self-conscious look around the bleachers.

I shake my head and place a hand on his arm. "This is between you and Jesus. No one else has to be a part of it. Not even me. So, you can say it out loud or pray silently, with your eyes open or closed. The important thing is you talk to God honestly."

He gives me a short nod, leans forward, elbows on his knees and drops his head. I sit back and let him have this moment for himself. Praying silent prayers of my own. Reveling in how random and amazing this moment is. It's one that I've been praying for off and on since I was old enough to understand that we all need a Savior and that Henry had never made that decision. I'm more than a little surprised and blown away by the fact that he's making his choice right here, in the gym, but I'm so excited.

After a few moments of silence, Henry sits back up with a smile. "I did it. I prayed."

"That's…awesome. I'm so…excited for you." The happy tears I've been holding back for the last few minutes start to leak out when I lean over to give him a hug.

"Am I supposed to…I don't know…feel different?" He asks once I pull away.

His question calms my emotions a bit. I have to keep it together to be able to answer. "Some people do. Some people don't. Sometimes it's an instant feeling of change and sometimes it takes longer to settle in. However, it happens for you, just know God heard you and he's so, so excited about your decision."

"I feel…lighter. Maybe?" He says it like he's unsure if that's possible.

Before I can swallow the tears that are yet again bubbling up, I hear my mom's voice.

"Clara, are you okay?" She's on the other side of Henry coming towards us, having just returned from her run to the restroom with absolutely no idea about the sacred, life-changing event that just happened.

I nod, searching for the words. "He…" I point to Henry, hoping he'll say something, but he doesn't. "He's really my brother now. Forever."

Not the most eloquent way to say it, I know. I can tell based on the confused look staring back at me. But I'm so excited, I can't come up with anything other than a ridiculous *brother in Christ* reference. So instead, I stare back at her with a smile and tears slipping down my cheeks.

Then she gets it. I know she gets it. I see it in her eyes when the meaning of my words finally clicks for her.

She turns to Henry, who's been glancing back and forth between us since my mom walked up, and gives him a fierce mom-hug. I can't hear what she says to him after she pulls away because the game started again and the crowd is getting louder by the second, but whatever she said, I see him discreetly wipe a tear or two as she continues past me to her seat.

Once seated, she reaches over and squeezes my hand. In an instant, it becomes clear to me that I'm not the only one who's been praying for Henry all these years. As a matter of fact, I would bet she's been praying for him longer, and with more consistency, than I have. Without saying anything, our eyes on the court, I know we are both celebrating in our hearts over Henry's decision.

With so much joy already pulsing through us, it's not hard to get swept up in the adrenaline-fueled atmosphere of the game as we cheer our boys on to a victory. After the game ends and everyone files out of the gym, Mom, Henry, and I find a quieter part of the commons area to wait for Dad and the twins. The large room quickly empties of everyone but the players' families and friends that are still lingering, spread out across the room, waiting for their boys to make an appearance. As usual, my brothers and my dad are the last ones to come out of the locker room.

"Nice game guys." I high-five each of the twins. They both got a decent amount of playing time tonight, considering they're sophomores and this was an intense game.

"Thanks." Cam accepts a hug from Mom before following Carter toward the door. My parents, Henry, and I follow behind them.

"That was a fun game to watch, Coach." Henry says to Dad as we push open the doors and receive a blast of cold air to the face.

"Yeah, I'm glad we were able to pull off a win. Definitely an exciting night for the team." My dad nods in agreement.

"You know, Dad. You guys winning isn't the only exciting thing that happened tonight."

Dad glances over at me. "What do you mean?"

"Henry has something to tell you." I push Henry a little to get his attention.

He nods in agreement, but not without shooting me a nervous look first. "Right. Um…I…how did you say it earlier?" He looks to me again before finding the words he's looking for. "I surrendered my life to God."

I look over to see my dad's reaction, only to realize he's not walking next to us anymore. Glancing back, I spot him a few steps behind us. It appears Henry's news quite literally stopped Dad in his tracks. Dad shoots a glance at Mom, I assume to check to see if she knew because she gives a short nod and a smile.

I watch as Dad glances at his feet and looks back up at Henry with tears in his eyes. "That is *by far* the most exciting thing that's happened tonight." Dad reaches out to shake Henry's hand, but then pulls him into a strong man-hug. "Henry, buddy, we have been praying for this to happen since the first time you tracked mud into our house back in pre-school. I think I can speak for all of us when I say this is truly an answer to prayer."

"Thanks." Henry smiles a real, genuine smile.

"Do you need a Bible? I have plenty. I would be happy to give you one. Or help you find one you like."

"Thank you, sir. I actually have one already."

"Really?" I didn't know that.

Henry gives a small smile. "Adam gave me one a while ago when we were hanging out. Said it was a Christmas present from him and Dana."

I laugh. "That's great."

"Alright. I need to head out. You guys have a good night." Henry waves to the boys, who are leaning against Dad's car. I happily accept the hug he offers before he heads toward his car at the back of the lot.

Once we get home, I head straight upstairs and pull my Bible off my nightstand and my notebook out of my purse and curl up on my bed. I flip quickly to the New Testament and begin to search for the passage that's been hanging out in the back of my mind this evening.

I find the parable I'm looking for at the beginning of Luke 15.

> So he told them this parable: "What man of you, having a hundred sheep, if he has lost one of them, does not leave the ninety-nine in the open country, and go after the one that is lost, until he finds it? And when he has found it, he lays it on his shoulders, rejoicing. And when he comes home, he calls together his friends and his neighbors, saying to them, 'Rejoice with me, for I have found my sheep that was lost.' Just so, I tell you, there will be more joy in heaven over one sinner who repents than over ninety-nine righteous persons who need no repentance.

I dig around in my nightstand's drawer for a pen and copy the last sentence into my notebook. Below the verse, I take a few moments to pour out all of the excitement I'm feeling tonight. It's pretty awesome to know all of Heaven is celebrating tonight, and I got to be a part of it.

Chapter Fifteen

Whether due to my spiritual breakthrough at small group the other night or Henry's decision to give his heart to the Lord last night, I get to work Tuesday morning bound and determined to find a way to connect with James. Which is probably why I've spent half of the morning discreetly staring at him, trying to figure out what to do.

Something El said weeks ago comes back to me. She told me to try to get to know him again, see how he's changed and grown in the last few years. I thought it was a good idea when she said it, but then he went and decided to do things on his own, and I got annoyed and didn't bother trying.

"What is your deal today?" James exclaims as I subtly watch him.

His outburst startles me and causes me to knock an empty cup from yesterday off my desk. "Good grief! Was that really necessary?"

He narrows his eyes and argues. "You have been staring at me all morning. Is *that* really necessary?"

I stare back, not really sure what to say.

"Seriously, do I have something on my face, or what?" He self-consciously wipes his hand across his face.

"No, you're good." I shake my head, trying to stall until I can come up with a good excuse for why I've been watching him all morning.

"Okay, so what gives?"

I put on my most innocent expression. "I have no idea what you're talking about."

"You were staring at me."

"I wasn't staring at you. I didn't even realize you were over there. I was just…thinking."

"About?" He's not buying it.

"Trying to come up with new content to post the week after next." It's the first thing that comes to mind, but it's not a bad answer, even if it's not the actual answer.

"You come up with anything?"

I shrug. "Not so far. Just trying to brainstorm."

"Alright, then." He turns his attention back to his computer.

I decide to bite the bullet and find a way to connect. "Hey, what are you doing later?"

James looks at me, so confused. "Working. Although, I have a meeting with the lawyer at the end of the day."

"I meant after work. Do you have plans tonight?"

"Not really. Why?" He's answers cautiously, like I'm trying to pull something over on him.

"We should hang out."

"Who's we?"

I give him a confused look. "You and me. We're the only people in here. Who else would I be talking about?"

"I don't know." He shakes off my question.

"So…you want to hang out?"

He gives me another hesitant look.

"I promise I'm not going to try to kill you or anything."

James laughs. "That possibility hadn't crossed my mind, but now I'm feeling a little wary about hanging out with you."

"Oh, come on!"

"What's with this sudden need for us to hang out? We don't ever hang out."

"I know! We only see each other at work, and that's lame. We use to hang out all the time. We could go to the new putt-putt place. Have you been?"

He shakes his head. "No, but you hate putt-putt."

I wave off his argument. "I don't hate it. I'm just not very good at it, so you make fun of me. That's the part I'm not a fan of."

"You're serious?" James is being so stinking skeptical. I would give up except I feel like hanging out in a non-work environment might be the key for me to connect with James again.

I nod. "As a heart attack."

He shakes his head at my response. "Clara, I mean this in the nicest way, but you're so weird."

"Thanks. So, are we hanging out later?"

"I guess." He glances down at his button-up and tie. "I will probably need to change. I don't think I want to wear this to go play mini-golf."

"Yeah, I'll go home and change after work too."

We settle on a time to meet and turn our attention back to our work. This time, I actually try to come up with content, although I'm working on content for the website not social media posts like I said earlier.

During my chat with Leah last night, she said she is making progress getting the website designed, so I decided I should try to make some progress on the information that will be posted on each page of the website. Coming up with the right text for the website is more difficult than I expected. Thankfully, the menu page of the site is fairly simple since all I have to do is re-type and format the information we have on our menus. If only all the other pages were that simple.

Midway through the lunch rush, Danny sticks his head in the office and catches my attention.

"We have a bit of an issue."

"What's going on?"

"One of your beloved cooks, who shall not be named…" He winks at me, as if I didn't know he was talking about himself, "…just dropped a jug of milk, which broke and exploded all over the floor."

"Okay…" I wait for him to continue because while that's not the best news, it's not that big of a deal as long as it gets cleaned up. I assume there's more to the story.

"It was the second to last jug of milk."

"Ah." That's what the real problem is.

"You know Cheeseburger Soup is our soup of the month right now, which we need milk to make…"

"So, you need to me run and get more?"

"Desperately. We're almost out of the batch I made earlier. It's been going quickly today."

Nodding my head, I pull my coat on and grab my purse. "Anything else you need me to grab?"

Danny hands me a list. I assume these are all items we go through quickly and are low on. Our food delivery comes the day after tomorrow, so I will only need to pick up enough to hold us over until the bulk delivery comes.

It doesn't take me terribly long to get to the grocery store nearest Jimmy's. It also doesn't take long for me to fill the cart with the items Danny requested because we need multiple of each item. The gallons of milk alone cover the entire bottom of my shopping cart, so by the time I get up to the counter the cart is packed.

The cashier gives me a funny look as she rings up all the items.

"It's for a restaurant." I offer an explanation for the ridiculous amount of food I'm buying.

The only response I get is a look that tells me she doesn't care, so I shut my mouth and wait patiently to pay and get out of here.

Once I'm back at Jimmy's, it's been almost an hour since I left, despite my best efforts to be quick. I unload the groceries on my own because both the kitchen staff and the servers are pretty swamped and James has already left for his meeting.

James disappearing like that would've driven me nuts a week ago, but in the spirit of showing kindness, I choose to say a prayer for his meeting instead of getting upset. Honestly, I feel a lot better this way.

I settle back in at my desk and am deep in thought, for real this time, when a phone call interrupts me. A quick glance at the caller ID makes me smile.

"Hey, Sharon!"

"Hi, Sweetheart. How are you?"

"I'm doing pretty good. How are you?" James' mom is one of the kindest people I've ever met and I love getting to talk to her.

"I'm so glad to hear that. We are having a fantastic time down here in Arizona. It's been so lovely. We're thinking of staying a little longer than planned."

"Bummer for us, but that sounds like fun for you and Dean."

"It will be. Plus, we'll get some extra time with his mom."

Hearing about Dean's mom reminds me I never asked Dean about interviewing her for promo videos. "That's great. Actually, I had something I wanted to run by you."

"What's going on?"

"I had an idea. James was sort of fifty-fifty about it, so we decided we would ask you guys. But things have been busy so I forgot."

"I'm intrigued."

"Well, I was trying to come up with some ideas of how to boost interest in the new location and drive up traffic on our website. One thought I had would be to have James, or Dean, interview Dean's mom about what it was like when they first decided to open Jimmy's. Get some perspective and history about the diner before the new one opens."

"Oh, Clara! I think that would be a lovely idea. We'll have to figure out how to do it since she's down here in Arizona, but I'm sure we can make it happen. I bet she would love to talk about it."

"Really?!" I fail to contain my surprise and excitement at Sharon's encouragement.

"Absolutely. I think she would be happy to be able to tell some of her story."

"That's awesome! I'm so excited to hear all about how they started it. I don't think I've ever really heard anything of their story."

"I love it. So, how are plans for the new location going?"

"Uh…I think it's going well. All the business stuff is a little over my head. James is at a meeting now. I'm sure he could fill you in when he gets done."

"You're not at the meeting?" Sharon sounds surprised.

"No. I'm much better suited for planning the online announcement, scheduling social media posts, and maybe picking out paint colors once it's time. Meetings with a bunch of guys in suits about legal stuff and accounting are not my forte." I hear the words come out of my mouth before I realize how true they are. I want to be involved with opening the new restaurant, but a lot of the stuff James has been doing lately sounds awful to me, which makes the fact that I was so upset about not being involved a little silly.

"Oh, well, I suppose that makes sense. I must say, I've enjoyed seeing your posts on Facebook. You are doing a great job."

"Aww…thank you. That means a lot."

"Well, it's true. So, tell me, what do you think of the location? I know James said you guys thought it was perfect, but I want to hear your take on it."

Her question catches me off guard, and it takes me a second to figure out how to answer it. It sounds like she thinks I saw the location with James the day he made his decision. While I know that's not true, I don't think I can correct her without throwing James under the bus about not taking me with him, and I definitely don't want to do that. Even if I didn't like the location, I would want to talk to James about it first, not Sharon.

Which means I have to be careful how I answer. "The location is great! It's in the right area. The space is plenty big enough. And there's a lot of parking, which I know is something James was worried about with some of the other locations."

"That is true. That's a good thing." Sharon sounds like she's not convinced.

"It is." I'm not sure what else to say.

"Do you agree with James that this is the right location to move forward on? Or was there another one you thought would be a better fit?"

Once again, I make sure I choose my words carefully. "From what I've seen, I think it's a good choice. James had a pretty good idea what he's looking for, and I think this location meets all the criteria."

"Alright then." She still doesn't sound totally convinced.

"I just thought of something else I wanted to ask you."

"I'm all ears."

"I know there are some old photos of Dean's parents and early days of Rockton on the walls here, but do you have any other pictures of Jimmy from back in the day? I was hoping to find a good, candid picture of him for something I'm working on."

"I'm pretty sure we have some at the house. Allen has been checking on the house while we're gone, so I'll see if he can find the pictures and bring them over to you. I'm sure Dean's mom has some too. I could always look for some there."

"Either way would be great. Although, having Allen bring me the ones from your house might be faster and I am on a little bit of a time crunch."

"Okay. I'll give him a call later today."

We casually chat for a few more minutes before she has to get off the phone so she and Dean can go on yet another hike. I hang up the phone, still smiling at the idea of Dean turning into Mr. Outdoorsman since they've been in Arizona.

ᘎᘎᘎ

James never made it back to the office after his meeting, but he did text me to let me know our mini-golf plans are still intact. Sure enough, when I walk into the new putt-putt place, I see James waiting in a corner of the lobby on his phone. He spots me and holds up his index finger like he needs one more minute.

With a nod of understanding, I head up to the counter to pay and get my club. I take a second to look around. They only opened a couple months ago, and I haven't been to this place before tonight. On the other side of the entrance, there's a snack bar with a large seating area. It looks like they have the kinds of food you would get if you went to a bowling alley, although this one looks cleaner and better lit. The sound of James' voice behind me pulls my attention back to the front counter.

"Sorry."

I shrug as he steps up to pay. "No worries."

"I was talking to the lawyer. He thinks we can finalize the sale next week after…"

"Not to be rude." I interrupt him, knowing I'm being a little rude. "But can we talk about that tomorrow at work and make this a work free hang out night?"

James looks a little surprised by my request, but obliges. "Yeah, I guess."

"You ready?" I use the putter in my hand to point him in the direction of the first hole.

"Oh, I was born ready." He laughs and takes off in front of me.

We joke around a little as we work through the first hole, which James does better than me on. I came into this particular game expecting to be the loser. While I could wipe the floor with him if we were at a bowling alley, at mini-golf, James is definitely the better player.

"Hey, which small group have you been going to lately?" I'm not sure I ever heard which one he landed on after we decided he wouldn't come to mine.

"Uh…the one on Monday nights." He says as he lines up his next shot.

"And you're liking it? That's the one Conner and…oh, shoot. What is her name?! The pretty redhead who leads the group with Conner?"

"Andrea." James suggests.

"Yes! That's her name. Conner and Andrea lead the group you're talking about, right?" I step up for my first swing on this hole.

"Correct. They're cool people. I like them."

"Good, I'm glad!" And I am. I want him to connect with other people in the young adult group. Hopefully, having more friends at church will help cure him of his workaholic nature. "What are you guys studying? Do you do a book study? Or topic discussions?"

James is watching the guys at the hole ahead of us when he answers. "Mostly discussing the text from Sunday's sermons. You know, use the sermon as a guide for a passage and see what everyone else gets from it."

"That sounds good."

"Yeah…what about you guys?"

"We typically go through books of the Bible. Currently, we're on your book."

He looks up at me, eyebrow raised, from where he's lining up his shot. "My book?"

"Yeah, we're reading through James."

"Ah. That book. Are you liking it?"

I think before answering. I'm not sure now is the right time to talk about how much I was struggling with working with him, so I might need to avoid talking about what I've been learning during our study of James.

"I am. It's a great group of people who often challenge me to think differently. I feel like I've learned a lot as we've studied James."

"You know, even though I share a name with that particular book of the Bible, I don't remember ever reading it. I've read through the Bible a few times in my life, so I know I've read it. I don't remember it though."

"Well, I highly recommend it. It's a good one."

"I'll keep that in mind." James smiles as we walk to the next hole.

We're halfway through the mini-golf course when I work up the courage to ask James about something I've been wondering about since we started working together.

"Hey, can I ask you something?"

"Of course." He nods and leans forward to make his putt.

"What exactly happened at your last job?"

James hits the golf ball so hard it hits the outside edge of the hole and bounces over onto the walkway.

"Crap!" He exclaims as he moves to go get his ball.

"Easy killer. What was that?" I laugh. It's nice to know I won't be the worst player on this hole.

James shakes his head and places the ball at the tee again. "I don't know."

He takes his shot, not over-shooting it this time, and steps out of the way for me to step up and take my shot. I swing, making sure not to hit it too hard, and see I had a pretty good hit. James takes his place at the end of the hole where his ball is waiting to be tapped into the hole.

"Are you going to answer my question?"

He gently taps the ball and it rolls toward the hole, stopping half an inch from the hole.

"Seriously?!" Now he looks like he's actually agitated.

I give him a sympathetic pat on the shoulder and line up for my hit. I hit the ball a little harder than I mean to, but the ball rolls perfectly into the hole. "Yes!"

I turn to see James shaking his head at me.

"Oh come on! I'm not allowed to do better than you on one hole? I'm still losing by like seven points…"

"Strokes." He interjects the correct word.

"…and the chances of me catching up to you are slim to none."

"That's probably true. Get out of my way so I can get this terrible hole over with."

I step off the fake green grass onto the walkway and wait for him to tap the ball in. Thankfully, he doesn't overdo it this time, so the ball drops into the hole.

"Moving on." With his ball and putter in one hand, he gives me a little shove in the direction of the next hole. I give him a hard time about his one bad hole, knowing he can mock me for my lack of talent, but I'm totally okay with that as long as he stays in a good mood.

The two of us spend the next few holes reminiscing about some of the crazy things we did with our friends when we were in high school. The memories from summer church camp alone are plentiful enough to keep us talking and laughing while we finish our 18 holes of putt-putt.

We're playing our last hole when I realize James never answered my question about what happened at his job in Kansas City. I can't decide if he purposefully didn't answer or if we got sidetracked. Either way, I make a mental note to ask him again later. At the moment, we're trying to get our golf balls all the way up a ramp to the pipe on the end of it, so the ball will roll down the pipe and be returned to the front desk. Naturally, James gets his up on the first try and I don't. It takes me three attempts to get it, at which point, I'm happy to be done.

"Would you look at that?" James holds the scorecard up in front of my face.

I push his hand aside. "Yeah, yeah, yeah. I get it. You're a better mini-golfer than me. Congratulations."

"Thank you." He gives me one of his award-winning smiles.

"You want some ice cream?" I ask impulsively. Our hang out night has been more fun than I expected it to be, so I want to hang onto that as long as I can.

James laughs. "It's thirty something degrees outside and you want ice cream."

I wave off his argument. "It got up to forty degrees today. Plus, we're inside."

"Fine. But loser pays." He agrees, before heading in the direction of the snack bar.

"Rude!" I call after him, but I really couldn't care less about having to pay. I'm just glad he's up for having some fun tonight.

Once we're seated with our medium cups of ice cream, I decide to ask James my question for the third time.

"Now that you're not trying to focus on your shots, want to tell me what happened at your last job before you came back to run Jimmy's?"

He drops his head before he can take his first bite. "You're really not going to let it go, huh?"

"Nope." I pop a spoonful of ice cream into my mouth.

"Why do you care so much?"

I shrug. "I don't know much about your life after you went off to college and left us behind. I guess I'm curious about what actually brought you back to Rockton."

He rolls his eyes at my remark about being left behind, but then his expression sobers and I have a feeling I might get an actual answer. "You know, the funny thing is I was so excited when I got the job right out of college. It was essentially a glorified sales position at a start-up company that seemed amazing. Things were great for a while. The business was doing well, the guys I worked with were cool, and life was good."

"Until…" I prod when he pauses for too long.

"Until I got promoted." James says it simply, as if promotion is a bad thing.

"What happened?"

"My promotion put me over a bunch of the guys I had been working with, but it wasn't too bad. It was still a good job. Then, the boss, the guy who founded the company, started asking me to 'adjust' the numbers in my reports."

"Wait, he was stealing money?"

James shake his head. "No. He was trying to make it look like there was more money, more business, more success than there really was. Don't get me wrong, they were doing well. I guess he wanted it to look even better to investors."

"What did you do?"

"I said no." He shrugs. "It was the only thing I could do. What he was asking me to do was wrong. When I made my stance clear, he acted as if that was what he wanted to hear. Like it had been some sort of test and I passed."

I take another bite of my ice cream, waiting to hear more.

"So, I moved on as if nothing had happened. A month later, when the investors were in town visiting the office, I saw a copy of the numbers the owner had given them. He altered the numbers on his own. I honestly don't know how he did it. All I know is I wasn't interested in being a part of a company that was lying to the people supporting it, so I submitted my resignation a few weeks later."

"Wow. That really sucks."

"It did suck for a bit, but then I realized God was leading me to something else, something better at Jimmy's. So, all in all, I guess it was worth it." He takes another bite of his ice cream. "Now, all I have to do is make sure opening the new diner goes according to plan."

"I guess so." I scrape the bottom of my ice cream cup with my spoon, trying to make sure I got all the sugary goodness out of it.

"You ready to head out?" James stands and tosses his empty cup into the trash can nearby.

"Yup." I wipe my mouth with a napkin just to be safe and toss my trash. "This was fun. I'm glad we did it."

A small grin creeps onto his face. "It was, although I'm mostly glad it wasn't some sort of setup."

"What do you mean?" I watch him closely, but he doesn't answer immediately. "Wait, is that why you were being so weird about it when I asked his morning?"

He nods, holding back a smile. "Some of my friends in college developed a habit of inviting me to hang out, only to have some lovely young woman join us in an effort to set me up. The worst was when they would introduce us and then disappear for a while."

"Seriously? That's hilarious. I wish I could've seen that."

James shakes his head at my reaction. "Actually…you did."

"I did what?" I stare at him, trying to figure out what he's saying. Then it clicks. "Wait. Are you telling me the one time I saw you in KC…"

"Yup." He turns toward me as he opens the door to the parking lot for me. "I planned to meet up with some friends of mine downtown. I show up and they have this woman I've never met with them, which wasn't a big deal. We were going to walk around and check out some different art shows, so it didn't matter if an extra person joined us. Ten minutes later, I find myself at the back of the group with this lady. I paused for two seconds to give a group of people directions and turned to find my friends gone and this woman standing next to me."

"Shut up! This is so great."

He chuckles and pulls his coat a little tighter. "We took off after our friends but couldn't find them and they weren't responding to calls or texts. At which point I ran into you. Do you remember what that was like?"

I think for a second before my eyes go wide and my hand flies up to my mouth. "Oh no."

"Yeah. I'm at the point when I desperately want to go home, but I don't want to leave this woman by herself downtown because then I would be a complete jerk. Then I quite literally run into you and all your friends, and you start interrogating me about my date, who's name I could barely remember."

"I'm so sorry." I laugh even as the words come out. I really did give him a hard time that night. Asking all about the woman I thought was his girlfriend. Even when he was clearly trying to downplay the situation, I kept pushing. My friends and I had been having a fun evening, so I was pretty hyper that night.

"You sound very apologetic." He rolls his eyes.

I force myself to stop laughing for a few seconds. "No, really. I'm sorry. I just always thought you were being awkward because you didn't know my friends, and I was so energetic. I had no idea."

"I know. I was so mad at my friends though. I bailed as soon as we finally caught up to them."

"You should've stuck around. Who knows? Maybe she was the girl of your dreams?"

"I doubt it. In the very limited conversation we had, she said golf was the most boring sport in the world, if it could even be considered a sport."

"And she lived to tell about it?" I fake a look of shock and abhorrence.

"Shut up." He waves off my statement and heads to his car, which is three spaces down from mine.

"Good night!" I call.

"See you tomorrow."

I smile as I get in my car to head home. I know things probably won't change at work, but tonight was a good step in the right direction.

Chapter Sixteen

James and I are both surprised to see his brother Allen come through the door to the office Thursday morning.

"What are you doing here?" James stands up behind his desk.

Allen holds up a tote bag and places it on my desk. "Mom asked me to bring these over to Clara. She told me the sooner I could do it, the better, so I grabbed them last night on my way home."

I clap in excitement before I start digging into the bag. "Yay. I didn't think it would be so soon. I just talked to her Tuesday."

"What is it? And when did you talk to my mother?" James comes around to my desk.

"Photo albums!" I pull the first one out and hand it to James. "Thanks, Allen. I really appreciate it."

"No problem." He smiles and for just a second, I can see a resemblance between the two brothers. "Now, I have to get to work. I'll see you Sunday little bro."

"See ya." James barely looks up from the photo album.

I pull a second photo album out of the bag and start perusing it, looking for photos of Jimmy. Thankfully, Sharon has written a description, including names, for each picture either on the back of the photo or in the margin next to the photo. I slowly lower myself into my chair, captivated by the pictures from a different time. Likewise, James leans up against the edge of his desk as he flips through the book in his hands.

He looks up suddenly. "Why did Allen bring these over?"

"I asked your mom if she had any candid or fun pictures of your Grandpa Jimmy. She had Allen bring them over since they're out of town."

"And why do you need my old family photos?"

"I'm hoping to find one I could use as part of the announcement of the new diner. I'm not entirely sure how it would look or what exactly I want, but I thought it would be cool if it worked out."

James nods and continues to look through the book in his hand. "So, when did you talk to my mom?"

Because I'm so excited about getting the photos, I manage to refrain from rolling my eyes at him for asking a question that's already been answered. "Tuesday."

"You were asking for photos?"

"Yeah..." I nod absentmindedly before remembering another part of the conversation I had with Sharon the other day. "I also asked her about my idea to interview your grandma. She thought it was brilliant."

"I'm sure she did." The words are quiet, but his agitation comes across loud and clear.

My head snaps up. "What's that supposed to mean?"

"Nothing." With a shake of his head, he deposits the photo album on top of my desk. "It's a good idea. I'll see if we can make it happen."

"Thanks," I mumble as he heads back behind his desk. Something about his demeanor has shifted and gives me the distinct impression he's frustrated his mom liked my idea, but he agreed to ask his parents. No sense picking a fight with him about his mood when he's just decided to move forward with my plan.

I spend almost an hour paging through the photo albums, placing sticky notes on the pages with potentially useful pictures on them. In the end, I have eight photos to choose between. Well, I have one I really like and then seven more options in case the first one doesn't end up working with the design I have in mind. My next step is to get them onto the computer so I can manipulate the pictures digitally for the design.

We don't have a scanner here, so I try to take pictures of the pictures with my phone. Unfortunately, they don't turn out too well. Either they have weird shadows from me holding the phone over them, or there are glare spots from the overhead lights. In the end, I decide to sneak away from work and take the photo albums to my house to use Dad's scanner in our home office.

It doesn't take me long to scan the photos, and as soon I get back to Jimmy's, I set to work designing the graphic I'll post with the announcement. I'm no graphic designer, but my limited skills are enough to complete this project. I use different pictures, layouts, and fonts to create multiple possible posts. Since this news is a big deal for James, I have a feeling he'll want this announcement post to be perfect. Which is why I'm creating a variety of choices for him to choose between, even if I am partial to the ones with my favorite picture.

My favorite picture is one of Jimmy sitting on a stool in the diner, leaning against the front counter laughing. He's looking almost directly at the camera, but not quite. It's a great picture and I'm hoping James likes it enough to use for the announcement post.

"Hey, come over here." I call to James when I've got enough options I'm happy with. There are six different ideas total, and I want him to look through them before I choose one.

James makes his way over to the side of my desk, bringing a stool with him. Slowly, the two of us go through each design I've created and hone in on our favorites.

"I think we should use this one." James points to one of the designs with my favorite picture. "But, can we change the font or something?"

We spend the next few minutes going over the possible changes for the design he liked, to make it better. It doesn't take us very long to come up with a look we both like enough to use.

"Will you read this and tell me if that sounds good?" I show him the text I've been working on this week to post along with the announcement photo. I watch as he leans in and his eyes scan the couple of sentences, hoping to catch his reaction, but I can't read his expression.

He sits back on the stool and crosses his arms in front of him. "Sounds good to me. It's factual, without giving away too much information."

"Okay. Are we on track for me to post this next week?"

James nods. "We should get the approval for the re-zoning on Friday. Then, we can sign all the official paperwork on Monday."

"Okay. Perfect." I nod and make a note to schedule the post for Wednesday. A sense of contentment fills me as I turn back to my computer to put the finishing touches on the post. With the exception of him being weird about my conversation with Sharon, James and I have been getting along really well this week. I definitely think hanging out together outside of work was a good idea. I'm glad we did it, and I want to make sure it's not a one-time thing.

Naturally, things get busy over lunch and throughout the afternoon, so I'm all ready to leave for the day before I remember I haven't actually scheduled the announcement post for next week yet. With my jacket on and my purse over my shoulder, I sit back down at my computer and log into the website I use to schedule our social media posts ahead of time. I do a quick copy and paste of the text and upload the final photo design and enter the time and date for when it should post. Closing out of the website, I wave to James and head home to get ready for small group.

ꟼꟼꟼ

Somehow, at small group on Thursday night, El managed to convince me to join the setup team for the young adult activity this weekend. Once a month, our young adult ministry, Thrive, has an event when all the small groups come together for a night. It's a night for young adults who aren't in a small group to check out the groups and get to know some people in a more relaxed and fun setting.

For February, we're doing a Family Dinner and Hang-Out night. Often, there's more to these nights than hanging out at the church, but every couple months, Stephen and Leah want a night to get everyone together to simply spend time together and get to know one another better.

Apparently, El thinks I should join the event planning team for our young adult events since volunteering with the youth group didn't end up being my cup of tea. I'm not totally convinced helping with the ministry I'm a part of is what I want to do either, but I'm willing to give it a shot. Which is why, after working all Saturday morning at the diner, I end up at church helping El, Leah, and a number of guys clear the multi-purpose room so we can set up the tables and chairs for dinner tonight.

Once the tables are arranged correctly, we set out to decorate the room a little—simple plastic table clothes, bowls of chocolate candies as centerpieces, and some balloons scattered around the room. I'm helping El set out and fill the bowls of candy when Leah takes a call on her cell phone and waves me over.

"Clara, will you come with me to pick up the food for tonight?"

"Yeah. Are you sure you don't want one of the guys to help you?"

Leah nods and heads to the door, pulling her jacket on as she walks. "We still need to set all the chairs out, so I'll let them do that."

"Alright, let's go." I grab my jacket off the back of a chair in the lobby and follow her out to her SUV.

"So, how's work going?" Leah asks as soon as we're on the road.

"Pretty good, actually."

A quiet laugh escapes Leah. "You sound surprised."

"I am. Things have been so weird between James and I the last few months, I wasn't really sure I wanted to keep working there."

"That's hard. Is it better now?"

"I think so. James and I hung out the other night after work. It was good to reconnect as friends. Plus, Jesus and I have had some serious chats about my attitude and how I respond to certain situations. I'm a work in progress, but I'm feeling hopeful."

"Good. I'm glad to hear it.

We continue to chat as we make our way to one of the best barbeque places in town. The food is ready and the staff helps us load it into the back of the vehicle, taking extra care to make sure it won't slide around too much on the drive back. Thanks to a text I sent her, El is waiting at the door with a kitchen cart for us to load the food onto when we pull back into the parking lot.

Based on the number of cars in the parking lot when we get back, I would say this event has officially started. With extra people around, it doesn't take long to get all the food set out on the tables with serving utensils.

More people arrive over the next few minutes, so we don't have to wait very long before Stephen gets everyone's attention and says a prayer over the food. I help Leah and El keep the food trays full as almost one hundred people dive in and fill their plates. For the most part, the three of us have fun doing our job, even though I basically feel like I'm still at work. Which makes me think I'll have to find some other area of the church to volunteer in because I don't want to join the young adult event planning team going forward.

The good part about hanging out near the food for the first part of the evening is I get a chance to say hi to pretty much everyone. I saw all of the people in my small group come through the line at one point. I was even pleasantly surprised to see James come through the line with Stephen.

"Has she heard the good news?" Stephen elbows James as they load up their plates in front of me.

I can't tell if Stephen is talking about me or not, but I respond anyway. "Good news?"

James looks up at me excitedly. "The re-zoning was just approved."

"Seriously?!" My hands involuntarily shoot up in the air in celebration. "That's awesome."

"Yeah. I didn't realize how worried I was about it until I heard the verdict."

"Well, I guess now all that's left is to sign the papers to buy it."

James shakes his head with a smile. "And you know, renovate the building and actually open the diner."

I wave off his statement. "Meh. That's easy-peasy."

"Wait until I have to be at the new location all the time and you're in charge of the diner, then we'll see how easy you think it is."

"Eh…I'm not too worried about it." Once again, I brush off his attempts to make this good news into stressful news. The best part is, I'm honestly not stressed about it. Three weeks ago, this would have freaked me out, but right now, I'm just happy James and I are getting along and I'm looking forward to doing more at the diner while he's working on getting the new one up and running.

James laughs at my determination and takes off after Stephen with his plate. A few minutes pass and I'm putting out more rolls when I realize someone else is talking to me.

"Thank you so much for setting all this up. You guys did a great job." The kind words are soft-spoken, but sound sincere.

I glance up, ready to wave off the thanks, but the speaker catches my attention. I recognize the red-head that's smiling at me as the leader of the small group James has been going to, so I move a little closer to strike up a conversation. "Of course. We had a bit of fun doing it. You're Andrea, right?"

She nods vigorously, her red hair swishing back and forth. "I am. I'm sorry, I don't remember your name."

"No worries. I'm Clara. I only know yours because I was talking to my friend James the other day, and he mentioned your small group."

"Oh, okay." The crease on her forehead tells me she's unsure who I'm talking about. "Sorry, I'm drawing a blank on his name too."

Glancing around, I spot the table where James is sitting and point. "He's the one sitting next to Stephen."

She follows where I'm pointing and nods slowly. "Right, I remember him. He came to the group a few times last fall. We haven't seen him in a few months, but we were glad to have him when he did come."

Now, I'm the one that's confused. "Wait. He hasn't been to your group in months?"

"Nope." Andrea turns her attention back to the food table. "I remember Conner reached out to him the first week he didn't come, but I'm not sure if Conner ever heard back from him."

"Weird..." I mumble the words as she walks away with her full plate. I can't help but feel a bit hurt and confused. James very clearly told me he was going to their small group, and I can't figure out why he would lie.

I don't get to dwell on it very long because El reappears at my side talking about something that happened with one of her students this week. I try my best to focus on what she's saying as we move from behind the table to the front to grab some food and take a seat at a table with Sam, Adam, Dana, and Jules. The guys leave not too long after we sit down. They've already eaten—at least two platefuls—and are ready to make the rounds.

I'm almost done with my food when I spot Henry walking into the room out of the corner of my eye.

"Is that Henry?" El whispers from her spot next to me.

Suddenly, I realize I never told the girls what happened with Henry Monday night at the basketball game. I grab El's arm with excitement as I remember. "I totally forgot!"

"You forgot you invited him? That's kind of pathetic. You must be really out of it." El laughs.

I shake my head. "No, I didn't invite him."

"Well, that's rude. Who didn't you invite? And am I invited?" Jules voice sounds from across the table.

"That's not what I mean. Nobody is being invited anywhere." I start to correct the misunderstanding.

Jules interrupts me. "Dana is inviting us to her wedding. Right, Dana?"

Dana, who just got back from getting a refill, responds to her question. "Of course. I thought we covered that already. Hey, did you guys see Henry is here?"

"Really?" Jules follows Dana's line of sight to where Henry is talking to the guys. "What's he doing here?"

I shoot an exasperated look at El and drop my head into my hands. "Ahhh!!!"

"What's wrong with you?" I hear Jules ask.

El places a hand on my back and gently rubs it in small circles. In a quiet voice she says, "Is there something you want to share with the class, Clara?"

Dropping my hands back to my side, I give her an annoyed look. "Is that your teacher voice?"

"No, that's my a-student-is-having-a-breakdown voice."

"Gee…thanks." I'm not sure I like what she's implying.

She just laughs. "Seriously though, you were trying to say something about Henry before these two dragged us down their rabbit trail."

"I was going to tell you that…" I pause, mainly for dramatic effect, "Henry got saved the other night."

"Wait, what? Seriously?" Dana looks almost as excited as I was. I have a feeling she and Adam have been praying for Henry a lot lately. The other ladies sound off with similar exclamations.

I nod, affirming the validity of the news. "Monday night at my brothers' basketball game. Out of the blue, Henry brought it up and asked how to do it. He prayed right there in the bleachers."

"That is awesome! And I'm going to go tell him." Jules takes off to the other side of the room leaving the rest of us behind.

"You know what I love about God?" El's question seems like an odd jump in topic, but Dana and I roll with it.

"What?" We respond in unison.

"The fact that he's not constrained by location or circumstance. He's everywhere. And he's always ready to love us, whenever we are ready to accept his love. Whether you're in a church, at a basketball game, in a prison, or on your deathbed in a nursing home. He's always there. Waiting for us to want him as much as he wants us. And I think that's really beautiful."

Neither Dana nor I say anything immediately. I let El's words sink in a little bit. Dana responds first though.

"You're right. God's grace is truly amazing." Dana leans over and pulls El into a hug. "Thanks for reminding us."

Dana excuses herself to find her fiancé, and El and I head over to start cleaning up the food. I stop and pull Henry away from Leah, Sam, and Jules.

"Have you gotten something to eat yet?"

He shakes his head. "I don't want anything though. I had lunch late and I'll grab something when I get back to work in a bit. I'm just here to hang out for a little while."

"Alright." I grab his arm as he starts to walk away. "I'm glad you got to come by tonight. I know it's a busy night at work."

"Thanks." He wraps his arm around my shoulder and gives me a quick side hug before wandering back to the group.

Out of the corner of my eye, I see Stephen hop back up onto the stage and grab the microphone. "Wasn't the food great?"

There's a round of applause and cheers from the large group of young adults still sitting around the room.

"I guess you enjoyed it. I'm glad, but even more than I want you to enjoy the food, I want you to connect with other people. The heart behind this month's event is to simply get to know each other better and spend time together as a family. Because the church is a family. Leah and I are so grateful we get to be a part of this family with you guys, we love you."

"Love you too, big guy!" Sam shouts from the back of the room, producing a ripple of laughter from the group.

Stephen laughs and rolls his eyes. "Thanks. Anyway, I wanted to let you know you are welcome to hang out in here, there are a number of games on the tables in the lobby, the gym is open, and we may fire up a movie here in a little bit. So, hang out, have fun, and keep an eye on the food tables because dessert will be appearing shortly."

I spot a few of the younger guys slip out the side door toward the gym that's attached to the multi-purpose room as soon as Stephen comes down off the stage. At least twenty people clear their tables and head out to the lobby to hit up the game stash. Quite a few people stay in their seats and continue their conversations.

A few people come over to help El and me as we load the leftovers onto the cart to take back to the kitchen. As soon as we get it put away, one of the guys helping us asks about the dessert.

El grins as she answers. "I think the plan is to wait a little longer before bringing it out."

"Darn." His shoulders droop as he leaves us behind to finish cleaning up in the kitchen.

"I guess helping was his way of getting to dessert faster." I whisper to El.

She chuckles and moves to help one of the girls find the right drawer for the freshly washed utensils from tonight.

When we return to the multi-purpose room, we take a seat at a table with Sam, Jules, James, Leah, and a few other people I recognize but don't know very well. Henry is sitting at the next table over with Stephen and Adam having what looks to be a pretty intense conversation.

As I listen to the conversation floating around the table, my mind can't help but wander to my chat with Andrea earlier about how James isn't a part of their small group. The more I think about it, the more upset I am he lied about it. I don't notice I'm chewing on the inside of my lip until I break the skin.

An elbow in my side pulls my attention away from James to El, the perpetrator. I raise my eyebrow, silently asking what the elbow was for.

"What gives?" She whispers so as to not interrupt the conversation at the table.

"What?" My response matches her volume.

"What's with the staring?" She nods toward James.

I shake my head. "Sorry, I was just thinking."

"Okay. Don't hurt yourself."

"Thanks." I stick my tongue out at her and turn my attention back to the table to see James walking away to take a phone call.

Not even five minutes pass before I receive another elbow to my side.

"Ow…" I make eye contact with El again to find out what I did this time.

One again, her voice is quiet. "Looks like you're not the only one with a staring problem."

I follow her eyes toward the door to the lobby, where James is standing at the door talking on the phone staring at me. Actually, he's more glaring than staring.

"Does he look upset to you?" She asks quietly.

Her question confirms my analysis. "I was going to say angry."

El reaches over and gently pats my hand. "Good luck."

"Thanks." I wait until he ends the phone call before I stand and make my way over to him.

If there was any doubt in my mind he was mad at me, his cold, harsh words convince me. "We need to talk. Outside."

I grab my jacket and follow him through the lobby out to the parking lot. "What's up?"

He's quiet for a few seconds before saying anything. But when he does, his words pack a punch. "I'm not sure what's worse. The fact that you went over my head about something that should have been between you and me. Or the fact that you lied about it."

I couldn't have been more surprised if he told me he was quitting to join the next expedition to the moon. I can barely wrap my head around what he just said, which is why all I manage to stutter is a weak, "What?"

"What? Did you think I wouldn't find out?" James is a pretty mild-mannered guy normally, so this is the closest I've ever heard him get to yelling.

"I quite honestly have no idea what you're talking about."

He crosses his arms across his chest and stares at me, shaking his head. "So, you're going to keep lying? I really expected better from you."

"Whoa." I hold my hands up in defense. At first I was feeling confused, but now I'm offended and mad, which causes me to snap. "First of all, I don't know what you're talking about. I didn't lie to you. Second, since when are you a pillar of honesty? Last I checked, I'm the one who looked like an idiot tonight when I was talking to Andrea about how much you're enjoying their small group because you don't even go to their group! Imagine my surprise, especially considering that story about how you weren't willing to falsify documents to keep your boss happy. Or was that whole story a lie too?"

James looks legitimately surprised by my counter accusation. But he doesn't get a chance to respond because the door squeaks open behind us.

"Everything alright out here?"

I turn to see Henry standing just outside the door. He's got his hands in his pockets and he looks relaxed, but I can tell by the tone of his voice he's ready to step in if I need him.

"We're fine. Move along." James visibly tenses up as he cuts off my response.

"I wasn't asking you." Henry takes a step closer and pulls his attention from James to meet my gaze.

"I'm good. It's just work stuff." I force a tight, joyless smile to stretch across my face.

"You sure?"

"Positive. Have a good night at work. I'll see you tomorrow." I nod, trying to convince him to leave.

"Okay. I'll see you in the morning." He slowly steps back and starts to make his way to his truck. I wait until Henry is inside his truck to turn back to James.

Chapter Seventeen

I take a deep, calming breath and say a quick, silent prayer for wisdom. "Who was on the phone?"

"What?" Based on his reaction, that wasn't what James was expecting me to say.

"We were fine until you got that phone call. Now, all of a sudden, I'm enemy number one. So, who called? And what did it have to do with me?" I make a point to keep my questions calm and free of accusation.

"My parents." His response is short but carries less hostility.

"Okay…so, what?" I think back over what he said about me going over his head and move forward with the only line I can think of to connect the two subjects. "Are you upset I asked your mom about the video idea? Cause you said you wanted to run it by your parents. I didn't think I was going over your head or cutting you out. And I told you, so I…I don't understand what you're upset about."

"What I don't understand?" He pauses and takes a deep breath, like he's trying to keep himself calm. "I don't understand why I just got chewed out by my dad for not bringing you with me when I went to look at properties and had meetings about the new location."

"Oh." It's the second time I've been rendered speechless by James tonight.

"So, you did complain to them?" Apparently, he's taking my silence as confirmation.

"No. I didn't. I mean, your mom asked me about how the process was going and I told her you had a better handle on it than I did, but I wasn't complaining about not being involved. As a matter of fact, I made a point to not say anything about how I wasn't involved with choosing the new property."

He looks like he's trying to figure something out. "If you didn't complain to them, then why is my dad freaking out on me?"

"I have no idea." I take his lack of response as an opportunity to continue the conversation. "I mean, do I think it would have been cool to go with you to look at properties? Yeah, I wish I had been involved, but I didn't go running to your parents. I promise."

"Okay." He nods his head slowly. He's still thinking, I can see it on his face.

"Want to head back inside?" A shiver runs up my back as I ask. The weather has warmed up lately, but the sun has already disappeared and tonight's breeze is making the temperature of 42 degrees feel much colder.

He tosses a self-conscious look inside and shakes his head. "No, that's okay. You go ahead. I think I'm going to head home. I'm not really up for dealing with everyone."

"Okay. James?" I wait for his eyes to meet mine. "Are we good?"

A small nod is his first response. "Yeah. I'll see you Monday."

"Yes, Monday. When you get to actually buy the building for the new diner." I try to cheer him up with a reminder that plans for the diner are still moving forward.

He nods again and slips off across the parking lot. I head back inside, but the events of the last half hour left me feeling drained. Or maybe I'm exhausted because I worked this morning and then spent all afternoon and evening prepping for this party. Either way, I only last another twenty minutes at the hang-out night before heading home and dropping into bed super early, praying for a good night's sleep.

Thankfully, I fall asleep quickly and sleep deeply. Unfortunately, I fell asleep without setting an alarm, so I don't wake up until about ten minutes before my Sunday school class starts. Instead of hurrying to get here for only part of the lesson, I take my time showering, picking out an outfit, and getting breakfast. Even though I take my time, I'm still going to be a little early for service, so at least I'll have some time to chat with people.

My phone starts ringing as I pull into the parking lot. "Hey, Henry."

"Hey. Are you there yet?"

His abrupt question catches me off guard for a second. "At church? Yeah, I just pulled in."

"I'm almost there. Where should I go?"

"What do you mean? You were just here last night."

"Can you just tell me where to meet you?" His response is short and for the first time, it dawns on me he might be nervous.

For a half a second, I consider giving him a hard time about it, but I think better of it and decide to simply answer his question. I wait in the parking lot for him to arrive. From the moment he gets out of his truck, he's fidgeting with his shirt, then his hair, then his phone, then back to his shirt. It's weird to see him nervous, but even weirder is the fact that he's wearing dress clothes. He's pretty much always in t-shirts, hoodies, athletic shorts, and jeans. On the rare occasion where t-shirts and hoodies won't do, he normally goes with jeans and a flannel shirt, so seeing him in slacks and a button-up is messing with my brain a little.

"Good morning." I offer him a hug when he finally gets close enough. "You look nice."

He accepts the hug then runs his hand down the front of his shirt again. "So, this is okay?"

"Yeah, it's good. But, you could've worn jeans and t-shirt. No one would care."

"But it's church. You're supposed to dress up."

I nod. "Dressing up is good, if you're comfortable with it and you want to, but it's not required. Although, it is kind of fun to see you like this. I didn't even know you knew what dress clothes are."

"Aren't you hilarious? Can we go inside now?" Henry gently pushes me toward the door.

"Of course. We're a little early. Do you want the full tour?" The first service is still going, so there are only a handful of people out in the lobby when we walk in. On our left is the door into the multi-purpose hall we used for the event last night and for our young adult Sunday school class. The doors are closed, so I'm sure they are still going as well. "I know you saw this area last night, but you haven't really seen the rest of the church, right?"

"I haven't. At least not in a long time. Did I come to something here when we were kids?"

"Probably. I think you joined me for some kids' church fun, which is through that entryway." From where we are in the lobby, we can see into the check-in area for elementary kids. The kids' church area is next to the multi-purpose room. We pass that and I point to the next area. "That hallway leads to the church offices and if you go past them, there's a set of stairs that lead to the second floor, which has a bunch of classrooms. We used to have our Sunday school class up there, but we recently outgrew it. Next up, the most important area."

"The bathroom is the most important area?" He laughs at me.

"The sanctuary can seat over 1,500 people. Having enough bathrooms for all of those people is very important. Plus, it's always good to know where the bathroom is."

"Okay, weirdo. Keep going."

We continue walking through the lobby that wraps around the outside of the large sanctuary. "Past the bathrooms is the hall leading to the little kids' area. Actually, let's walk down this hall. I want to show you something back there."

We head down the hall, and right as I'm about to lead him away from the kids' area, down the back hallway towards the office, I spot someone I know behind the nursery check-in desk.

"Hey, pretty lady!"

Dana waves enthusiastically when she sees us approaching. "Hey guys, what are you doing?"

"I'm taking Henry on a little tour of our lovely church."

"Nice." She turns and looks at me. "Speaking of our lovely church, I hear you're looking for an area of the church to volunteer."

"I am. Sort of." I try to shrug it off, but she keeps watching, waiting for me to continue. "I don't want to volunteer just to say I'm volunteering. You know? I want to do something I'll actually enjoy. I just haven't found what that is yet."

"Makes sense. No pressure, but we could always use a few more people back here with the little kiddos. It's a lot of fun."

"You know, I worked in the nursery when I was in high school. I didn't mind it at the time, but that doesn't not sound like the right fit now."

"So you're saying you don't like kids?" Henry jumps in to give me a hard time.

"No. I'm saying I don't think this is the area God is calling me to volunteer in. That's all."

Dana nods her head like she understands. "No worries. I wanted to suggest it since Leah mentioned last night that you're trying to find your niche."

"Thanks. One of these days, I'll find the right area to utilize my gifts. Until then, I guess I'll have to keep praying about it."

A young couple walks up to the counter with two nursery-aged kids, so Henry and I let Dana get back to work. I lead the way down the side hallway and around a corner to the hallway leading to the church offices and find the door to the office unlocked like I had hoped.

Henry follows me in hesitantly. "Are you sure we can be in here? There's no one here."

"We're fine. Come on." I make my way past the main reception area and the maze of offices and cubicles the pastoral staff and volunteer leadership use. "Here we are."

"It's an office door. In a room I'm still not sure we're allowed to be in." He whispers his rebuttal.

"We're fine to be back here. Stop worrying. I practically grew up here, no one cares. This is where my mom works."

"So, this is where Mama Evans spends her days, huh." He leans over and peers through the window into the dark office. "It's nice."

"I think so too." A deep voice from behind us says.

I spin around to see Pastor Bill standing directly behind us looking particularly stern. I'm surprised to see him back here because I didn't realize the first service had ended, but I'm not even a little worried about him actually being upset. Before I can say anything, he continues.

"What might I ask are you two doing back here? Trying to break into my office?"

Henry's face goes white at his words.

I, on the other hand, start laughing. "Yes. That is exactly what I was trying to do. Break into your office. I was hoping to steal some chocolate from your desk."

Henry elbows me in the side and I realize he has no clue Pastor Bill is kidding. I elbow him back before explaining. "Henry, he's messing with us. This is Pastor Bill. My mom is his assistant. And his office really is the best place to find chocolate."

Pastor Bill, who has been giving us a hard look this whole time, finally cracks a smile and sticks his hand out to Henry. "That is true. I love chocolate, but I'm always happy to share. No need to let this one talk you into breaking in. I'm Bill. Nice to meet you…"

"Henry. Henry McKinley." He finally finds his voice as he returns the handshake.

Not to be ignored, I hop in the conversation. "Henry and I grew up next door to each other. Our parents are actually still neighbors."

"Ah…" A look of recognition crosses Pastor Bill's face. "Did I hear you recently got saved?"

Henry nods, still looking a little uncomfortable that we got caught back here.

"Welcome to the family, son. If you ever have any questions, and you will have questions, don't hesitate to ask. Myself, or anyone else on staff—I assume you know Stephen?"

"Yes, I do."

"Good. Good. It's good to meet you, Henry. Now, I need to run in there really quick to grab something before the next service starts."

"See you later." I throw a wave his direction and pull Henry toward the side entrance into the office, which is locked from the outside but not the inside.

"I told you we shouldn't be there." He mutters as soon as we're in the hallway.

"And I told you we were fine. Pastor Bill has been here almost my entire life, and my mom has worked for him for years. I promise he doesn't care."

"Whatever. Let's get out of here before he comes out."

"That I can do." I lead the way back to the lobby, which is now packed with people leaving first service and people heading into second service. We work our way toward the section where the young adults sit and find our friends. Stephen gives both of us a hard time for skipping out on Sunday school, but I brush it off. I enjoyed catching up on my sleep too much to allow him to make me feel guilty. The next ten minutes pass quickly as we all talk. Henry gets introduced to a ton of people by the time the music starts and we make our way into the sanctuary.

Worship is great today, and I'm a little bummed when it ends and Pastor Bill gets up to preach. While he's working on his introduction, I open my Bible to the chapter listed on the bulletin and a laugh escapes me.

El, sitting on my left, gives me a quizzical look. I point to the passage heading, but she doesn't understand. I wave off her unspoken question for now. I can answer her after service is over. I turn my attention back to Pastor Bill, who is now reading the scripture for today—1 Corinthians 12, which is all about how different people have different spiritual gifts and how the church needs all of them. I scribble notes the entire time, which is not normal for me, but I feel like he's speaking directly to me today.

Unity in Diversity

- gifts all come from the same God
- spiritual gifts given to one person benefit all
- Which gift do I have???
- Human body has many parts, but works as one body. So should the body of Christ.
- All parts are important (except maybe that extra kidney...jk)
- No one can say your gifts aren't important
- We need each other – to survive as a body

By the time the sermon is wrapping up, I have three full pages of notes.

"If you're here today and you don't know what your spiritual gifts are—what part of the body you are—I would invite you up to the front to pray. I've asked the worship team to come up and play for a few minutes. Our prayer teams will be up front as well. Come, spend some time with the Lord."

The music that began while he prayed continues as he steps off the platform and begins to walk back and forth across the front of the church. I want to head down to the front, but I'm almost dead center in the middle of our row. Instead, I kneel where I'm at and pray.

Today's message was so perfect for me. I've been confused about things at work and about where I should volunteer at church.

Heavenly Father, things have been crazy lately. I've had so many questions about what I'm doing that I don't know how to answer. You have been so faithful to lead me these last few weeks and months. Work has been rough, but you've guided me through it. I feel like I'm coming out on the other side so much more confident that I am where you want me. Now I'm asking for more direction. Where should I serve in church? I'm not entirely sure what my spiritual gifts are, but I want to use them for you. I want to be who you're calling me to be. Please continue to lead me.

I stay on my knees in worship for a while, singing along with the worship team, but no immediate answer comes. Despite the lack of answer, I feel at peace with the situation. Normally, I would be stressed out and upset about not hearing from God on the issue, but today I feel so overwhelmed by the truth that he knows me, I don't need to worry about it right now. God will reveal it to me in his time. At the right time.

When I finally get up from my spot on the floor, I see most of the sanctuary has cleared out. El is sitting at the end of our row and I make my way over and take a seat next to her.

"You know when you go to church and the sermon seems like it was written specifically for you?"

She gives me a knowing smile. "Yeah…"

"I can't decide if I think it's awesome or super creepy."

A laugh bubbles out of her as she slaps her hand over her mouth and nods for me to follow her out. Once we're out of the sanctuary, the laugh is released full force. "Clara, you can't say things like that!"

"Sorry, I didn't realize I was so funny."

"You basically just said God was super creepy…in church."

I toss my arm around her shoulder. "I guess I did. Oops."

"I don't know why, but that struck me as really funny."

"I do what I can." We laugh as we walk across the lobby to join our friends.

The rest of my Sunday passes quickly between hanging out with some of my small group and doing my laundry. I even spend a little time online searching for a place to live. Once again, I'm not finding much of anything, which I take to mean I need to be patient. I'm choosing to believe God has a plan for where I should live, where I should serve at church, and how things are going at work. I'm just hoping I have the ability to wait for him to show me what it is.

ꟼꟼꟼ

"Are you okay? You don't look so good." I ask as soon as I walk into the office and see James Monday morning.

"Gee, thanks."

"No, I just mean you look like you don't feel good."

He brushes off the apology. "I haven't gotten much sleep the last few days."

"That's never fun. You should take a day off or something, get some rest. Things are about to get crazy with plans for the new location, so you should get it in before it gets nuts."

"That's probably not going to happen. I have a lot to get done in the next few months. I doubt I'll be able to take time off. Even if I tried to take a day off, I would be thinking about my to-do lists the whole time."

"Alright, suit yourself. But I am happy to cover for a day or two if you need it."

He nods that he heard me, but he's too focused on whatever he's doing to really respond. I choose not to take it personally. He's stressed about the big news for today. Speaking of which… "Hey, I know this might be weird, but if you could have someone take a picture of you signing the papers today, we could potentially use it for when we announce the actual location in a few weeks."

He gives me a skeptical look.

"Pretty please."

"I'll try to remember to ask Mr. Simmons to take a picture."

"Thank you, thank you, thank you. I'll let you get back to whatever it is you're doing now."

He gives a slight nod and turns back to his computer. It seems like today is a good day for headphones. At least until he leaves.

The lunch rush is once again busier than normal today. I'm not sure if it's because the weather is getting a little warmer and people are more willing to leave their house or office for lunch, or if it's because of the advertising and promoting we've been doing online. Maybe it's a combination of both. Either way, if this keeps up, I may have to start scheduling another person to work the lunch shift on Mondays.

Although on this particular day, I'm happy to be out front. As much as I want to respect his space, James' silence is starting to weird me out today.

Putting on a smile, I approach the third table from the door, which holds one of our regulars and her adult daughter. "Hey, ladies. How are you today?"

"We're doing fine, sweet girl." The older lady at the table pats my hand.

"Can I get you a refill or anything?" I point to their drinks.

"No, we really are fine. How are you though? I saw the big announcement on Facebook. So exciting!"

I blink slowly, trying to process her words. "I'm sorry, you saw what?"

"The announcement about the new location. You guys must be so excited. It's such a big change."

"Oh…yeah. That announcement." My words barely come out. Today is Monday. The announcement wasn't supposed to post until Wednesday. Slowly, the realization sinks in…I must have messed up the date when I scheduled the post last week. And now everyone knows. I suck in a deep breath and try to find a better response because all I can do about it now is move forward. "Sorry, I didn't realize that was announced today, but we are very excited."

"Where exactly will it be?" The mother asks.

"You know, we're not quite ready to release that information. You'll have to wait a few weeks to find out."

The older woman smiles and pats my hand again, I guess that's her thing. "Well, we wanted to tell you how excited we are for you guys. I knew Jimmy and Lois way back when. I'm sure she's pleased as could be to see her grandson taking over and expanding."

"That's so great you knew them. From what I hear, she is pretty excited about this change."

She continues talking for another couple minutes all about how she first met Lois. It's an interesting story I would love to hear, but I can see a couple other tables that need assistance out of the corner of my eye. Her daughter must notice too because she kindly interrupts her mom and sends me off to do my job.

I hurry to clear a couple of tables that have just been vacated, then I turn to check on the tables on the opposite side of the room. Of the eight tables I check in with, two need refills, one is still waiting to have his order taken, and three want to talk about the big news.

When there's finally a break in the lunch crowd, I slip down the hallway that houses the bathrooms and a side door into the kitchen. Instead of entering either, I simply lean up against the wall and pull out my phone to check the Jimmy's Diner Facebook page.

I'm blown away by the number likes, comments, and shares on the post. It's by far our most popular post ever. Still hanging out in the hallway, I start scrolling through some of the comments it's gotten. Mostly, they are from people saying they're excited to have a Jimmy's Diner closer to where they live or people congratulating us. There are a few questions about the specifics of where and when it's going to open. I make a point to type out quick responses to those people telling them more information will be released in the coming weeks. There are a handful of not-as-positive comments, but for the most part, people are kind and supportive. Which makes me feel at least a little bit better about my mistake.

"Clara?" I look up to see Scout standing a few feet in front of me with an expectant look on her face.

Shoving my phone back in my pocket, I head towards her. "What's up?"

"Can you help me out? I've got an…upset customer out here. I was going to ask James, but…" She gives me a look that perfectly communicates what she's thinking—she would rather ask me than James. I don't really blame her. The staff think he's intimidating on his good days, and I wouldn't really say today is one of his best days, given how stressed he seems.

"Of course." I head out behind her to help her deal with the issue.

It doesn't take long for me to resolve the problem, or at least smooth things over enough that the guy is willing to pay and leave. A glance around the room tells me the lunch rush is ending and I don't necessarily need to be out here at this point.

Plus, a glance at the clock tells me James will be leaving soon for his meeting to sign all the documents to make the purchase for the new location official. If I head back now, I can catch him and let him know about the mix-up with the announcement post.

"How's it going, Danny?" I call over the hum of the kitchen equipment.

"Pretty good. It's been a busy day, but that makes the time pass quicker."

"Do you know if James is still here?"

"I haven't seen him leave." Danny glances over to the large digital clock by the door to the front. "He's probably getting ready to leave soon."

"Alright." I smile and head into the office. James is still here. He's sitting at his desk with his back to the door, which is a little odd. My guess is he's thinking about what he's about to go do.

"Hey. I know you're about to head out, but I wanted to mention…I may have accidentally set the announcement post to publish today instead of Wednesday." He looks up at me, eyes wide, at my confession, but I wave off his concern and open Facebook on my phone. "But it's okay. You should see some of these posts. People are so excited! They can't wait. They are totally supportive. It's awesome! So, I know I screwed up and I really am sorry, but at least we know our customers are pumped about the new location."

I'm a little breathless when I finally stop talking because I couldn't seem to slow down my motor-mouth. I guess, despite the positive response, I'm still a little worried James will be upset about my screw up, and it was a screw up. So, here I sit, waiting for him to respond.

But he doesn't say anything. He turns back toward the wall he was staring at when I walked in. I wait another couple seconds and right as I'm about to say something, he stands.

"I have to get out of here." His words are strained and croaky.

I watch as he quickly exits the office and heads in the direction of the back door. His response leaves me too stunned to move for a few minutes. I honestly think him yelling would've been easier to handle. Getting up to close the office door, I notice something on his desk. There, right by his computer mouse, are his keys and his phone. I wonder why he hasn't come back in for them yet. He clearly won't get very far without them. I shake my head as I grab them and head out the door to find him.

However, the scene in front of me when I open the back door stops me in my tracks. "Danny!"

Chapter Eighteen

I rush out the door to where James is leaning the left side of his body against his car, barely holding himself up. His arm is clenched up toward his chest like he's in pain.

Getting to his side, I slip an arm around his waist and try to help him onto the ground. I have no idea what happened, but clearly something is wrong. It seems like he's having trouble breathing. Danny comes out and takes over.

I pull away, willing my arm to stop shaking, only to realize I wasn't the one shaking, James was.

"Bud, what's going on?" Danny asks.

"What happened?" I search his face for some indication of what's going on.

James doesn't respond. Instead, he keeps attempting to breathe, but it looks like he can't. His eyes are wide with fear.

"Clara, call 9-1-1." Danny's voice is calm, much calmer than I feel.

I take a few steps away and tap the screen of my phone to place the call. I force myself to inhale slowly once, twice until I hear an answer on the other side.

"Something's wrong with my friend. He can't breathe, he's shaking, and he's in pain. He needs help."

The operator responds with a few questions about the situation and our location and after hearing my responses calmly tells me an ambulance is on the way. I stand back and watch as Danny talks to James in an effort to calm him down.

I stand just behind him, my arms wrapped around myself.

Lord, I don't know what's going on here, but you do. Please be with James right now. Take away the pain. Help him to breathe. Please just…

"What's going on?" A voice from behind me interrupts my silent prayer.

I spin around to see Wendell and Josh standing in the back doorway. The looks on their faces and Wendell's question forces me to think practically.

"Something is wrong with James. We called an ambulance. Can you just keep things going in there until Danny can come back inside?"

He nods and slowly backs up toward the kitchen. I start to close the door behind him, but think of something.

"I'll be right back." I call to Danny as I slip back into the office. I hurry to grab my purse from behind my desk and loop it over my head before I head back outside. I drop James' phone and keys, which are still in my hand, into my purse as well. If James is going to the hospital, I'm going with him.

A few long, agonizing minutes later, I can see the ambulance out front. I told them on the phone to come around to the back of the building, so I'm standing on the side of the building waving to them. I point the ambulance around to where James is and follow on foot.

By the time I catch up, they've got James on the stretcher with oxygen and are loading him into the back of the ambulance. On top of everything else, it looks like he's dripping sweat. It's barely forty degrees out right now, so that's not normal.

"Can I come?" I ask the EMT closest to me. She gives me a quick nod and points to where I should sit. I turn to

Danny before following her instruction. "Can you stay and take care of things?"

He's supposed to leave soon when Laura comes in for her shift, but I would feel better about leaving if I knew he was here.

"Of course." He nods and waves me to the ambulance.

"Thank you." I hop in and sit quietly as the other EMT checks various medical things on James.

It looks like James' breathing is finally getting back to normal. At least, normal enough he can choke out two words. "Call…Allen."

"Yeah. Okay." I nod vigorously as I pull my phone out, but then I realize I don't have Allen's phone number. I start to look up the main number for the hospital, hoping I'll be able to be put through to the financial office where Allen works, and then I remember I still have James phone. I navigate to Allen's number and tap the screen to call.

"Hey, baby bro, what's up." Allen answers, obviously expecting James.

"Hey, it's Clara." I choke back the worry that's been taking over the last few minutes. "I'm with James. We're on our way to the hospital."

"What happened?" Concern threads his voice.

I give him a brief summary of what happened, which is especially short since I don't really know what happened.

"I'll head over to the ER and meet you guys."

"Thank you." I end the call and give James the best smile I can muster. "He'll meet us there."

James gives a quick nod and relaxes back into the stretcher and closes his eyes. James may drive me nuts half the time, but seeing him on a stretcher in the back of an ambulance has me ready to burst into tears. The EMTs don't seem as concerned now as they were when they first showed up, so I'm taking that as a good sign.

I hop out when we get to the hospital and follow the stretcher into the ER. Sure enough, Allen is standing at the nurses' counter inside the door. Allen walks up next to the stretcher and with a hand on James' arm, leans in to say something to him.

I'm a few steps behind, but I still catch some of what he says. "I talked to the doctor…knows your situation…still wants to run some tests…to be sure."

All of the worst-case-scenarios I've been pushing out of my mind come bubbling back up. I had mostly convinced myself this was a fluke thing and James would be fine while we were riding in the ambulance, but Allen's words make it sound like something is really wrong with James.

James's response is weak but he seems okay. I stand in the middle of the lobby watching as he's wheeled down the hallway with Allen beside him. Suddenly, I feel out of place. I look around and decide to sit in one of the chairs out here to wait. I'm not sure how much time passes as I stare at the wall opposite my chair, but my ringing phone pulls my attention away from a spot that desperately needs to be repainted.

"Hello." I answer without looking at the caller ID.

Leah's voice sounds on the other end. "I just got to Jimmy's to go over the website design, but Danny says you had to take James to the hospital?!"

I rub my hand across my forehead. I had completely forgotten Leah was coming by today, even before everything happened with James. I was so distracted by the accidental announcement and the meeting James was supposed to have—which is something else I'm just now remembering. I'm going to have to call Mr. Simmons or the lawyer to reschedule the meeting. A sigh escapes before I can stop myself.

"Hello? Clara? What's going on? Is James okay?" Leah sounds scared.

"Yeah. Sorry. It's been a crazy little bit. To answer your question, I'm not entirely sure what happened. I think James is okay, but I'm not sure about that either."

"Okay. Where are you?"

"I'm in the waiting room of the ER. James was taken back. I guess they're going to do some tests. Allen's here. He went back with them."

"Are you okay?"

Her question immediately elicits tears. I choke them back. "Yeah…I'm fine."

"You don't sound fine. You sound like you're crying."

"Well…" My response is halted by the tears that don't want to go away.

"Hang in there. I'm going to head over."

I shake my head. "No…you…"

"I'm coming. Now, try to relax. I'll be there in a few minutes."

I hang up the call and once again force myself to breathe slowly. It seems like only a couple minutes before I spot Leah coming in the door to the ER. I stand up and accept the hug she offers. A few more tears escape before she pulls away and we sit down together.

"Do you want to talk about what happened or are you more in need of a distraction?" She asks cautiously.

I take a deep breath and try to calm myself down. "Let's go with a distraction. Do you have one of those?"

She nods and leans over to pull her laptop out of her bag. "I sure do."

I wait semi-patiently and try to push the fearful thoughts from my mind. Thankfully, I don't have to wait very long before Leah turns her computer toward me.

"What do you think?"

I focus my eyes on the screen and my jaw almost hits the floor. She's got the design for the website pulled up and it looks amazing. "Oh my gosh. Leah!!"

"So, you like it?" She's biting her lip.

"This is perfect. Thank you. Thank you. Thank you." I throw an arm around her shoulder and pull her into an awkward hug over her laptop.

"Yay." Leah claps her hands in front of her when I pull away. "I can't wait to see what everyone else thinks."

"James is going to love this." Saying his name reminds me why we're having this meeting in a hospital waiting room instead of at the diner.

"It's not live for other people to view it yet, but you can click on all the links and see the different pages, complete with the content you sent me the other day."

I shake my head, trying to get rid of the worry, and move the mouse to click on the first link. Slowly, I read through each page of the website, amazed at how good it looks. "Seriously, Leah, I knew you were good, but this is perfect."

"Thank you."

"And…added bonus, it was a really great distraction." Almost an hour has passed since James and Allen disappeared down the hallway into the depths of the Emergency Room.

"Good, I'm glad." She glances at her watch. "I hate to do this, but I should probably go. Stephen and I have a meeting with a couple at church in like twenty minutes, I could try to put it off…"

"No. It's okay." I wave off her suggestion. "You go to your meeting. I'll text you when I find out anything. I should probably make some calls anyway."

"You sure?" Leah looks torn. She wants to stay here with me, but she also doesn't want to bail on her meeting.

"Positive." I give her the best smile I can muster. "I'll be fine. Like I said, I need to check in with Danny and I should probably call Mr. Simmons to let him know why James never showed up for their appointment."

"Okay, but promise me you'll call if you or James need anything."

"I promise."

"Alright. Here." She reaches over and takes my hand. "Lord, we pray you will give the doctors wisdom as they try to figure out what happened with James. We ask you to take away the pain he's experiencing and heal his body. You are a mighty God. You're our Healer and our Comfort. Please comfort James and Clara and his whole family. In your name we pray, Amen."

"Amen." I whisper as best I can despite the tears that have started again. I quickly wipe them away, so Leah doesn't get too worried.

"Love you, girlie." She pulls me into another hug.

"You too. See you later." I wave and watch her disappear back to the parking lot.

Settling back into my horribly, uncomfortable seat, I pull out my phone to call Danny. The call is short and simple. I let him know James was breathing easier and looked a little better when he was taken back for tests. I left out the part about what I overheard Allen saying. No need to worry Danny if it turns out I heard Allen wrong.

Danny did mention he tried to call Dean and Sharon, but didn't get an answer. I guess he left a voicemail asking them to give me a call, so now I wonder if I should try to call them or wait for them to call me.

I'm staring at the two cell phones in my lap trying to decide which to use: mine to call Dean and Sharon or James' to call Mr. Simmons, when I hear my name.

Looking up, I spot a nurse looking around for a response. I wave to her and hurry to slip the phones into my purse so I don't drop them as I stand. "I'm Clara."

She offers me a kind smile. "Mr. Harper asked me to find you and show you back to his brother's room."

"Oh. Okay." I follow as she leads me down the ominous looking hallway and around a corner. She points me down another hallway, and I see Allen standing outside room 127 halfway down with his phone in his hand, like he's texting.

"Hey." The word barely comes out, but it's loud enough to get his attention.

"There you are." He smiles. "I thought we might have lost you for good, which would've been a shame. We like you."

I don't really respond because I'm so taken aback by his relaxed, almost cavalier, attitude.

Realizing his mistake, he tucks his phone in his pocket and faces me. "James is going to be fine. I have to head back to work to put out a fire, but he asked me to send you in before I head back to my office."

"Okay…" I follow his direction and enter the hospital room as he disappears down the hall. The lights in the room have mostly been turned off and James is leaning back, the head of the bed is propped up to keep him in a slightly reclined position. It looks like he's sleeping, but his eyes open as I step closer. My voice is quiet when I finally say something. "Hey."

"Hey." James utters quietly, convincing me he feels as tired as he looks.

I pull the one chair in the room closer to his bed and take a seat. "How are you? Allen said everything's okay…"

James nods in affirmation, but I'm still confused. "Do you have my phone?"

"Um…yeah." I pull it out of my purse, along with his keys, and hand them over to him.

"Thanks. I need to send a quick text."

I nod, thinking he's texting Mr. Simmons about the missed meeting. James is nothing if not punctual, so I'm sure it's driving him crazy that he missed the appointment. "Oh…right. I was about to call Mr. Simmons when the nurse came to get me."

"No, I was texting my dad. I figure by this point, you've probably called him a few times."

I shake my head and offer a smile. "You really need to get over this whole thinking I'm in cahoots with your dad thing."

He laughs, which allows me to breathe a little easier. If something were really wrong, he wouldn't be laughing right now. I don't think.

"I'm never going to live that down, am I?"

"Eh…we'll see. The fact that we're having this conversation while you're lying in a hospital bed might evoke some mercy on my part." I shrug.

"I'll take what I can get." He exhales another deep breath, making me wonder if he's as okay as he's acting.

"Speaking of you being in a hospital bed…" I pause to see if he'll jump in. He doesn't, so I continue. "Are you sure you're okay? Because you looked really not okay back at the diner. And chest pain, shortness of breath, sweating…those are textbook signs of a heart attack."

I finally say out loud the fear that's been weighing on me since I first saw him holding his chest. He's young and in good shape, but he could have a heart condition or something that would cause it.

"They are also textbook signs of a full-blown panic attack." He meets my gaze when he says this and waits for a reaction.

A sigh of relief is my first response. The idea of a heart attack was really freaking me out. And after everything that happened with Henry's dad last summer, the second possibility rolling around in my brain was of some sort of tumor or growth in his chest. I have no idea if that's even possible, but that's the super scary place my mind went to while I was sitting in the waiting room. I don't want to say any of that though, so I go with a simple response.

"Okay, what…what caused it?" I think back over the day and my stomach drops. My eyes go wide. "Is this my fault? Is this because of me?"

"No, no, no." He shakes his head. "This is not your fault. It's not anyone's fault. It…it…I don't know. I guess it's how I'm wired or something.

I'm hesitant to believe him, after all, the panic attack happened right after I told him about screwing up the announcement about the new location. What if he was so upset…

"Stop." The strong directive interrupts my mental freak out. "I can see the wheels turning inside that crazy brain of yours, Clara. Listen to me when I say, this was not your fault. Do I need to have a doctor come in here to tell you?"

"No…" My response sounds sheepish even to me.

"Good."

"So…how long do you have to stay here?"

"Not too much longer, I hope."

"You want me to stick around and give you a ride home?"

He grins at me. "With what car?"

I start to reply before realizing he's right. I don't have a car here. Both of our cars are still at the diner. "Well…I can get a ride to go get my car and come back."

"You don't have to."

"I know, but you're my friend and I want to. Plus, Allen is your other option, and I'm way nicer than him."

James laughs. "You might be right. He's already started giving me a hard time."

"Then it's settled. I'm going to get a ride back to the diner, and I'll be back to give you a ride home when they say you can go." I pull my phone out to call my mom for a ride. While my dad is probably done teaching for the day, I'm betting he and the boys are still at school for basketball practice. Mom is clearly the better option right now.

Once I explain everyone is okay, she's happy to come pick me up and give me a ride from the hospital to the diner. James and I chat while I wait for Mom to get here.

His doctor even makes an appearance, looking over James' chart. "We should be able to get you out of here and on your way soon. We're waiting for the results of the second test we ran. I don't anticipate any issues with it, but I want to be sure."

"Sounds good. Thanks, Doc."

"I am recommending you take a couple days off. I know work isn't totally to blame here, but a few low-stress days won't hurt."

"Yes, sir." I can tell James has no intention of following the Doctor's advice. I however, plan to make sure he doesn't darken the door of the diner for a few days.

As the doctor slips back out the door, my text alert notifies me that my mom is here. "I'll be back in a bit. Don't go anywhere."

"Ha-ha…very funny."

I wave and head out.

I find my mom's SUV pretty quickly and spend the ten-minute drive back to Jimmy's filling her in on what happened. I also let her know I probably won't be home anytime soon. I have a few things I want to wrap up at the diner before I head back over to give James a ride.

"How's he doing?" Danny asks as soon as I step in the back door.

"He's okay. The doctor says he'll be fine. He should be released in about an hour. I'm going to head over to give him a ride home."

"I'm glad to hear he's doing better. Do they know what happened?"

"Yeah. And it's under control. He can explain it when he comes in, which won't be tomorrow. The doctor has prescribed a few days off, and I intend to make sure he follows that advice."

"Sounds good." Danny nods and turns back to whatever he was working on. Technically, he's okay to leave since Laura is here as our primary cook, but based on the number of food containers sitting out on the prep table he's at, I would guess he's been busy prepping things for later in the week.

I wrap up my work at the diner as quick as I can, and I'm packing up to leave when I see Danny outside the door, holding something.

"What's that?" I try to slide past him, but he holds up the bags in his hand like he's trying to get me to take it.

"Food for James. I doubt he'll be up for cooking himself food, and he should have good food."

I peer into the large, rather full bags and smile. Apparently, Danny's idea of good food is comfort food. No matter, I'm sure James will appreciate it. My phone goes off with a text from James telling me he's ready to go, so I accept the bags without protest and drop them on the backseat of my car.

When James slides into the passenger seat of the car, he smiles. "It smells good in here."

"I think Danny cooks when he's worried." I nod toward the bags in the backseat. "And that isn't just normal diner food either. He's made all your favorites and there's a ton of everything."

"I guess I won't have to cook this week." He leans his head back against the headrest and doesn't say much else for the rest of the drive to his apartment, other than to give me directions since I've never actually been here before.

James sits up suddenly when I pull into the parking lot of his apartment complex. "I don't have my keys. I left them at work earlier."

"I've got them." I call as I climb out of the car. "Grab that food, will you?"

"You don't have to walk me in. I'll be fine, Clara. I promise." He complains as he gets out.

"What makes you think I'm coming in to check on you? I'm only in it for the food. I don't know if you know this, but I didn't get lunch today and I just spent almost half an hour smelling that stuff. I want some." I walk toward his building.

"Fine." He laughs and shakes his head as he grabs the bags of food and walks up the path behind me.

With a little help, I figure out which key to use to get inside the building and then which one to use to get into his apartment.

"Sorry, it's kind of a mess. Obviously, I wasn't expecting company."

I look around the space that's cleaner than my room currently is and laugh. "You do realize I live with twin teenage boys, right? This place is practically spotless compared to any room they spend time in."

"Good point. Now, let's eat. I'm hungry." He starts unpacking the bags to identify what sort of deliciousness is inside. We both find something to eat and take our plates to the living room to eat. Mainly because he doesn't have a kitchen table and chairs to use.

"Dude, you've been living here for like eight months. Why don't you have somewhere to eat?" I carefully lower myself on the couch and tuck my legs under me.

"What are you talking about? I can eat right here." He waves a hand over his living room, which is pretty sparse except for the couch and a coffee table that's acting as a TV stand for his 50" TV.

"This place is depressing." I say as I dig into my food.

He glances around thoughtfully. "It is a little empty in here."

"Well, at least you have a nice large elephant to take up some space." I watch him to see if he gets what I'm saying.

The confused look he gives me tells me he doesn't.

"You know…the elephant in the room." I don't have to wait very long for him to get what I'm asking.

"You want to know about my panic attack."

I shrug and take another bite. "I mean, I might be a tiny bit curious about why I had to call an ambulance for you today."

"Fair enough. What do you want to know?"

"Is that the first time you've had a panic attack?"

"No. I had them off and on growing up, but they got really bad my first year of college. Over time, I've learned how to manage them. I hadn't had one that bad in a while…maybe ever, and I couldn't stop it. None of my usual coping tools worked. Normally, if I can't get myself calmed down on my own, I call my dad, but by the time it was bad enough for me to need to call him, I realized I didn't have my phone, which made it worse. A lot worse."

"I'm sorry. That sounds awful."

James grins into his plate. "It definitely wasn't pleasant."

"So, what causes them? I mean, I know you said it wasn't anyone's fault, but the panic attacks, they have a trigger or something, right?"

"It depends on the person and the kind of panic attack, but yeah, mine typically do." He gets quiet for a second. Part of me wants to ask what the trigger is, but something inside me says to wait. To be patient and let him tell me. So, I take a few more bites of my dinner while he thinks.

"Fear of failure." He spits the words out like he hates them. Again, I feel like I should just wait. Eventually, he goes into more detail. "That's the way the doctor put it after my first one way back when. Fear of failure. Like, I would get so worked up about doing well and passing classes, I would get really bad anxiety that eventually turns into a panic attack. Which is probably why they were so bad my freshman year of college. Everything was new. I was so worried I would screw up."

"And now?" Given that he's not in school anymore, I wonder if the same triggers it.

"Now…" He releases a deep sigh. "Now, it's the same basic fear I guess. I'm afraid of failing. Or, in today's case, I'm scared about having to admit I have failed."

"How so?"

"You know the meeting I was supposed to have today?"

I nod, wondering where this is going. He didn't miss the meeting until after the panic attack happened.

"I got a call right before I was supposed to leave, while you were still out front. It was Mr. Simmons. They backed out of the deal. We can't buy the property. All the plans I've worked on for months—they're gone."

Chapter Nineteen

"Wait, what?" I drop my fork onto my plate and sit up straight. "They can't do that!"

"They can. And they did." He shrugs. "I'm honestly still trying to wrap my head around it."

"What happened? Why did they back out of the deal?"

"Based on what Mr. Simmons told me, I'm not sure they ever planned to go through with it."

"Seriously?!"

A dejected nod is his first response. "Yeah. Remember how I told you the property was initially listed together, the warehouse and the office building?"

"Yeah. They were splitting it. That's why you had to apply to have it re-zoned for a restaurant."

"Well, I guess they had some company expressing interest in buying the whole thing, but the other company was being wishy-washy and not offering enough money. So, the owners said they would pursue other buyers to light a fire under the other company."

"And they just strung you along the whole time?"

"Basically. They didn't say it outright, but that's the impression Mr. Simmons got when he spoke with their representative."

"Wow. They suck."

James nods his head and takes another bite of his dinner. "Now I have to start over again."

"Any chance I might be able to join in on the fun this time?" I ask hesitantly.

He gives me an apologetic smile. "Of course. Dad and I chatted about that today when he called, after you left the hospital."

"Oh yeah? What did he have to say?"

"That we hired you for a reason: to help me open the new location. I shouldn't limit you to the social media and marketing aspect."

"I always knew I liked that guy."

James smiles and gives me a short nod before his expression turns serious again. "Clara, I'm sorry I shut you out of it so much. I honestly didn't even realize I was doing it. I was so focused on making it happen and moving forward, I guess I had tunnel vision. It didn't even dawn on me that you would want to come along. Anyway, dad and I talked, and I promised him to loop you in on all of it from here on out."

"Yay!" I clap in excitement.

A comfortable silence falls between us as we continue to eat. I'm excited I'll get to be a part of the new search process, even though I feel bad the first property fell through. It's frustrating to say the least, but more than anything, I hate that James is blaming himself for this.

"James, you said earlier that you failed, but that's not true. You didn't fail. They failed at being decent human beings. You shouldn't be upset with yourself about this. I mean, yes, it sucks that you spent all this time on it, but it happens. We make plans that don't work out. Things we want fall through. It's not your fault."

"Yeah. I think, deep down, I know. In the moment though, it was too much, and I couldn't get a handle on it."

"And then I came in announcing I had already told the whole world about the new location."

"Like I said, it's not your fault." He gives me a pointed look before continuing. "But, yeah it was all too much. I got too overwhelmed. I went outside thinking it would help me to get some fresh air, but it kept getting worse."

His breathing seemed to get a little difficult there for a second, and it makes me nervous. "How are you feeling now?"

"Tired and still hungry." He stands and heads back to the kitchen and the piles of food still on the counter.

"The doctor said you would be tired." I stand and follow him to the kitchen with my now empty plate. "He also said you should take some time off."

"I don't need to."

"You haven't taken a day off since we started working together."

"Neither have you."

"Yes, I have. I took a couple days off back in October—around my birthday—because my friend was visiting."

"Oh right."

"Seriously, what's so bad about taking a day off? You could sleep in. You could hang with your niece and nephew. You could watch movies all day…"

"Alright, alright." He cuts me off before I have to think of more suggestions. "I'll take tomorrow off, but then I'll be back Wednesday morning."

"Deal." I stick my hand out to shake. He rolls his eyes, but accepts the deal anyway.

Once we sit back down in the living room, I decide to keep this open communication thing going. "Can I talk to you about something? Or are you too tired?"

"If you need to talk, we can talk."

"So, we sort of touched on this already, but I wanted to reiterate it and explain a little more. About us working together going forward—I need you to communicate with me more. Not just about the new location, but in general. For the last few months, I've been feeling like I'm not…like you don't really want or need me working with you…"

"That's not true." James interrupts me.

"Thank you for saying that, I really do appreciate it. But there was a point recently when I was ready to quit and find another job because I felt like nothing I did mattered. Then Jesus and I had a little discussion and I realized that was the wrong thing to do."

A look of concern briefly flashed on his face, so he looks relieved when I finish explaining. "Glad to hear it."

"Anyway, I think we could both do a little better moving forward of working together."

"I agree. We have been a bit out of sync, which is probably more my fault than yours. I tend to get closed off when I'm stressed instead of reaching out and getting help. Can I make a request though?"

I nod for him to go on.

"If something is wrong, I need you to tell me. Obviously, I can get too focused on certain things and not pay attention to what's going on around me, so I need you to call me on it when it starts to happen. No ignoring it and hoping I'll realize it on my own."

"I can do that."

"Okay. Anything else?"

"A couple things. Why did you say you were going to Collin and Andrea's small group?"

He lets out a humorless laugh. "I don't know…I was caught off guard when you asked, and it was the first thing that came to mind."

"Cause the truth was so hard to come up with?" I push the matter.

"No. I felt lame. You're always talking about how great your group is and how much you enjoy it and how close you've gotten with the people in your small group. I didn't connect with anyone in the groups I tried like you have with your small group. And I couldn't exactly come to yours when

I gave up on the other ones I had been to. I mean, I was the one who said we should be in different small groups."

"And I agreed. At the time. I don't anymore. It's stupid for you to try to find another group when you already have friends in this one. You should join us on Thursday nights."

"You sure?"

"Yes." I give him an ornery smile. "If I get sick of you, I promise I'll let you know."

That gets a real laugh. "I'm sure you will."

"So, you'll come this week?"

"That sounds good."

"Cool. That brings me to the last item I want to talk about." I stare at my hands for a minute before jumping into this one. I was fairly certain we would be able to agree on the first two things, but I'm less confident about this one. I take a deep breath and go for it. "You don't like Henry."

"And you want to know why?"

"Uh…not necessarily. I want to know how to fix it. Or rather, I want to ask you what needs to happen to change that. He'll probably be coming to small group and Sunday school whenever he can, and I don't want there to be all this weird tension. You two are some of my best friends, and I hate that you don't like each other."

"Honestly, I'm not sure I'm ever going to like him. How about I try to be civil and see how things go?"

"I think it's a good start. I'm totally putting you on the spot right now, but will you at least consider talking to him to see if you can work it out?"

James grimaces. "I'll think about it."

"Works for me."

ꟷꟷꟷ

"Hey. Long time, no talk." I say as soon as Kenzie answers her phone Wednesday evening. We've barely managed to connect in the last few weeks.

"I know. I'm sorry! I miss you. I've just been working a ton, and when I'm not at work, I'm doing church stuff. Most of the time, I'm so exhausted I barely manage to keep myself fed and bathed."

"Well that's kind of gross."

"Whatever. You know what I mean. Anyway, how are things there? Is James okay?"

Kenzie and I were texting yesterday while I was at work, and I got her caught up on everything that happened on Monday. "I think so. He still seems kind of tired, but other than that, I think he's doing a little better."

"Good. I'm glad. Panic attacks are rough. I've seen quite a few of them at the hospital, and they tends to wear people down pretty bad."

"Yeah. I'm just relieved we were finally able to talk about some things."

"Talking is definitely a good idea. I'm happy you guys were able to work out the issues."

"Me too. Even today, I noticed a difference in how we were working together."

"That's awesome."

"How are things with you?" I hate being all happy about work being better for me when I know she's still struggling with her job.

"Fine. I'm hanging in there. Trying not to focus on the negatives."

"That's a good plan."

"Oh! Guess what?"

"What?"

"Liz is getting engaged today."

That wasn't what I was expecting Kenz to say. Liz is a friend of ours from college and Kenzie's current roommate. "Really? Didn't they just start dating?"

"It seems like it. They've been together since July, so I guess that's like seven-ish months."

"Wow. It still seems fast. Do you think it'll be a long engagement?"

Kenzie lets out a chortle. "No. I would bet they're married before June."

"Seriously?" I can't contain my surprise.

"Oh yeah. Liz and I have a lease through June, so it would be logical for her to move out before she has to sign another lease. And…it's Liz. She's always been one jump before looking, if you know what I mean."

I nod, even though she can't see me. "I do know what you mean. I still think it's crazy she's getting engaged so soon. Wait, how do you know it's happening tonight?"

"Oh, he invited me to the surprise engagement party he has planned. I'm actually getting ready to head over there now. It's at his parents' house. A bunch of their mutual friends will be there. Mostly people I don't know, but I feel like I should go since Liz is my roommate."

"That's nice of you. I guess Liz getting engaged means you'll have to find another roommate, huh?"

"Ugh! Don't remind me. I have enough stress in my life without having to go through that process." Kenzie pauses, and I would bet anything it's because she's looking for her keys. Her voice is hopeful when she starts talking again. "Any chance you want to move back to Kansas City and be my roommate?"

"Do I wish I was your roommate again? Absolutely. Am I interested in moving and finding a new job again? Not really. Sorry."

"It's okay. I had a sneaking suspicion you would say no, since you and James are finally getting along." She says over the noise of starting her car.

"You could always move here." I throw out the unlikely suggestion before actually thinking about it.

She laughs. "I'm sure your parents would love for me to move in."

"I meant we could get a place together, you goof." It would make it more affordable.

"I know. Sorry, but remember when I said God keeps telling me to stay where I am?"

"Yeah…doesn't mean I have to like it. I want you to be my roommate again."

"I miss you too, kid. And don't worry too much, you'll find a place."

"I hope so." Thinking about my desire to move out reminds me of my other big New Year's goal for this year. Now seems as good of a time as any to bring it up. "I have another question for you."

"Okay, shoot."

"Since you won't move here, will you at least consider taking a trip with me?"

"Sure!" She sounds happy to oblige my desire to travel.

"Really?"

"Of course! Where are we going?"

A laugh escapes me. "I have no idea. I just want to go somewhere. I've barely been out of state—I don't think the Kansas side of Kansas City really counts."

"Yeah…not so much. Do you have any ideas about where you might want to go?"

I pause to think about it for a minute. Despite the fact that traveling has been on my list, I don't have much of a clue about a destination. "Um…we could go visit my Aunt Lil. She's been telling me to come visit for a while."

"Okay. Sounds fun."

I'm not done thinking though. "Or we could go to a beach? I've never seen the ocean."

That one really gets her attention. "Let's do both."

Her enthusiasm makes me smile. "When?"

"I don't know yet, but we'll figure it out. Look at your calendar and find a couple dates that work for you. I have vacation time to use. So, as long as I give my supervisor enough notice, I'm sure we can make it work."

"Cool." This is the most excited I've felt in a while.

"I have to go, but we will talk more about this later."

"Sounds good."

Kenzie sounds as excited as I am. "This is a good idea, Clara. I can't wait!"

"Have fun at the party. Tell Liz I say congrats."

"Will do. Bye."

I immediately pull out my notebook and start jotting down ideas for trips because it feels like the only thing I can to at this moment to get closer to making that goal a reality.

Trips to take someday:

- Go visit Aunt Lil
- Go to a beach, see the ocean
- Adam and Dana's wedding in Indiana
- Liz's wedding
- New England – historical cities and places
- NYC – someday!
- Old England. I would love to visit the country that gave us Jane Austen and C.S. Lewis and Julie Andrews

ꟷꟷꟷ

Based on the lack of cars outside, I think I'm one of the first people to get to small group on Thursday night. As usual, I slip off my shoes and make my way into the living room. Adam and Dana are sitting at the dining room table having what looks like an intense conversation. Instantly, I feel like I'm intruding, so I start to back up.

"Hey, Clara." Adam calls.

"Hi." I cautiously step closer. "Sorry, I can…"

Dana ignores the suggestion. "No, it's fine. Come on in."

Against my better judgment, I join them at the table and spend the next few minutes trying not to feel like an awkward third-wheel. It doesn't really work though. I'm relieved when Sam comes bounding down the stairs and livens the group up a bit.

It's not long before Leah, Stephen, and El arrive and the conversations start flying. If I hadn't walked in on their debate when I first got here, I never would've guessed something was up with Adam and Dana now.

"Clara." El calls from the kitchen, waving me to join her. When I do, she points out the front window. "What's going on out there?"

I follow her gaze to the front yard, where James and Henry are apparently having a chat. "I have no idea."

"Are you going to go out there?"

"No. I want to see what happens first." I move to the side of the window, so I can't be seen from outside, and keep an eye on the two of them with El by my side. A few minutes pass and I'm beginning to regret telling James I didn't want to know what his issue with Henry was because now I really want to know.

"Should I go out there?" I whisper to El, although there's no one else in the room. The fact that I'm spying on them through the window makes me feel like I should be discrete.

"Maybe…oh, no. Wait, it looks like they're coming in." She bolts away from the window.

Sure enough, the two of them shook hands and are heading toward the door. I follow El and rush through the kitchen back into the dining room, where we pretend we haven't been spying on James and Henry.

Sam makes quite a bit of noise when he sees Henry coming in. I guess you could say he's excited to have him here again, which makes me smile. Henry makes his way into the living room and takes a seat on the couch with Sam. The two of them are talking like they haven't seen each other in five years, instead of a couple days. I should probably just be happy that they get along.

I lean over to look around the corner toward the door, wondering what happened to James.

"Looking for something?" His voice sounds on my other side and I about jump out of my skin.

"Why do you always do that?" I smack him on the arm.

He simply laughs and moves to high-five Stephen, who's sitting at the dining room table. Leah and El have moved their conversation onto the open couch. Before joining them, I duck back into the kitchen to refill my water glass.

"I thought about what you said." James says behind me. Thankfully, I heard him come in, so it doesn't scare the crap out of me this time.

"Yeah? Does that mean you're going to stop sneaking up on me?" I ask with a smile, fairly certain he'll never stop, but it's worth a shot.

"No." He shakes his head slowly, like he's trying to buy himself some time. "About Henry."

"And?"

"And…we talked. Although, I'm pretty sure you already knew that." He shoots a pointed look to the window where El and I were standing a few minutes ago.

I give him the best confused look I can come up with. "I have no idea what you're talking about."

"So it wasn't you watching us from the window?"

I shake my head slowly, trying desperately not to smile.

"You're a terrible liar, Clara. Luckily for you, I don't care if you were watching us. It might make it easier for you to believe when I say I think we've buried the hatchet."

"Yeah?"

"Yeah. We cleared the air. I mean, we won't be having sleepovers or braiding each other's hair anytime soon, but we've moved on."

"Cool." I resist the urge to ask him about it and decide to just be grateful. I slip my free arm around his waist. "Thank you."

"No problem." He returns the hug before heading back into the dining room. I'm not in the kitchen by myself very long because Jules materializes next to me shortly after James disappears.

"Hey, girlie." She says cheerily as she gives me a hug.

"Hey. How are you?"

"I'm doing pretty well. How about you?"

I shrug. "I'm good."

"How are things at Jimmy's?"

"Uh…getting better. James and I are finally on the same page, so that's been good."

"I bet." She turns to pour herself a cup of coffee.

I ask my next question cautiously because I'm not totally sure how she'll respond. "How are things with you and Sam? After you know…"

"…he chose to work instead of spend time with me on Valentine's Day." She finishes my thought for me.

I nod.

"We're okay. We were able to talk about it. I guess he volunteered to work so the guy who was scheduled could be off. Apparently, the guy and his wife have been going through some rough stuff lately, so he wanted to do something for her. Sam encouraged him to do it and offered to cover."

"Oh…that's nice."

"Yeah. It was nice of Sam to help his friend out, so I'm not upset about that. I think I was more upset he didn't really tell me why he did it…until a few days ago, when he finally realized how mad I was about him bailing on me. So I spent all this time being mad at him for something I didn't need to be mad at him for."

"That's kind of a bummer."

"It was. We had a good chat about it though, so I think we're in a better place now."

"Good, I'm glad." I offer her an amused look. "El will be very happy to hear it too."

Jules laughs. "She's so funny. I do love her support though."

The two of us head into the living room and join the rest of the group, which seems to be growing by the minute. Alex and at least six others—all people I don't know very well—have arrived, bringing our total to seventeen, which is probably the most people I've ever seen here on a small group night.

Having extra people livens the discussion and I love following along and listening to everyone's thoughts on the passage. It also means there are enough people here to keep the discussion going, so I don't have to say much.

Despite the extra people and the lively conversation, Sam wraps things up a little earlier than normal.

"Alright, I know we've closed the dialogue portion of the evening sooner than we usually do, but we have a reason. Without further ado, I will pass this off to my best buddy and his lovely lady." Sam directs our attention to Adam and Dana with his usual dramatic flair.

Adam and Dana are sitting next to each other on one of the couches and their expressions have reverted back to the ones they were wearing when I first came in tonight, which makes me suddenly feel a bit sick to my stomach. Dana has a sad smile stretched across her face as she nods for Adam to get started.

"As all of you know, this amazing woman and I are getting married in a little over two months. We are so excited for the wedding and sincerely hope you all will be there to support us. Most of you also know I will be graduating and getting licensed to be a pastor just before our wedding. The two of us have been praying I would find a job in ministry after I finish school. As much as I enjoy working for my dad, I know God is calling me to serve him in full-time ministry."

I glance at Dana looking for clues as to where he's going with this and see she's tearing up. Her words from our Valentine's Day party come back to mind, and I have a feeling I know what Adam is about to say, and I don't like it.

"A few weeks ago, we were approached about a position as the Discipleship and Young Adult pastor for a church about half the size of ours. After weeks of prayer and seeking counsel from our families, we've decided this is where God is leading us." He looks to Dana, as if expecting her to continue the story, but she's silently crying pretty hard at this point, which means I'm a puddle of tears as well.

Adam simply squeezes her hand and continues, choking back tears of his own. "The hard part is the church is in southern Indiana, pretty close to where Dana grew up. So, we will be leaving Rockton. We'll be leaving the church. But…hardest of all, we'll be leaving this group and all our amazing friends…"

Adam's monologue breaks off as he tries to collect himself enough to speak. The entire room is full of people wiping their eyes and trying to hold in their tears.

Dana collects herself before him.

"I can't even begin to say what all of you have meant to me over the last few years. This group has been a constant source of support and encouragement when I need it…I have grown so much because of you all. Leaving you will, by far, be the worst part of this move." Her head drops as a fresh wave of emotion hits her. She wipes the tears and looks up at us again. She offers the biggest smiles she can manage. "You're all invited to come visit. It takes just under four-hours to drive, and my parents have plenty of extra room for guests…"

Adam wraps his arm around her shoulder and pulls her close to him. "I know you guys can't tell right now, but we really are very excited about this opportunity."

His attempt at humor lightens the mood for a second, but the news is still so fresh no one seems ready to laugh. Sam stands up, drawing the attention of the room.

"I know this is hard. Trust me, I struggle being apart from Adam for five minutes, so I can barely wrap my head around what it will be like when he's four hours away." His joke goes over slightly better than Adam's did. "But, before we do anything else, I would like for us to pray over these two amazing friends. Adam, Dana, can you come over here?"

The two of them stand and join him. Sam throws one arm around Adam's shoulder and waves the rest of us out of our seats with his free hand. We create a large cluster around them and Stephen starts off the prayers. A few more people follow his lead. I pray along silently because I can't seem to stop the tears from flowing. Sam closes the prayer time and the cluster breaks apart. Everyone is wiping their eyes and trying to get close enough to hug both Adam and Dana.

Sam steps back and climbs up on the couch. "The good news is Adam and Dana will still be around for a little while. This isn't their last week or anything. We've still got them for about two months. I don't know about you, but I plan to squeeze in all the hang out time I can with them before they skip town. Also, because I don't know how else to cheer up a ridiculously sad group of people, I have ice cream in the kitchen for anyone who wants some."

This declaration garners more laughs and lifts the mood a bit. Sam and a few others slip into the kitchen to get the ice cream started. I hang back, waiting for a chance to talk to Dana. Finally, the people remaining around her head toward the kitchen, and I walk over and pull her into a tight hug.

"I'm really going to miss you." I whisper into her hair with tears running down my face.

"Ditto."

I finally pull away. "But, I'm also really excited for you guys. It sounds like an incredible opportunity. I will definitely be praying for you guys."

"Thank you." She wipes her eyes for probably the millionth time tonight. "And like Sam said, we still have a couple months. We'll have to plan a few more girls' nights before I leave though."

"Oh, definitely. That's a must."

"And you'll have to keep me updated on everything after I leave." She gives me a mischievous grin and continues at a lower volume. "Especially now that Henry's a Christian."

"Stop. I told you…" I shake my head at her suggestion that there's more than friendship between me and Henry.

"I know, I know. I'm just not sure I believe you."

I laugh. "Whatever."

"I also want updates when you find your own place, if that doesn't happen between now and when I leave. And your search for the right place to volunteer and use your gifts. I want to know about all of it. You promise?"

"Absolutely."

"I don't know about you, but I'm ready to drown my sorrow in a bowl of ice cream."

I nod and start to follow her to the kitchen, but I spot James standing by the front door trying to catch my attention. I tell her to go ahead and I'll be there in a minute.

I meet James at the front door where it's a little quieter.

"What was she saying about finding your gifts?" He asks with brow raised.

"Oh, ever since that Volunteer Fair thing at church a couple weeks ago, I've been trying to figure out what the right place is for me to get involved."

"And you haven't come up with anything?"

"I've ruled out a few things, but I haven't found the right fit."

"Really? Am I allowed to make a suggestion? Because I have a pretty good idea of what would be a good fit for you." He looks super sure of himself when he says this.

"If you're going to suggest helping with the youth group, being on the Thrive event planning team, or working in the nursery, I can save you the trouble." I tic the places I've already thought about off on one hand as I talk.

He shakes his head with confidence. "None of those are what I'm thinking of."

"Then what's your suggestion?"

"You know, it's getting late. I'm going to head home."

"Come on, you're not going to tell me?"

He shrugs. "Maybe tomorrow. Speaking of tomorrow, why don't you come in late? That way, you can stay and hang out as long as you want."

As annoyed as I am that he won't tell me what he's thinking, I don't want to pass up the offer. "Really?"

"Yeah." He nods.

"Thank you."

He nods. "See you tomorrow. Mid-morning."

I wave as he disappears out the door. Time to drown my sorrows in some ice cream. A few people bail out as soon as they finish their ice cream, but the core group settles into the living room again to hang out. For the most part, we manage to keep the tears to a minimum. Instead, we stick with light-hearted funny things, with a sprinkling of Sam's crazy antics to keep us awake.

It's almost midnight by the time Jules, Dana, Henry and I leave. El and Leah and Stephen left around eleven saying they had to be up early and were already out too late. Had James not given me a reprieve from my early start, I would've bailed by then too.

I give Dana one last hug in the driveway and head to my car. Henry is walking alongside me since his truck is parked behind mine.

"Hey, aren't you supposed to be at work tonight?" I turn toward him.

"Normally, yeah. I would've gone back to work a while ago, but I took the night off. Adam asked me to make sure I could stay for the whole group tonight."

"Oh…"

"I have to say, that was not the reason I was expecting."

"Right?" The mixed emotions of excitement for them and sadness for me come flooding back and I notice how tired I am. "I think I'm going to call it a night. I'm beat."

"Okay, see you later, kid." Henry waves as he backs toward his truck.

I slide into my car and head home feeling extremely grateful for the time I've had getting to know Dana this last year.

Chapter Twenty

The more I think about it, the more I'm going to miss Adam and Dana. Which is why I'm sort of thankful the days following their announcement are insanely busy. Friday was a crazy day at work and I wasn't even there for the full day. Then the boys had a basketball game.

I got up fairly early Saturday morning to help my mom get ready for my brothers' 16th birthday party. Their birthday isn't for a couple days, but they have a game the day-of and next weekend. So today seemed like the best option.

"Delivery!" El pokes her head in the screen door about an hour before the party is supposed to start. I wave for her to come into the kitchen since my mom's hands are currently full.

El is here because my mother was worried about having enough desserts for all the friends Cam and Carter invited. Being the amazing friend that she is, El spent most of last night and I would bet the better part of this morning making some of her specialty cookies.

"Wow! Oh, Eleanor, these look amazing!" Mom is almost in tears when she opens the large container of cookies. After wiping her hands on her apron, Mom pulls El into a tight hug.

Mom's been emotional all day because her babies are turning 16. El, the lover of hugs, graciously accepts the hug with a smile.

"These do look amazing." I back up my mom's opinion once I take a peek in the box. It's full of cookies cut out and decorated as baseballs, bats, gloves, and baseball hats. They are some of the cutest cookies she's ever come up with, especially since the hat cookies have STL written across the front for the St. Louis Cardinals.

"Thank you. They were a lot of fun to make." El pulls the box closer to her and starts laying out the cookies on the platter Mom handed to her.

Before too long, the boys come bounding down the stairs and each snag a cookie from the container.

"Thanks, El." Carter says as he takes a bite.

"Yeah, these are cool…and delicious." Cam echoes with a mouth full of cookie, which earns him a glare from Mom. They both disappear out the backdoor before they get in trouble for snitching cookies. Thankfully, the craziness of Missouri weather means it's in the upper 50s today, which means the boys and their friends can hang outside for most of the party.

Before long, their friends start arriving, and even though half of them stay outside, our house automatically gets louder. It's a full house with most of their friends from baseball, a number of kids from the youth group, and other family friends from church. Even Mr. and Mrs. McKinley came over; he's not using his cane tonight, so that is a good sign.

The party's been going strong for almost two hours when I spot El sitting on the steps watching the crowd inside.

"Hey, what are you thinking?" I ask as I take a seat next to her.

"You are incredibly lucky, you know." Her words are so quiet, I can barely hear them over the noise of the party.

"What do you mean?" I take a sip of my Dr. Pepper and set it on the step next to me.

She nods toward the living room where my parents are sitting talking to Mr. and Mrs. McKinley. "You have an amazing family."

"Oh, yeah. I do know that. They're a little much sometimes, but I'm still pretty grateful to have them." I nod in agreement and smile at her. "You're welcome to borrow them anytime you want."

"I don't think that's how it works." She gives me a sad smile.

I turn to face her. "Believe me, I know I have been really blessed in the family department. I know not everyone has that. But I also know family isn't just the people you're related to. Like Adam said the other night, our friends and our church are family also. They're the family you get to choose."

"I suppose that's true."

"It is. Plus, I know your family situation wasn't great when you were a kid, but that doesn't mean you can't still have this." I point her attention back to where my parents are sitting. "You never know. Twenty years from now, maybe we'll be sitting in your living room celebrating your kid's sixteenth birthday."

"You think?" She sounds doubtful.

"Absolutely." I nod definitively. "What I'm saying is the way you grew up doesn't have to dictate what you'll have in the future. We serve a big God who has plans for us that we can't even begin to imagine, so don't get so focused on the past that you can't move forward when he reveals those plans."

She nods slowly and turns to me with a small smile. "Now if only I could speed up those plans a bit."

I laugh. "I know it's been hard lately, but keep reminding yourself that God's got you. And remember his plan will always be better. Take me for example."

"You don't have a boyfriend either." Her eyebrows scrunch up. "Unless there's something you forgot to tell me?"

I shake my head. "Nope. No boyfriend for me. I meant about work. I was completely sure leaving Jimmy's was the best move for me, but God had other plans. It involved me being patient and obedient, not that I was super good at it, but it turns out this is better. Leaving Jimmy's because I was angry would've burned some bridges I really didn't want to burn. Staying and waiting for God's timing was frustrating in the middle, but now I'm really glad I did. James and I are getting along way better. It was worth it. And when God brings some amazing guy who loves Him into your life, it will be worth it too."

"Thanks." She throws an arm around my shoulder and pulls me in. "I needed that reminder. But, I do need you to promise me something."

"What's that?" I'm intrigued.

"Promise you'll be there for my kid's sixteenth birthday party, whether that's in twenty years, or thirty. Promise you'll find the time in your busy schedule being the General Manager of the Cardinals to come to my kid's birthday party."

Her ridiculous suggestion for where I'll be in twenty years makes me laugh, but the request it holds makes my heart happy. "I promise I'll be there for all the important birthdays and graduations and weddings."

We sit in silence and people watch for another few minutes before El turns to me with another question. "So, I take it you haven't found your own place to live yet?"

I shake my head. "That's another one of those waiting-on-God things. I'm praying and looking and praying and looking. And believing God will lead me to the right place at the right time."

"Don't you sound all mature?"

I shrug off the suggestion. "I've just had a lot of practice lately trying to figure life out on my own. It's not super fun."

"Like when you allowed yourself to be roped in with helping in areas of the church you didn't actually want to help in?"

"That's a good example. I tried to figure that whole thing out on my own."

"Any luck yet?"

I turn to her with a smile. "Actually, yes."

"What? When did that happen?"

"Thursday night after group, James said he had the perfect suggestion. It took some doing, but I finally pulled it out of him at work yesterday. And surprisingly enough, I think he might be on to something. I emailed the leader yesterday to find out more information."

"And? What ministry did he suggest?"

"I'm not telling. You'll have to wait and see. It will be good practice for you." I tease.

Her mouth falls open. "You're really not going to tell me?"

"Nope. It's going to be a surprise."

"You stink." She sticks her tongue out at me.

"Yes, but you love me anyway." I give her a big smile and a hug.

"Yeah, I guess I do."

ฃฃฃ

The next few weeks fly by as James and I start looking at other properties for the new location. It's a little intimidating to know we're responsible for the success or failure of this venture and the amount of money that's on the line with a deal this size, but I've enjoyed getting to be a part of the process.

Turns out all those episodes of *Fixer Upper* and *Property Brothers* I've watched have helped me develop an eye for potential. Where James can see the financial aspect of the work that needs to be done, I'm much better at picturing the end result. So, we've made a good team as we're looking at various properties.

We haven't found the right place yet, but we're determined to take our time and not jump into anything too quickly. We want the next location we spend time and money on to be the right location.

In the meantime, I'm trying to coach him on how to appear friendlier and more approachable when he's talking to the staff. So far, I think it's working. He's relaxed quite a bit in general, so they're getting to see more of his fun and goofy side and not just his business-oriented side, which helps. I've even convinced him to have a staff outing some Sunday night when the diner is closed so the whole staff can hang out.

Naturally, he decided we're going to go to the new putt-putt place again, so I'm sure that will be plenty embarrassing for me. Oh well.

The best part is Dean and Sharon got back this week and will be joining us for the hang-out night. I've only seen them once since they returned to our lovely little hamlet, but I'm so pumped for them to be around more. Not that I think we need the help. I'm just excited to be able to see them on occasion. I really missed them while they were off hiking through half of Arizona.

James' suggestion for which ministry I volunteer with was even more spot on than I thought and I've been looking forward to getting started ever since I heard back from the ministry leader. Which is why on the second to last Sunday of March, I slip out of my Sunday school class twenty minutes early to man my new post at the welcome center in the middle of the lobby.

The woman I'm supposed to work with today is on the inside of the large circular desk when I get there and she happily welcomes me to the team. I'm excited to get started.

"So, this is where you disappeared to." El says when she spots me a little bit later.

"Ta-da." I hold my hands out on either side, showing off my new gig.

"You were right. This is a good fit."

"I know! I can't believe I didn't think of it on my own."

She rests against the edge of the counter. "I want to know how James came up with it."

"I asked him. He said it was the first thing he thought of since I seem to enjoy getting to chat with all the different people who come to Jimmy's throughout the week. And he's right. I help the wait staff out front a lot with the basic tasks, and I love it because I get to talk to all kinds of people."

"Good. I'm glad you found your spot."

"Hey, Clara. Ellie. Have either of you seen Adam?" Henry interrupts our chat.

"I have." El kindly points him in the direction she saw Adam last and Henry disappears.

"I don't think I've ever heard someone call you Ellie before."

"Yeah…it's been a long time since someone's called me that." She's still staring off in the direction she sent Henry, and her response is an absent-minded one. El turns to me with a soft smile on her face. "When I was little, my grandma would call me her little Ellie-bean. My dad called me Ellie too."

"If you don't like it, you should tell him. Trust me, he wouldn't use it again if you really hated it."

She shakes her head. "No, it was kind of nice."

"Okay. Well I should probably get to work here. I'll see you later."

El waves as she heads past me in the direction of the bathrooms.

The first few people who come by the desk are looking for information about Sunday school classes. I give each of them a pamphlet listing all the options and give them a map of our large church building so they can find the classes easily.

A couple people, including my mother and Sharon, stop by just to say hi. My partner at the desk turns to me when yet another family friend walks away. "You know, some people work this desk in hopes of meeting more people at the church, but it looks like you already know pretty much everyone."

I laugh. "Well, I grew up going to church here, and my mom is on staff. So, I do know a lot of people, but I don't think I quite know everyone."

"That makes a lot of sense. Do you mind if I slip out to use the restroom? I think I've had a little too much coffee this morning."

"No problem. Service is starting any second now, so I'm sure it will slow down pretty quickly."

She starts to exit the closed in desk area, but stops and turns around. "I'm sure Tom told you this when he trained you, but we're out here for the first fifteen minutes of service. I try to slip out five minutes early to be back here for the end of service."

"Sounds good." I nod. Tom did tell me, but I appreciate the refresher.

I'm resting against the inside of the counter listening to the worship music that's just started when an older woman I've seen around the church for years stops in front of me.

"Hi there, can I help you with anything?"

"Oh, no need. I'm waiting for my ride." She points toward the doors on the end of the building with the covered drop-off and pick-up spot just outside.

"Okay. How are you today?" Even if she doesn't need help, I feel like I should chat with her while she waits. It's not like I have anything better to do.

"I'm having a lovely day. How are you…" She leans a little closer to read my name tag. "…Clara?"

"I'm doing well…" I let the fact that I don't know her name hang between us, hoping she'll offer it.

And she does. "My name is Sandy. I like the name Clara. It's a pretty name."

"Thank you. I like it too."

She keeps staring at me. "Any relation to David and Joanna Evans?"

I nod. "They're my parents."

"Oh, I just love them. Your daddy is so funny, and your momma is so sweet every time I stop by the office."

"Don't let my dad hear you say that. I don't need him thinking he's any funnier than he already does. I have to live with him."

"It can't be that bad."

"Eh…depends on the day." I laugh. "I'm just kidding. I can handle his lame jokes most of the time. It's a small price to pay when they let me live with them for free."

"It's good to have family around."

"Yeah. I'm ready to spread my wings a little, find my own place, but I'm definitely grateful for them."

Her eyes get big when I say this, but she doesn't say anything.

"Everything okay, Miss Sandy?"

"Everything is better than okay. I love seeing God work." She lets out a little chuckle. "You and I need to talk."

Her statement catches me off guard. I thought we were talking. "Okay."

"My renters just told me this week they're planning to move out in a few months. They're a lovely young couple who've been renting from me for years. They found out they're expecting their second child this fall and will need more space. So, I've been praying all week that God would show me the right person to live in the house when they leave. It's you."

Surprised by her declaration, I'm not really sure what to say. On one hand, this could just be a crazy old lady spouting off random ideas. At the same time, I don't really want to dismiss her if she really might have a place for me.

"Do you have a pen?" Miss Sandy pulls an insert out of the bulletin and turns it over. When I hand her a pen, I see she's writing her phone number down. "Clara, I see my ride has pulled up outside, so you give me a call sometime this week and we'll get together to talk it over."

She hands me the slip of paper before walking away.

Still feeling a bit stunned, I slip the paper into my purse and pull my phone out to text my dad. Miss Sandy seemed to know him, so he can tell me if she's crazy or not. Without telling the specifics of our conversation, I ask my dad about her.

I'm just walking into the sanctuary for the service when I get a response from my dad.

> **Sandy Cartwright. She and her husband were missionaries for many years. Amazing people of faith. She's quite the prayer warrior too.**

I smile as I read the text. My words from my conversation with El a few weeks ago come back to me. I serve a big God who has plans I could never anticipate. If James and I hadn't worked out our issues, he never would've suggested me volunteering at the Welcome Center, and I wouldn't have met Miss Sandy. God had a plan for me staying at Jimmy's that was much bigger than I could have ever imagined.

A tear slips down my face as I take a seat at the end of the row where El saved me a spot. Worship is wrapping up, but the music is still going. There's a reverent atmosphere when Pastor Bill walks up on stage.

"Isn't God good?" He asks.

I can't help but laugh. Yes, God is good.

SPECIAL THANKS

To every single person who bought and read my first book, THANK YOU! You're all amazing, and I'm so grateful for your support.

Ricky: Thanks for being my only sibling who will read my books, even if you're a little demanding when it comes to wanting more. ;) Also, you're rocking it in school, in case you didn't know.

Tay and Spence: Even though you will probably never read this book, thanks for always answering my sports questions and making sure the sports references makes sense.

Kelley: I have loved watching you finally get to be a mom! Thanks for always listening when I need you, even if kids are screaming in the background.

Emma: Girl, God is doing some big things in and through your life, and I'm so thankful I have a front-row seat for it!

Annie: I love that we live near each other again (for however long it lasts)! You have always been such a blessing and encouragement to me, but especially during the process of writing and finishing this book. Thank you so much!

Cara: You literally saved the cover of this book. Thank you so much for stepping in and making the cover photo happen. I appreciate you—your photography skill and your friendship—more than words can express!

Rachel: Thank you for all the feedback and encouragement the last few weeks and months as I've tried to nail down all the details of this book! Your words have been life-giving through this crazy process.

67425917R00176

Made in the USA
Columbia, SC
28 July 2019